I0780419

© 2025 by Joshua Spiegel & Kristen Spiegel. All rights reserved.

**Published by Grayline LLC**
**732 S 6th ST STE**
**V Las Vegas NV**
**89101**

Editing by **Kristin
Noland, Noland
Editing
www.nolandediting
.com**

Cover design by **JD&D Book Cover Design www.jdandj.com**

ISBN 9798218786281

First Edition: 9/2025

Printed in the United States of America

No part of this book may be used or reproduced in any manner whatsoever without written permission except in the case of brief quotations embodied in critical articles and reviews.

# The Other Side of The End

Is there ever truly an end if the will is strong enough?

The end. So, finalizing and satisfying for some, yet others cannot accept the concept, festering in denial and grasping for a different outcome. The ambitious consider this end merely an interlude; the dangerous use this quiet time to ponder, fueling their insanity.

And that is where our tale begins... at the end.

# Chapter 1

Something stirred deep in the tower's heart. Something that once held the land captive in fear and doubt. A threatening presence long forgotten, reduced to nothing but a pile of old, musty clothes near a dried-up cauldron.

Decay and weather corroded the once steadfast stones. Winds and rain chipped at the withered castle, leaving only a broken memory. Occasional lightning from the gathering storm was the only light that graced this forsaken place.

The walls had long since cracked, weather-beaten and reclaimed by nature. Mold and musk perfumed the air, giving the once-brilliant black marble floor a slick green blanket of resin.

In the center of the room, a starved obsidian throne, ivy choking its imposing glory, and next to it was a matching table with a clouded glass orb, cracked and dulled with age. The crystal ball forsaken and dormant.

Broken metal candle sconces clutched the walls, holding half-melted candles. Torn green and black tapestries waved gently in the icy breeze hissing through the shattered windows, and a haunting ambiance held fast in the air.

This was the way it had been since Dorothy had left. A room and fortress long discounted, yet some stayed, even with their lady's passing. The castle's depths and the small outside structures provided the only glow, yet no creature entered the upper rooms since they killed the witch.

A faint sound floated up to the massive steel gates that stood steadfast, closing off the only path in and out of the immense castle. The black metal structure was the one stronghold that endured for all these years, impassable, but the whispers in the wind reached through like creeping bony fingers.

To the faithful inhabitants, it sounded like the evening howls of the wolves on the side of the mountain outside the castle gates. There was no reason to pay the noise any mind, so the bustling of the weary soldiers and goblins continued.

Those who remained did so out of faith, but faith had been dwindling for years. They moved between their huts and the lower parts of the castle, performing the same nightly rituals, a mix of routine and loyalty pushing them to survive.

Next to the fire, a soldier took a cloth to his bladed staff. He diligently cleaned his weapon, just as he and his fellow soldiers had cleaned it every night since her death. The goblin milling about placed a plate of food at the soldier's feet and hurried away to deliver the other plates to those at their duty stations.

The howl sounded again, but something different grasped tightly around the mournful melody. The intelligence behind it gave the soldier pause. His gaze shifted from the blade to the gates. Many eyes lifted and found the noise peculiar as bodies ceased their nightly routine, all focused on the howl echoing off the mountains. The unexpected nature of the sound left them in a state of uncertainty.

The energy of the sound commanded their attention. The brave stood with their weapons as others found shelter within the huts.

The wind carried the sound closer. A tone, chilling even to the inhabitants of such a dark place. It washed over them like an icy flood, drowning their ease. The devoted army and followers felt the foreboding wail sweeping up to the dead and dormant broken windows in the tower looming above. Just moments later, an eerie silence followed. Even the wind ceased, leaving them in a state of heightened anxiety.

Silence fell upon the abandoned throne room; confused shouts from the inhabitants below could not penetrate the strange quietness that held the room like an invisible hand.

Echoes of the howl reverberated off the stone walls, but a voice replaced the morose cry before it faded.

"Rise..."

Silence followed the deep, melodic voice. The throne room remained still, and the tapestries hung stiff and steadfast like dead oaks refusing to fall.

"Rise..." came the command again, but with an energy pulsing and forcing the words into fruition.

Next to the cauldron, something moved. A forgotten spark, long extinguished, revived, animating the pile of old clothes.

"Rise!" the voice bellowed, the echo vibrating the air around the throne.

The clothes took shape, climbing toward the heavens as a soft, mournful wail turned into a scream of agony. Gray hands reached out as a head pushed through the clothing—a tangible body formed under a tattered black dress.

The cloth wrapped around a slender, gray-skinned woman with long, flowing black and gray hair. The torn dress hugged the familiar form like a long-lost friend.

She collapsed onto the ground, her hair covering her face as she panted on the marble floor. Her eyes focused on an object next to her hand—a pointed black hat that had seen the wear of time and had remained untouched for years.

"A witch I once was… feared… wicked they called me…" She lifted her eyes to the tapestries above, sitting on her knees. Her hands shook as they came to her face, her fingers touching the aged skin. She began to get her bearings. She moved her shaking hands in front of her eyes. Her skin was gray, but time and death were bound to take a toll on the physical form.

"Wicked does not describe what I am capable of now…" Her seething gaze moved from her hands to the crystal ball.

A bit of her energy returned, and she dragged herself to the steps of her marred throne. Each movement was agonizing, but something deep within forced her to move.

Using the stone steps, she pushed herself up. The witch's legs were weak, but she mustered enough strength to carry her weight. Legs steadied and eyes focused on the wooden door, stumbling forward. Nearing the doorway, she lifted her hand and made a flicking motion toward it. Green sparks flew from her fingertips and shattered the door into slivers.

A goblin rushed in, and before he slammed into the old woman, she caught him by the throat and raised him to eye level.

Weakness returned to her limbs, causing her to stumble backward. She braced her shoulder against the doorway and slammed the goblin into the wall. Her eyes remained cast down, and anger rose in her chest.

"How long?" she demanded.

The goblin struggled and gasped. When he wiggled out of her grasp enough to speak, his voice shook. "Y-years! We thought you were dead! I heard a noise and came running—" The witch threw him against the opposite wall, just outside the shattered door. He landed with a thud and sank to the floor, unconscious.

Staggering toward the clouded orb, the witch let out a sharp cry as her eyes traced the jagged fractures running across its once-pristine surface. It was utterly useless; the glass clouded and dulled. Repairing it would take far too much time. Her head lowered, and she fell onto the steps, breathing labored and weak.

A melodic chuckle sounded, and she turned her gaze to the ceiling. A moment of silence passed before her eyes darted around the room.

"Who dares intrude on these dark grounds?" She asked, searching for the source of the laughter.

"I'm glad that time and death have not stifled your passion."

The witch pushed herself into as much of a sitting position as possible. Her rage was budding as she scanned every dark corner for the form to which the deep male voice belonged.

"Where are you?"

"That will become relevant later. Until then, I must reserve my energy."

The witch paused in her pursuit of the voice, her thoughts lingering on the statement.

"You're in my fortress. It is relevant now," she spat.

A pain surged, collapsing the witch to her knees. Her body contorted, leaving her with no control. She grabbed her head and shrieked. Her hair flew forward as she clutched her slender fingers to her temples, screaming for relief from the assault.

The pain ceased, but the ordeal had cost her the bit of strength she had, leaving her curled up on the steps.

"All you need to know is I have brought you back, and I can just as easily return you to where that girl sent you."

Rolling onto her back, she asked the tapestries, "Why bring me back?"

"You wasted so much potential by dying. I brought you back for a chance at redemption." The voice stopped, and the last word hung in the air. "Do not make me regret my choice."

"I am no weak-willed servant! You may wish you had chosen one more obedient."

"There, there, wicked one, your fire will have a place and time to burn, but first, there is one I have to join you. A sister in ideology and an equal in power. You will find her company as useful as I have."

"I already have a sister," she spat the venomous statement into the ground. The worn woman's thoughts circled around the idea of an ally, and she allowed her emotions to simmer.

"Who is she?" the witch asked begrudgingly; a tiny surge of energy rushed through her. She rose to her knees, placing her hand on the crystal ball.

"The mistress of another world."

The witch growled. "How does that benefit me here?"

"Because you will use your remaining power to unite your worlds."

"Worlds?" The witch laughed. "You ask the impossible."

"I don't ask, I command, and you will use every part of your being. If you disobey me, you've seen what's waiting for you." The voice paused. "Or does my gray beauty need a reminder?"

The witch's gaze moved to the surface of the dormant crystal. She could barely make out her worn appearance in the clouded glass. Wrinkled features matched with sunken and dull eyes, which mirrored the state of her crystal ball. Gray streaks marred her black hair, matching her aged skin. She dared not test the entity further and gathered her resolve.

"I will obey your command, she answered resentfully." "If you are powerful enough to revive the dead, why do you need me and this other?"

The voice responded in a tone denoting the sternness and seriousness of the following words: "We each have our part to play; this is yours, and do not question my power again."

The witch hit the ground, writhing in pain. Just as she felt she might have pushed too far, the pain suddenly stopped. "I am not a cruel master. I give you a great opportunity that anyone in your situation would appreciate.”

She stared at what she could see of her reflection in the cracked and clouded crystal ball. So many years had passed in death, but the taste of vengeance sat vibrant on her tongue.

“Kill Dorothy.”

“Kill Dorothy,” the voice echoed.

The witch reveled in the thought of revenge against the girl who had taken her life so many years ago.

The crystal ball sparked with life for a moment. Vengeance is a prospect that is not so easily attainable, especially in a world driven by magical chaos. She narrowed her eyes and turned her gaze skyward.

“And what am I to give for such a chance?” The strained words rattled in her throat.

“Your loyalty and obedience. A small price to pay for what I am offering.”

She knew this being could easily decide to place her back in the depths from which he plucked her. The lure was an excellent one. The offer pulled at her core. Despite the stone-cold expression on the witch’s face, she weighed the options of servitude and being able to fulfill something she longed for.

“One to my left,” the booming voice rolled, “the other to my right, my hands to rule a new land. A... collective vision, if you will. Power and a chance at redemption.”

The witch caught a faint movement behind her reflection, returning her gaze to the crystal surface. Red flickered, and a shape formed, but it was far beyond the glass. The depths of the ball seemed to expand inward, showing a surging energy waiting to be released.

“There is still some magic left within you. Find it. You’ll need it for what is coming, but first,” A dull shimmer flourished on the ball’s surface. “Information can be rather powerful, wouldn’t you agree? You have missed so much. Let me enlighten you. Allow us some time to recuperate from our recent efforts, hmm?”

The witch placed her long black fingernails on the ball. As her skin graced the glass, a spark of green electricity leaped forward, grasping at her hand. As time lifted from the old item, a small section cleared, and magic pulsed through it again.

The red shape sharpened, and a new power surged through the witch, guiding her movements. A green glow emanated from the ball. She placed her palms firmly on the smooth surface, and it began sapping her strength.

"This will kill me."

"Your power still sleeps. You must awaken it. Now, do as I command."

The witch focused entirely on the swelling light before her. The ground trembled slightly as the light surged through her. She kept her gaze locked on the blurred red figure. The crystal surface softened into a clear liquid, and the witch's breath caused ripples on her reflection as she leaned closer. Another spark of green electricity flashed through the ball. The currents reached like small green limbs to embrace the old woman.

She dipped her fingers below the surface. She shivered from the chill but continued her search, reaching for the unknown.

# Chapter 2

Dorothy's eyes snapped open, her breath rapid in her chest, her head twisting from one way to the other. She tried to gain a sense of control over her surroundings. The clinging nightmare finally dissolved into a more solid reality. The dizzy feeling faded as consciousness returned.

Her fingers gripped the sides of the brown leather chaise she was lying on. Touch was the only sense that was registering in her mind, and she felt the smooth and dimpled leather under her fingertips. Sight shortly followed, with objects close to her taking shape.

Gazing intently forced a figure out of a shadowy hiding spot. She squinted, pushed her weight onto her elbows, and leaned forward to help her focus return. Across from her sat a man with robust features and a demeanor that stated he would rather be elsewhere. His salt and pepper hair matched well with the wrinkles around his eyes, which were lowered as he wrote on a small pad.

"I'm upping your dosage, Ms. Gale," he said, with a cold bite to his tone. Dr. Boyde had never been the type to have a proper bedside manner, but he was the best in the city, and after many years of failed treatment, Dorothy needed a specialist.

"Again? But I thought—" Dr. Boyde's hand ceased its scribbling. His icy gaze moved up to Dorothy's meek eyes.

"If you know so much, why are you paying me? I'm upping your prescription," he said with a finality that quieted any further inquiries about his methods.

But why did it have to be more pills? They never seemed to work anyway. She thought.

Dorothy sighed as Dr. Boyde's last pen strokes sealed another unwanted decision. She begrudgingly walked over with a defeated hand out. He shoved the paper into her palm and gestured for her to return to the chaise.

Noticing tiny droplets of moisture on its surface, she reached over and plucked a tissue from the box on the small table and dabbed the sweat from her brow, patting down the leather shortly after as well. She still felt a nagging foreboding; a constant itch she couldn't scratch. The dreams had been worsening, and she could not ignore that fact.

"What was it this time?" she asked, taking a seat.

"I haven't heard you speak of this 'witch' in over a year." Dr. Boyde folded his arms over his chest and gave her a judging glare. His disappointed sigh concluded his statement. "I thought we had worked past this already."

"I-uh…" Dorothy looked at her fingers fidgeting with one another. Only in the second hypnosis session, she didn't know what she had said or seen either time, but each time, impending dread woke her.

He walked over to his desk and played the current session back. Dorothy's eyes widened only a few moments in; her strained whimpers and cries made her squint and look away—some of what she saw while under hypnosis returned to her.

Vivid images of the witch's old decaying castle, an army waiting for a commander, and ... that voice.

"Next week. Same time. And I expect you to be taking the new dosage." He reached over and clicked off the recording. "Make your next appointment with Stacy."

She rose without a word, made for the door, and pushed it open. It felt heavier than usual. She slipped out, moving emotionlessly to the secretary, who had just as cold a regard as her boss.

The woman shoved a reminder card into her hand and gestured to the door. She barely said thanks before the secretary lowered her head, as if she had forgotten another human being was present.

The large doors to the office opened, and the next patient came through. Dorothy slipped out in the person's wake and went to the massive foyer of the high-rise. Dr. Boyer's office was in the better part of the city, and the décor of the building looked like that of a high-end hotel.

She walked past the front desk, where a secretary and a security guard were deep in conversation. Men and women in suits scurried by her to the gold and green elevators in the center of the building.

She should consider herself lucky. She would not have been able to afford her psychiatrist if not for her aunt and uncle, who were paying for each session. It helped that Dr. Boyde was an old family friend and gave them a nice discount on his hourly rates.

Dorothy reached for the glass doors as the doorman opened them for another man in his mid-fifties. She tripped and, maneuvering her body, narrowly avoided crashing into the gentleman, who did not even give her a second glance.

She clutched her purse under her arm as she found her footing. Her eyes scanned the sidewalk before glancing at her wrist to check the time. Only twenty minutes to get to her shift at the cafe. The bus stop she needed to get to her waitressing job was conveniently only two intersections away. The session overran, putting her behind schedule, and her bus stopped earlier than she wanted.

Dorothy felt with each step down the stairs that her legs turned to stone. The combination of the lingering unease from the session and the loathing she had for the job she needed to survive made her wonder how anyone with her level of social anxiety, along with traumatic experiences that may or may not be real, could keep going with a smile on their face no matter how unenthusiastic it may appear to others. However, determination kept her shoes shuffling through the crowded walkways.

She tilted her head to view the dark clouds above just in time to have a raindrop hit her cheek. She held her small purse tighter to her chest and looked at her work uniform. It's not exactly something to wear in any weather, especially in the cool, rainy fall.

The thin material was excellent during the summer, but even the blue and white sweatshirt she wore over the rest of the uniform only did so much. Her dress hung just above her knee, and the white tights she usually wore had to be discarded a few days ago, so she would be stuck bare-legged in the oncoming storm. Her apron held some old, stubborn stains that refused to lift, which got the owner of the diner on her, but she could barely afford the necessities and replacing it would have to wait until she paid the rent.

A sigh left her lips. Only one bus would be at the stop in time for her to make it to her shift, so she broke out in a full-on sprint. At the first intersection, a car nearly struck her; the driver was not paying attention. The man honked at her, though the crosswalk glowed green for pedestrians.

In the middle of the second intersection, the bus zoomed past her. The rain fell harder, so Dorothy put her purse over her head and picked up the pace. Thankfully, the next light turned red, and the driver stopped. She bolted to the corner, using the few extra seconds she had to catch up; her chest heaved with exhaustion.

The light flipped to green, and she took off again. The bus was quick on her heels, yet she closed the distance to the bench. She turned and frantically waved to the driver, who seemed not to notice anything other than the road ahead of him.

The bus did not slow. She waved more viciously to get his attention, but the bus slid past her. A harsh squeal of the brakes brought some hope. She jogged to the open door and stumbled up the stairs, her hair disheveled and plastered to her cheeks from the pouring rain.

The man barely acknowledged her with a half nod before shutting the double doors behind her and hitting the gas. She slipped a bus pass from the front zipper pocket of her purse and hovered it over the small machine. It beeped and flashed green, showing at least one thing would go right this afternoon. Take the small wins where you can.

Dorothy grasped the metal poles as she found a seat. There wasn't much of a crowd at this time of day, so finding a spot wasn't too tricky. She flopped into a seat close to the back and allowed herself a moment to take a deep breath and sink down. Her reflection in the window showed off tousled hair, which caused her to grab a white rubber band from the purse in her lap, along with a travel brush. She pulled her hair back into a ponytail. It at least helped to make her look less like a drowned rat.

Another sigh escaped her, and she leaned close to the window, watching cars and people move from one destination to another. Most did not acknowledge any other presence except their own, which was not uncommon. She was guilty of it, but that was merely a reaction to how she was often being forgotten. There was no room in this world for the quiet and reserved anymore. Society brushed people like Dorothy under the rug, deeming them obsolete and exploitable by the more aggressive.

She shook the thoughts from her head and lost herself in the rain streaking down the window.

Just up the street from the little cafe—a hole in the wall, but one of the most popular eating spots in this busy section of town, well known for their French onion soup and gourmet sandwiches—Dorothy pulled the line to stop the bus. The large vehicle slowed and squeaked to a standstill.
The doors opened, and she stepped onto the sidewalk.

Tilting her purse over her head in the downpour, she rushed toward the building that was one door down from the bus stop. She pushed open the cafe's glass door to the sounds of the late afternoon rush. Dishes clanking, loud chattering, and busy servers rushing about, taking care of unappreciative customers.

"Dorothy!" An older woman rushed up wearing the same uniform, though she looked well put together. Her apron was sparkling white despite being there for a few hours. Her white hair was short, curled, and clean.

"Hi, Nancy. Sorry, I'm late." The older woman shooed the apology away with a wave, took Dorothy by the arm, and ushered her into the back room.

"Don't worry about it. Jimmy isn't here. He doesn't need to know. Get yourself situated and give Erica a break when you're finished straightening yourself up, okay? Don't forget to clock in."

Dorothy was grateful to have a manager like Nancy, though the owner, Jimmy, was harsh. Most of the workers were relieved during the days he spent elsewhere.

The older waitress smiled at her, brushing a wet lock out of Dorothy's face before turning and rushing back out.

After ensuring her ponytail wasn't a chaotic frizz ball at the back of her head, she straightened her uniform and dried off. She tucked her purse into a locker, slid the lock into place, and grabbed a pad and pen. She pushed open the door with a deep breath. It was just another day.

"Hey, where's my food, little girl?" a plump man bellowed across the cafe. Scrambling behind the counter, pouring drinks, Dorothy looked up, her long fawn-colored locks tangled. Strands shot out in wisps all over. She looked even more frantic as she gathered the items on her tray.

She wasn't unattractive, but the day's stress had taken its toll. Between her tousled hair and the food stains on her white blouse and apron, she looked just short of a woman holding a cardboard sign at a streetlight.

"Hey, girl!" the man yelled again, his voice that of a person who enjoyed the misery of the less fortunate.

Dorothy briefly caught the man's impatient gaze. "I-I'm sorry, sir. Just one moment." She stepped through the double doors leading into the kitchen.

A moment later, she burst out with a tray holding a plate of unappealing food, but to some, like the man, it was a Friday night date meal.

She rushed past the other tables. No one gave the exasperated waitress a second glance. They carried on their conversations and meals as if she were a gnat escaping a crack. She set the plate in front of the chunky man.

His expression soured, and his eyes moved over her with a judging glare. "What the hell took so long? The food here isn't good enough to take twenty damn minutes," he spat as he picked up a fork in his meaty hand and stabbed one of the butter-dipped potatoes swimming in the oil and sauce of the limp steak next to it.

"I'm so sorry. The cooks were busy, and I had to look up how to make it myself," she said as she wiped her free hand onto her apron, spreading another greasy smear over it. "If anything is unsatisfactory, I'd happily make it again for you, sir."

His slimy expression broke into a lopsided grin. "Oh, is that right?" Leaning in to read her name tag, "Dorothy," he said, and lifted the fork with the potato skewered on the end. He placed it into his fat palate and squished the whites of the potato through his uneven teeth. After swallowing, his gaze moved from Dorothy to the food on the table.

He lifted the plate and dumped its contents on the floor before meeting her wide, doe eyes. The food slid, making an unsavory "plop" on the fake wood flooring.

"If you'd be happy to remake it, let me grant you the luxury of such a pleasure, doormat." The salivating slob belched as he dropped the plate onto the pile of spreading food. "I'm glad I could make your day, sweet cheeks."

"I'll find the busser to clean that up, sir, and I'll see if the cooks are available. I'm sorry again." Dorothy tucked the tray under her arm, slowly turned, and headed back toward the kitchen.

The man folded his plump hands over his swollen belly with a victorious smirk. Nancy slapped her hand hard onto his tabletop. The glasses and silverware clinked and clattered. The slob almost jumped out of his chair as Nancy's face came into view.

"What have I told you about harassing my servers? One more time, and you're gone, understand?" She waved at Dorothy to get her attention. "Dorothy, take a break. You don't need to worry about this swine. I'll take care of him personally."

Dorothy paused, her hand on one of the double doors to the kitchen, and gave a weak nod. As she slipped through the kitchen door, she heard her manager using colorful language to describe her displeasure with the customer.

Nancy gave her an intermission. Someone else would come along and see her as a doormat. It was only a matter of time, but at least someone picked her off the ground and hung her to dry occasionally. Dorothy slipped out the back door and stared at the bricks of the opposite building in the alley; a numbing white noise buzzed in her mind, accompanied by the heaviness of her heart.

About ten minutes passed before the back door to the cafe opened, and the older woman came out. Dorothy sat on the steps leading to the alleyway, her eyes cast downward as her fingers brushed absently over the food stains on her shoelaces. The faint smell of garbage from the restaurant's dumpster added to her destitute situation.

"Honey, you've got to thicken that skin of yours, or these pigs will walk all over you," Nancy said, closing the distance between them. She sat next to Dorothy and rested her elbows on her knees. She looked at Dorothy. Her eyes were dry. Most of the girls came bursting back here in tears. "Are you okay?"

"I'm fine," Dorothy said with a halfhearted shrug. "I've heard worse."

"You're too nice to be in a place like this. You sure you want to stay here?"

Dorothy did not answer right away but gave a single nod. "A job is a job right now. It would be worse if I didn't have it."

"Tell you what, we're covered for the rest of the evening. Why don't you dip out a couple of hours early, hmm? Take it on fresh tomorrow and whatnot?" Nancy put a motherly hand on Dorothy's shoulder.

"Okay," she whispered, slipping out from under her hand. She disappeared into the building momentarily, then returned with her small purse under her arm.

The older woman watched Dorothy turn the corner and sighed, shaking her head. "How that poor girl has survived life so far is a mystery."

Dorothy went unnoticed on the bus ride home, as usual. It never upset her. It gave her time to think and reflect on her day. People scrambled around her, bumping into her without ever uttering an apology. She might as well have been one of the metal poles.

She sighed, looking down at her purse in her lap, lying like a loyal dog. Her eyes squeezed shut momentarily as her old friend popped into her head, the only being who cared on this plane of existence. Toto had passed long ago, and it was just her and her dingy apartment across town.

A man in a business suit rustled his newspaper, jostling the vision of Dorothy's dog from her mind. Her gaze landed on the front-page headline.

*Extreme weather warning: expect intense storms in the coming week.*

She tilted her head and squinted, but the angle at which the man kept the paper made it impossible to read the article. However, she could see a picture of the expected forecast and cloud patterns over the counties.

Dorothy leaned her head against the window. She secretly wished for another tornado to pick her up and carry her far away, but such a vivid dream would probably never happen again, especially since she was no longer a child. It seems those things happen before people discover what life is like.

She stared out the window, not seeing anything, though the rain streaking over the glass attracted her attention occasionally. The water pattern sparked her curiosity. Moving like exposed veins, shifted into unnatural shapes—spires of a familiar city that many had tried to convince her did not exist.

Dorothy squinted, mostly in shock, as the liquid streaks outlined the Emerald City. She closed her eyes and took a deep breath before opening them again. The water had returned to normal.

She turned away, trying to force the image from her mind and let her gaze move about the surrounding people. Distracting herself only lasted so long, and her eyes returned to look at the street to prolong the diversion. She jumped back as her reflection disappeared, replaced with a gray, withered face.

Her chest rose and fell rapidly, eyes darting around to see if anyone had noticed her reaction or seen the same image. She went unnoticed and was grateful.

Dorothy reached up and grabbed the line. She was still a few lights away, but preferred walking plus the shops from here to her apartment offered some covering with their awnings. Getting wet was better than risking the chance for her imagination to play more.

The bus squealed and barely stopped, but she could stumble down the steps and onto the sidewalk. She dashed towards cover, her head tucked to shield as much as she could from the rain.

She paused under the first large awning and took a moment. The awning belonged to a bookstore that specialized in old and rare books. She'd been there a few times—the smell of the aged pages was always comforting. The bookstore only became crowded during Christmas, but it was not busy today. It was a miracle they stayed open.

She leaned down to get a better look at an old copy of a leather-bound book. The cover was bare except for a title written in silver stitching: *Crossings, A Tale of Realms.*

Dorothy furrowed her brow. She knew it was probably more than she could afford, but hoped the next time she stopped by, it would still be there.

Her eyes lingered on the worn cover long enough that she did not notice the couple approaching her. The woman bumped into her rudely and told Dorothy to watch where she was going.

Disappointed in the inability to pick up something as simple as a book, her aggravation rose, but she extinguished it. There was little to be done about it, and getting upset was pointless.

An image in the shop window caught her attention. She braced herself, hoping it was not another vision, but the gray face took over her reflection again. She stumbled back, gripping her purse. It was like a horrible car accident. She wanted to look away, but her body froze in place.

But… there was something more—another humanoid figure with no features. A red blur danced in the background of the familiar face: an ominous omen or just the mind of a crazy woman?

Dorothy immediately turned toward her apartment. Maybe Dr. Boyde was right.

# **Chapter 3**

Cheshire's lips curled into a mischievous smile as the woman's exasperated expression waned from the glass. He observed Dorothy until she rushed off down the rainy street and tilted his head toward the mirror with an ornately carved wooden frame gripped in his gloved hand. The glossy dark finish of the wood dully reflected the moonlight peeking through the dead leaves of the trees that had seen life many years ago.

His smile widened, showing his brilliant white canines, as he dismissively tossed the mirror on the ground. The image of the city street faded into Wonderland's night-drenched sky.

The sly cat's gaze shot to the sparkling specks in the abyssal maw of the night. His indigo eyes lingered on the creeping black clouds swallowing the stars, and he let forth a content-filled sigh.

It had been some time since little Alice had skipped through these now-dead trees and found herself in one of the most trying predicaments a small girl could. Cheshire pursed his lips with an amused spark in his eyes as he focused on the eroded stones of the crumbling structure before him.

What had been bustling with chaos sat dead and forgotten, left to be reclaimed by the forest. The only foliage remaining was the choking vines that squeezed vitality from everything they touched. So, seeing a sudden brush of movement from within the dull, clouded windows caused the cat to squint at something that was nothing more than a blemish of the past.

Since the queen's defeat, Wonderland had flourished, including Cheshire himself. However, beings who thrive on chaos can only be content with "happily ever after" for so long, bringing him stalking around the old castle. Well, that was his line of work, to be in places he should not be.

Another flit of movement, delicate yet slow and deliberate. It could not possibly be the old queen, could it? There were rumors she still stalked the palace grounds, mainly bound to her throne room. Parents told tales to their children of the defeated mad queen who talks to the wind, but they were stories.

He knew the actual events well. After Alice left, the queen deteriorated, and the people of Wonderland seized her power. People left her to become nothing but a joke. She'd slipped further into self-loathing and madness. It was hard to believe someone such as herself could delve further into insanity, but she proved it was possible.

Individuals brave enough to venture to the outskirts of the palace grounds had seen her on rare occasions, walking amongst her dead garden, the roses long since wilted and brown with necrosis. Then the queen vanished, and all signs of life vacated the haunted land.

Cheshire craned his neck to better view the stone ledge at the bottom of the stained-glass windows. He took a few long and lithe strides to a dead oak just outside the once-colorful glass. Each delicately decorated window displayed vibrant colors at one point, but only a dim shimmer and streaks remained, darkened with time and by a lack of proper care.

Even though his current physical state was more humanoid than feline, he gracefully moved up the trunk to a low-hanging limb thick enough to support his weight. The cat preferred his recently adapted humanoid form. Though he maintained his dark gray striped fur and feline facial features, his body was that of a toned middle-aged man.

His vigorous, lanky frame made his physical prowess far more intimidating. He usually wore form-fitting black attire to blend into the darkest of places. Strapped to his belt were shining, bladed reminders of not crossing him or getting in his way, and the calf-high boots he "acquired" from a magic-peddling merchant made it almost impossible to hear or track his movements. Strange-looking vials of liquid, dark green and purple, and most likely something dangerous to encounter, separated his daggers.

He slid into a seated position on the branch, one hand bracing himself on the stone wall and the other planted firmly on the branch next to his thigh. He found a small shard in the upper corner of the window and leaned forward to get a glimpse inside.

Another flutter of movement, the dulled silk of a sleeve. With sharp eyes focused, he saw which arm the sleeve belonged to. It had to be the old queen. There would be no one brave or stupid enough to be flitting around inside. Cheshire was positive; he was the only one to come this close to the structure in recent years. He guessed the dull pink silk was once red, and ivory surrounded the splashes of color, like white left out in the sun for too long.

The cat slinked down the tree, landed quietly on his feet, and gracefully sauntered with curiosity to another window closer to where the throne used to sit. Leaning against the stone wall, he peeked in. He could barely make out the decaying throne, still stubbornly in place.

He went unnoticed by anyone who might have been inside, which made it easy for him to watch. The broken old figure stood before the body mirror built into the wall.

That mirror was part of another story heard in the shadier taverns across Wonderland. Traveling musicians and criminals alike performed the beautiful yet haunting song.

*Beware the hearts of the fair.*
*The old queen is no longer there*
*Gone to insanity*
*Commune with vanity*
*In the mirror, she stays*
*Waiting for the end days*

The corner of Cheshire's lip curled into a half-smirk. "So... it is true," he whispered as he headed back toward the hand mirror that reflected flashes of light from the thickening clouds overhead.

A blast of thunder rumbled deep within Cheshire's chest. His hackles raised as a flush of foreign energy crackled through the air. Most would run for shelter, but his smirk grew with each sauntering step. A bright red flash from within illuminated the outer parts of the castle, and the blazing light breathed life back into the crumbling structure.

He folded his arms over his chest, a bemused look on his face. His gaze shifted between the dying trees and the dead plant life. He caressed his chin, brushing his dark gray-and-white-striped fur as he weighed his options. He couldn't waste this opportunity.

Cheshire narrowed his eyes, the brightness assaulting his senses. The flash subsided, and he clicked his tongue. With a raised brow, he looked to see if he was the only witness.

"What an interesting turn of events." He chuckled and glanced about again. One could never be too careful.

Most did not care to get involved in the cat's personal affairs because of the reputation he gained following Alice's departure. No longer a mere feline talking in riddles but a well-feared and respected criminal or savior, depending on who told his tale, though "criminal" was most often wrapped on people's lips when referring to him.

He made a move but caught his reflection and stopped to admire it. His fur complemented the white accents around his indigo eyes and up the bridge of his nose. Time had been kind to him, but he could not say the same for others. His gaze focused on the outline of the old queen pacing inside the throne room.

"Funny thing about some memories... They never die." He chuckled as he stood over the glass, his reflection framed by the clouds and the few remaining stars.

The cat glanced up, wary of the pulsing light, which was nowhere near as blinding as it had been before.

With all he had experienced in his many years, this, by far, was the most exciting thing he'd seen in the peaceful times since Alice left. The queen's loyalists scattered and hid. Other issues had surfaced since then, but none ever compared to the Queen of Hearts.

He tilted his head back to view a sizable hanging stone. It would only take a little encouragement to break it from the structure.

Cheshire turned gracefully to the mirror in the dead grass. He peered down at himself; the glass fogged as his image changed, evolving into a woman with long blond hair and blue eyes that stared back at him. He clasped his hands in front of him, chuckling with amusement.

"Ah, there you are," he said, a satisfied tone lingering on his words.

He snatched a dagger from his boot, spun, and flicked it into the crack of the stone. Debris teetered and slid free.

His boots touched the mirror's flat, icy surface, and metallic ripples immediately formed. He slipped under the surface and disappeared.

The cat looked up from the other side of the mirror and saw the stone plummet to the ground where he'd stood just seconds prior. It shattered the mirror, ensuring that the cleverest sorcerer couldn't observe him even. Cheshire's grin formed an accomplished smirk before he turned, his lithe figure taking on a more diminutive feline form. He trotted off into the cosmos between worlds.

His cheerful hum announced his entrance. Occasionally, he added words to the song formed with mischievous intent.

*"Alice, how far did you roam?*
*But here comes a message. We're bringing you home.*
*The time for peace has ended.*
*Vengeance is virtuous, my dear old friend."*

# Chapter 4

Her dreams had been rather persistent for the past two months. Years had gone by, and Wonderland stayed a mental scar, an old trauma not covered up but dealt with in more direct and less conventional ways, and years of psychiatrists and pills had finally run out of their worth. Fed up, Alice had tackled her demons and pushed forward. It was no surprise when she woke to her phone buzzing relentlessly on her nightstand after days of dealing with said demons alone. She rolled over, groggy with a strange tune stuck in her head, grabbed the phone, and hit the connect button.

"This is Alice," she said, her voice still strangled by sleep.

"This is Dr. Lewis. How have you been?" He did well to hide the irritation in his voice, but she heard it buried behind his professionalism.

"Busy," she said. She swung her legs over the side of the bed and stood stretching, her white spaghetti-strap tank top rising over her toned stomach. Her powder-blue pajama pants gripped her waist, fitting more like yoga pants.

Dr. Lewis started immediately. It was the same spiel every time. Alice showed him the courtesy of listening to what he had to say. She listened to the same rhetoric he threw at her. She still picked up the phone for his calls for her aunt's sake, not hers.

Every few months for the past few years, her psychiatrist would call to follow up. It was because of her aunt's probing, but Alice was done with pills and leather couch therapies.

She gently placed the phone on her vanity, sat, and began her morning routine. Her index finger brushed over the speakerphone option.

"Your aunt is concerned, as am I, that you may need your prescription again."

Alice sighed at the phone screen. "I would like to know how you came to that conclusion."

"You are becoming more distant and less engaged with people, Alice. That's not what we would consider normal behavior."

"What's normal for you is not normal for me." She hit the end-call button and welcomed the silence.

She walked to her bathroom and turned on the water to warm it up before pulling the knob to the shower. The light in the room caught the silver shard around her neck perfectly. Her necklace glistened in the mirror and twinkled back at her. The necklace reminds her of things she shouldn't completely bury and forget.

Alice shook her head, bringing her trance to an end as warm fog covered her reflection. She tossed her clothes toward the hamper, but only the pants half made it in. One leg dangled over the tank top on the marble floor.

She showered with a brief pause, hurried to start her day, and gained as much distance from herself as possible from the rude wake-up she'd received. Alice never wore much makeup; the only accessory was the ever-present silver shard around her neck. After putting on a light layer of foundation, eyeliner, and mascara, she entered her bedroom and slid on her work attire: a white button-up blouse, a tan pencil skirt, and matching knee-high boots. She neatly tucked her necklace into her blouse, where it remained unseen.

Grabbing her purse and keys off the entry table by her front door, she brushed her eyes over the black couch with midnight blue stitching and accent pillows. The feeling that she was forgetting something crept into her thoughts, and she pursed her lips. She kept her high-rise condo clean and organized. Most of the time, it was spotless, so she should have seen what she might be forgetting.

A blue and gold dining set was arranged on the deep cherry-wood dining room table; all four chairs were pushed in and the overhead fixed dome light was dimmed. The kitchen was spotless. All was as it should be. When she looked at her bedroom, she paused.

Her vanity mirror caught her attention with what looked like a spark of light. It could have been the reflection of a passing car. But her apartment was high enough that a passing vehicle on the city streets below could not reach her bedroom. Alice preferred logic these days.

The door covered a good portion of the mirror, yet she saw two swirling indigo orbs.

She stood still, with no emotion, simply focused on the glass, deciding if this was an old trauma or something new. Her purse and keys slid from her shoulder to the entry table.

Over the past year, dreams of Wonderland seeped into her subconscious, but she shrugged them off as old scars trying to reopen and nothing more. These orbs, though, were too familiar to ignore.

She closed the distance between herself and the vanity and pushed open the bedroom door to see herself in the mirror. The tune she heard in her sleep returned to her mind and got louder with every step she took toward the mirror.

The indigo spheres shifted, melding together, slinking down, forming a feminine figure wrapped in pulsing green electricity. Alice placed her hands on the vanity top and focused on the unknown figure, delicate and enchanting. Why did the vision make her stomach drop?

A second figure formed. Red mist swirled out from the green, gracefully becoming another feminine stature but remaining intertwined with the first. Alice studied the scene before her, trying to decide if her dreams were bleeding into her waking reality again.

The two colors entangled, engaged in an ominous dance, before they faded, leaving her staring into her blue eyes. It was a strange spectacle, but she was not sure of what. Nor did she have time to contemplate the matter further.

Alice returned to her keys and purse, which waited by the front door. Plucking her keys from the table and throwing her bag over her shoulder, she glanced back at her dormant mirror. She opened the door and left the strange occurrence behind.

For a couple of days now, *I've been trying to get in touch with you. I'd understand if I were a co-worker or a friend, but*

Alice looked at the text that had just flashed across her home screen. She couldn't give it too much attention right then; the electronics store she managed had one issue after another. On top of everything, they were short-staffed for the day.

It was the fourth or fifth message from her boyfriend within three hours. She hadn't talked to him since their last date, which was... Saturday? If it were Saturday, she hadn't spoken to him in a week. Each stressful day after another made this week feel more like a nightmarish month. The holiday season was chaotic, and the next one was just around the corner. She brushed the phone to the side.

Customers packed the floor, and her employees rushed between each group in feverish attempts to keep everyone happy.

The earpiece she wore blared her name, calling her to a different section. Another issue in the computer department. She sighed, trying to keep straight one problem at a time. She wrapped up allowing a return transaction for one of her employees and hurried off to put another fire out. It seemed like she was always running around putting out fires.

She weaved in and out of the aisles, passing racks of merchandise and dodging people through the cell phone department. She was almost through the television section when someone backed into her from an aisle. Surprised, Alice tripped and fell. She braced herself at the last moment with her palms, but her knees smashed into the floor.

The man who backed into her apologized repeatedly. Though irritated, she kept a calm exterior, gathering herself. She stood, and a hand grasped her elbow. She looked up and saw the man's reflection on a hanging flat screen.

His features went from those of an average middle-aged man to those of a warped and twisted creature. His mouth shifted from a worried grimace to a wicked, sharp-toothed maw resembling a malicious smile. She almost pushed the man away but whipped her head around to the man's face.

He looked like an embarrassed man and not a shapeshifting monstrosity. Her eyes darted back to the reflection, but the image was gone—just a regular reflection, though Alice's own looked bewildered.

"I'm so sorry, miss," the man repeated.

Alice stood and ran her hands down her blouse and skirt, giving the man a professional, polite smile. "It's all right. It's busy, and things are bound to happen."

She stole one last look at the still-dark television screen. She needed a vacation. The stress and lack of sleep brought back all too familiar memories.

It only took a few minutes to correct the computer problem, but just as she finished, another call came from the front of the store.

As she approached the front information desk, her annoyance amplified. Her boyfriend stood at the desk, waiting for her.

"What are you doing here?" Alice asked calmly.

"I figured this was the only way to get you to talk to me."

"I was going to text you once I got off work. As you can see, we're a little slammed." Texting repeatedly is one thing, but showing up at work made her patience wane.

"Yes, I see that," he said, folding his arms over his chest.

He would not leave, and she was not about to make a scene.

"I'll meet you for dinner after, okay? But I need to get back to work." Static came over the earpiece again, then her name once more.

"Fine," he sighed, dropping his hands to his side. "I'll see you tonight."

Before going to the following department that needed her help, she paused and watched him walk out the door. One thing after another. If this kept up, she knew the incident with the disturbing reflection on the television would happen again. But that was a worry for a different time. Right now, she had another issue to deal with, and after work, she was going to the gym. The rest could wait.

# Chapter 5

"Status report, sergeant."

A female Pridyr stiffened to attention. The small ledge, tucked away deep inside the mountains, had remained relatively quiet, so the sudden voice made her fur stand on end like a cub caught in the meat cabinet.

"Captain Ralk," she saluted, her balled-up fist forcefully pounding on her chest as she dipped her head. She shot the other sergeant a look, making him follow suit; he did, but looked surprised.

With hands clasped behind his back, the captain stood. The harsh look of his humanoid lion features didn't seem to be disapproval but more the weight of the situation. The rumblings from the mountains, the change in the wind, and the fact that he could smell something was off — so had the General, who had ordered him to check on the two watching the crumbling castle.

"I'm concerned I could sneak up on the two of you so easily. Perhaps a leave of absence to the grunt training grounds would be in order." The captain's honey-colored eyes narrowed on the soldiers.

"Apologies, Captain. Our attention was fully on the fortress itself. We will be more aware of all surroundings in the future."

Captain Ralk's steely gaze lingered on them for a moment longer before shifting to the witch's fortress.

The mountains far west of the Emerald City concealed the old structure. Between the city and the mountains lay the lush Spectral Woods, well-known for their mysticism and strange black-bark trees. The captain looked over the tops of oaks, maples, pines, and scattered black-bark trees. Their leaves shifted colors from dark jade to indigo, giving off a shine as though bathed in moonlight.

While he had never gotten lost in the dense forest, many had. Others came face to face with a dangerous unknown creature. Plenty of paths led safely through the massive oblivion, but many adventurers and thrill-seekers would wander, finding themselves in peril. A few returned, but most were never the same. Captain Ralk rarely traveled to the poppy fields between the Spectral Woods and the Emerald City and stuck to the Great Pride Plains on the western border—the territory of the Celehawk Clan, a massive and fertile plain, thriving with life and tended by his lion-like people, the Pridyr.

Their domain, wedged between the Spectral Woods and the mountains that housed the witch's fortress, made it a perfect spot for them to maintain a watch over the dangerous border. Nights passed, years came and went, and no sound louder than a somber whimper came from the fortress or its desperate inhabitants clinging to the camps inside the massive metal gates.

An icy gust broke the captain's concentration. His eyes stung, and the rumbling overhead forced his gaze skyward. The gray clouds deepened to a worrisome charcoal. He inhaled, trying to sense the information on the chill, causing all their fur to stand on end.

"What's this now?" His nose twitched at an electrical charge in the air, one beyond the simple lightning and magic of the land. He'd never held this scent before, and it fed his unease.

The female sergeant's ear flicked toward a noise behind the fortress gates. She turned away from her captain and focused below.

Life breathed into the witch's old chambers, the tapestries moving as if someone had gently brushed them aside.

"Captain, in the witch's chambers above, look," the male sergeant said in an almost-whisper, his muscles tense. "Are we to believe this is just a breeze?" His eyes narrowed as he reached for his bow staff in the cracks of the rocks just behind him. The Celehawks made their weapons from the black bark trees, and their mystics blessed them, so when he contacted the weapon, it let off a slight indigo shimmer before settling back to its black state.

"Nothing with the witch is coincidence or chance," the female answered, her almond-colored eyes locked on the windows above them. Their post was far enough back and set into a carved-out section of rock that they could see the witch's chambers from the narrow pathway below, and no one had traveled the road since the witch's demise.

Though they could see much from their spot, jagged rock edges, unexplored caves, and other treacherous paths blocked some areas from view. Their focus stayed on the one path leading to the plains from the fortress gates.

With the usual hopelessness on their faces, the soldiers and goblins dragged through their nightly routine. A sharp wind kicked up again.

Captain Ralk growled deep in his chest, a low rumble of warning. The scent and unease continued to grow. Nothing about this was right.

The encampments burst forth with commotion, yelps of shock and cries of concern echoing off the stones. Goblins scurried to dark corners, and soldiers whipped about the tents and fires, grabbing their weapons.

"A goblin just went in," the male sergeant hissed, tightening the grip on his bow.

"It's going to the upper levels," Captain Ralk growled.

A green electric flash blistered the throne room.

"Go now!" Captain Ralk barked, and within a second the three were moving.

The female Pridyr gripped the sword at her side and slid down the narrow trail, slipping over boulders, until she found her footing and leaped down to the next boulder in a beautiful parkour ballet. Her mind remained steady, and though her heart beat frantically, it was not from the physical exertion of rushing down a mountainside.

The males covered the distance in a few leaps. The captain bounded on all fours, dashing ahead of his female subordinate. "Light the signal!" he growled over his shoulder as they hit the foot of the mountains.

The male sergeant reached into the pouch attached to his belt and pulled out a small green gem. As they rounded a large rock formation that carved out the border between the mountain path and plains, he breathed an incantation into his right hand, the left gripping the small shimmering item. A fire ignited in his palm, and he dropped the gem into the flame. He closed his fist and launched the gem up into the air. A flash of green lit the sky, signaling to the Celehawk village that the worst had happened. Flames from inside the wooden pike gates sparked to life.

A crack of thunder caused the three to slow down, turn, and look up toward the peaks. Clouds rolled over the plains, coming from the upper mountains. They halted, taking in the sudden storm as one bad omen followed another.

Despite the wind violently whipping their faces, they continued their retreat. The chill nipped at their backs as they closed the distance between them and the Celehawk village. The wooden gates opened, allowing the grateful soldiers in, and they took a moment to catch their breath.

Captain Ralk pointed to the water-skins hanging by the guard post. "Drink. This will not be easy to report. Once you're finished, come to the chieftain's hall." He took off down the main path as curious and tired Pridyr emerged from their cozy huts.

The female grabbed the waterskin lying on one of the food barrels that the Pridyr kept ready for their scouts, warriors, and guardians. She took a long drink before pushing it into the male's chest.

"Finish it and hurry. This news can't wait," she said in short, gasping breaths. Looking no better, he brought the waterskin to his lips and gulped the rest. He tossed the skin back onto the barrel, and they headed to the blazing tribal fire outside the chieftain's hall. Typically, this time of morning, the fire would glow embers.

Other warriors, scouts, and guardians joined them on their way to the hall, skirting around the blaze. Though the clan had trained for many years for this exact moment, all had hoped it would never come.

They reached the double doors to the large hall carved with the Celehawk Clan's crest. A half-corporeal hawk, with its lower portion more wraith-like, wrapped around a crossed spear and sword, wings outstretched, and its eyes peering downward on all who entered the hall. The female looked at her fellow warrior and sighed. She had a horrible feeling that nothing would ever be the same.

The two sergeants entered and crossed their right arms over their chests, pounding their fists to their hearts in a rushed greeting to their comrades. Other Pridyr settled into bench seats at the long tables as the sergeants walked past the five main tables in the center. She spotted Captain Ralk, who stood beside a pile of hot coals encased in a brick pit. The soft glow of the coals usually gave a homey warmth and was welcoming. It was a sobering reminder of their duty to their people, the Land of Oz, and the Emerald City tonight.

The sergeants took their places on each side of Captain Ralk and faced Chief Urvan and his chosen Lurisa. The aging chieftain sat on his ornate throne, the back crafted from a mix of carved wood and antlers from many successful hunts and stained with berries plucked from the Spectral Woods. He shifted in his cushioned seat, covered with many furs. His chosen's throne, though smaller, mirrored the chieftain's.

The three soldiers placed their fists over their hearts and dipped their heads.

"Sir, there has been a movement within the witch's chambers," Captain Ralk began, but paused as another member of the royal family stepped in.

Pridyr made way to make room for his approach to the thrones. The royal nodded politely to those he passed and took a spot close to the steps but out of the way. He leaned against the wall and folded his paw-like hands in front of him.

The captain gave him a nod before he looked back at the chieftain and continued, "A scent is on the wind. One like I've never encountered. It has the charge of our mystic's magic. But it is foul" He needed to continue, but once the words left his lips, they all would have to acknowledge what would come to be.

"We saw the tapestries within her chambers moving, and the encampment stirred. One goblin ran into the fortress. We have seen no one enter the upper rooms since the day after she died."

The hall tensed, the air heavy as the weight of the captain's words settled.

"There's more," he said and cleared his throat. He had to force himself to relay the rest of the information. "We saw two distinct green flashes from her chambers."

Chief Urvan's old gray eyes narrowed. The only things giving away his age were his gray and white fur peppering his once golden mane and his worn, scarred face. His body still moved fluidly as he stood. His hand fell to his side and gripped his sword.

He looked at Lurisa, whose signs of aging she displayed with far more finesse and fewer visible battle scars, at least through her flowing gold and red dress. Her fur was almost entirely white, with only hints of her youthful golden color. She nodded and stood, picking up a talisman from the table between them. The only thing visible was the gold chain that dangled from her grip.

Lurisa walked behind their thrones, lifted the red and gold tapestry holding the Celehawk Clan's crest, and disappeared behind it.

"General Ragnus." Chief Urvan's eyes fell on the Pridyr, who had entered late.

"Yes, father?" he said, coming to attention.

"I need you to return to the Emerald City. Relay this information to the Grand Magus, his council, and the Emerald Parliament. Also, let them know what our next move will be." He curled his hand into a fist and placed it on his heart, dipping his head to his son. Ragnus responded in kind and saluted the captain and his sergeants.

"General Ragnus," Captain Ralk said, lowering his head toward the chief's son. His sergeants saluted, and the general left the hall.

"I'll need you both to return to your posts, but take three guardians with you," the chief said. "I want to watch her fortress, so we don't end up with unwanted surprises. Captain, see that it's done."

"Of course, sir."

The three reached the hall doors by the time Urvan dismissed the rest, and the captain looked with concern and unease at the other two as they departed.

No one liked what this could mean, but someone had placed the pieces, and they had no choice but to play the game.

# Chapter 6

"This is merely just a practical application of magic. We'll delve deeper into this subject later in the semester. Are there questions before we finish up for today?" A middle-aged munchkin asked his audience in the large auditorium. The student's faces staring back were of all ages and beings—Pridyr people of the wilds, munchkins, and humans. One hand shot up.

"Yes," the munchkin pointed to the human teen male.

"Professor Grenin, will we cover realm transfer and shifting in this class?"

"Ah, the advanced class will cover the more complicated subjects next semester." He folded his hands in front of him. "Anyone else?"

Another hand on his right moved skyward, and he nodded to the female munchkin.

"When will Scarecrow be coming in for his guest presentation?"

"Remember, he goes by Lucian now."

"Forgive me, that's right, Lucian." Her cheeks turned slightly pink.

The professor chuckled. "It's all right, old habits and such. He'll give his presentation once he returns from his pilgrimage to Munchkin City. I'm expecting him back in about two weeks." He smiled and scanned the rest of the class for any more hands. Once satisfied with no more questions, he scooped up his papers and placed them in neat piles.

"If you have no further questions, the class is dismissed," he announced. He cleared his throat and grabbed the book from his desk. "Remember pages 257 to 280 for the next class. I'll see you all in two days."

The shuffle of students erupted in the auditorium, ruffling papers and chairs scraping the green marble flooring announcing student departures. The munchkin squire descended the stairs, passing students as they left, and Grenin pursed his lips as concern spread on his features. Only the council or parliament would send a squire. He didn't like those meetings.

"Squire Harold, what brings you to my classroom?" Grenin asked as he placed the last of his papers in a drawer and tucked the book under his arm.

"The Emerald Parliament just received an envoy. They are requesting your presence in the council chambers."

Grenin was about to head for the stairs but brought his gaze back to the squire. "An envoy." He wrinkled his nose. "Why would the Master Apprentice of the Magus Council have any dealings with an envoy?"

"He claims to know you, sir, and wishes for your presence at this meeting." The squire followed behind Grenin as he adjusted the book under his arm and began climbing the steps.

"That's... odd. Inform them I will be on my way once I drop this off at my office." He pushed the door open and held it for the squire.

"Oh no, Master Apprentice, please." Squire Harold held the door and gestured for the professor to walk through first. Grenin smiled at the respect and kindness and exited, his hand still slightly remaining on the door, allowing Harold to slip through as well. "I'll inform them at once, Master Apprentice."

Grenin nodded and turned toward his office in the east wing of the academy. With each step he took, his black leather dress shoes echoed down the halls. The other classes were in session, so he made it to his office unhindered.

He placed his palm over the golden doorknob, twisted it once counterclockwise, then half a turn clockwise. His middle finger tapped twice, then once with his thumb, followed by a whispered incantation. The lock popped open, and the Master Apprentice slipped in. The door shut on its own as he crossed the lush silver and green spiral rug.

Grenin glanced at the filled bookcases that reached from floor to ceiling, covering the walls as he made his way to his desk. It amazed his students that he had read every book that graced the shelves, even more than once. He appreciated the wallpaper's decorative floral pattern with its mix of emerald, obsidian and silver accents.

Brushing a chaotic mess of parchments off to the side as something that could be dealt with later, one parchment stood out, titled Seismic Tremors in and around the city. Grenin thought to himself I must get back to reading this one, but each disaster in time. He then placed the book on his desk.

His eyes glanced over the two loose papers shoved haphazardly inside the book, but more in-depth analysis would have to wait until after the meeting.

What envoy from any city or people would want to speak with him? He hoped it was not someone from Munchkin City regarding Lucian's visit. Not that the man would do something wrong; it was more that something unfortunate happened on his journey there. One had to navigate the Spectral Woods between here and Munchkin City. If he stayed on the yellow brick road, the dangers were few, but not nonexistent.

Grenin had taught the Scarecrow much over the years, and culture and social interactions were among the many subjects discussed and practiced, so a blunder on Lucian's behalf would be a less likely reason.

He gathered himself and stepped past his desk and to a silver-framed body-length mirror nestled between the door to his office and the first bookcase. He waved his hand over the glass, and the busy park replaced his reflection out in Emerald City's main square. Grenin wanted to see how busy the streets were and possibly steal a glimpse of this envoy. He didn't see an envoy; only a few people walked the roads between Oz University, the Reverie Citadel, and Myst Library.

The three main buildings created a triangle within the heart of the city. In the center, four brick roads met, swirling into a pattern with a plaque in the middle. A beautiful city garden surrounded the main square. Many of the city's occupants found the spot serene and memorable.

Years had passed since the people of Emerald City had gathered in that spot to watch the young girl Dorothy fly away with the man they knew as Oz. They built and placed the plaque the morning after, and have celebrated that day as a holiday ever since. The garden grew within the first week, thanks to the Magus Council. Over time, the yellow, blue, green, and red bricks almost disappeared as the garden expanded. They planted trees, added benches, and cultivated a few grassy patches, now used for picnics and by travelers.

The roads were still somewhat visible, circling the park like a colorful frame, a bountiful masterpiece for the heavens to smile upon. No matter how large the garden grew, the plaque remained in the center.

*"To mistake kindness for weakness is the great folly of evil. In memory of the day Dorothy liberated our world from darkness."*

The words on the plaque echoed in the back of Grenin's mind as he stood in his office. The peaceful scene faded back to his reflection.

Grenin adjusted his forest green tie, which complemented his black shirt. He glanced down at his black suit jacket, which lay nicely on the back of a chair close by, the buttons and stitching adorned with silver accents. His pants matched as well. He sighed as he plucked his jacket from the back of the chair. If this was an envoy and a meeting with the parliament and Magus Council, he better look the part of Master Apprentice.

He rarely wore the robes donned by the other magus in the Emerald City, but he wore the amulet—a symbol of magic all students attain once they pass their studies. The silver chain draped around his neck, with the gem resting on his chest, emanating a hint of an otherworldly green. His hands clasped behind his back; he rocked on the balls of his feet, his leather dress shoes occasionally squeaking.

But his reflection gave him pause. His dark brown hair was more silver-streaked, and his beard had grown in the past few years.

Leaving his reflection, he slipped his arm into his jacket and went to his office door. He flicked his index and middle finger. The doorknob twisted of its own accord, and the wooden barrier opened enough for him to walk through. Once he heard his office door shut and latch behind him, he pulled on the other arm of his suit jacket and headed down the hall toward the Reverie Citadel, home of both the Emerald Parliament and the Magus Council.

Grenin walked down Emerald Road away from the Oz Academy at the end of the avenue. He dipped his head in greeting to those he knew; others received a polite smile. His cheerful demeanor was a mask over the concern beneath.

As he neared the circle of colorful roads that wrapped around the oval of Gale Park, he glanced toward the other impressive structure built diagonally from the Reverie Citadel between the emerald brick road and yellow brick road.

The Myst Library reflected the citadel in its glass doors. Grenin paused at the steps of the Reverie Citadel and looked down the blue brick road, the magic district. His attention lingered before his gaze landed on the red brick road that split off from the main yellow brick road and snaked back into the residential district.

Figuring he had stalled enough, Grenin sighed and huffed it up the stairs to the citadel. The shadow of the central spire spread down the middle of the steps. He glanced at it, pulled open one of the green double doors, and headed down an ornately decorated hallway on the right.

The clicking of his shoes ceased, muffled by the rug covering the wood flooring. The well-kept black rug with thin silver trim cushioned his steps as he glanced at the beautiful watercolor portraits lining the corridor's walls, each of a different landscape from across the Land of Oz. Every door in the hall was hand-carved and boasted the talents of the artists who made them.

One landscape caught the eye of the munchkin as it did every time he came to this wing of the citadel. Placed next to the main meeting room's door was a mesmerizing painting of the citadel and the emerald spires behind it.

The Chimera Spires, which the city was so well known for, held a beacon of hope and prosperity for everyone. A welcoming light to the wayward traveler, a symbol of knowledge and mysticism for the students that flocked to the academy, a place of acceptance no matter who or what you were. The spires became symbols of these and more. The citadel's reputation included grand meetings, political strongholds, and potent theurgy practices; daily, visitors and members of the Magus Council and the Emerald Parliament filled the foyer. Today, something made the painting darker. An invisible shadow. It made Grenin uneasy.

Builders constructed the citadel around the first and primary Chimera Spire, and over time, the Magus Council helped construct more until the city continued to prosper to a magnificent degree. The Master Apprentice pulled his gaze from the painted spires and pushed open the door to the main chamber. He plucked a glass from the table next to the door, filled with an iridescent blue liquid. It gave off an appealing aroma of berries and honey. The munchkin felt he might need it for what was to come. He took a long sip and felt the warmth of a potent wine made by the Master Alchemist himself spread through his body.

Grenin walked about the room, glass firmly in hand. He sipped occasionally as his eyes brushed over the paintings. Deep mahogany frames wrapped each hanging piece, reminding all who entered never to forget where they came from and why they were there.

The Master Apprentice slipped his now-empty glass onto the table. Carved silver runic symbols in the center of the table emitted a soft pulsating glow, giving the room a spiritual feel. Despite the internal moral dilemma that occasionally plagued Grenin's thoughts, the reminder that certain negatives may lead to positive outcomes kept it from driving him insane.

He could not help but let out an amused chuckle at the painting before him. It was a story he remembered well, and in some depictions, he was staring at a younger, naiver version of himself.

He had been present and helped construct the first magical spire and all that followed. One of the first to be on the Magus Council, he had been involved in many beginnings within the city, both good and bad. The founders, visionaries, and prominent leaders of Oz—those who remember the pre-Emerald City era—were on the Magus Council or the Emerald Parliament.

These paintings were also reminders of the necessary evils that brought them the prosperity they enjoy today. Significant actions drove the world to be what it is. Many would crumble in response if he didn't maintain his composure and confidence.

The click of the chamber's doors caused the Master Apprentice to glance at a massive humanoid lion, ducking to avoid hitting his head on the door frame. A male and a female Pridyr entered close behind.

The female wore the dressings of a captain, and the male had the markings and armor of a Celehawk Clan guardian.

Ragnus met Grenin's gaze, his lips curled into a friendly smile. "Master Apprentice, it's an honor to see you again."

Grenin offered his palm in a warm greeting. "Ragnus, my old friend." Ragnus gripped the Master Apprentice's hand, and Grenin's gaze moved to his two companions.

"To think they used to call you cowardly." Grenin chuckled, and the chieftain's son laughed in return.

Only the Pridyr clans knew the reason behind the old title, and he kept his past as nothing more than a lesson learned. Ragnus's expression turned serious, and he cleared his throat.

"I wish this were a more social visit, but the news we bring is dire to the safety of the Land of Oz and its people. They sent us to the visitors' chambers. I can only assume the meeting is to start soon?" He gestured to his captain and guard to take their seats.

"Yes, I just have this pesky ability always to be earlier than I should be," Grenin said, moving to his chair on the right-hand side of Grand Magus's seat at the north end. It was customary for each leader of the governing bodies to sit at the end of the oval mahogany table. Their positions represented the similarities and differences between the parliament and the council. Guests sat in the middle, giving them the focus.

"Perhaps we should make this meeting more hospitable with proper lighting, yes?" The Master Apprentice flicked his wrist, waving toward a silver wall sconce with a green wax candle. The wick ignited, and a small flame appeared. Sconces between the paintings sparked to life, creating a more welcoming ambiance. The candlelight illuminated the floor's white and black marble, and the forest green velvet of each seat cushion of the mahogany chairs glistened.

Ragnus slid into the middle seat facing the door—a habit his father taught him at a young age and something he kept over the years. His captain sat on his right, and his guard on his left.

Grenin folded his hands on the table and leaned forward. "Allow me to entertain our esteemed guests with a drink?"

Ragnus gave the munchkin a smile and a nod. "Though I'm not sure your drink measure will hold against our resistances."

"Ah, let's have a shot at it, shall we? I don't believe we'll see anyone from the council or parliament here for a few minutes." He pushed away from the table and headed to a cabinet in the back corner.

He opened the two sides, showing off many oddly shaped glass bottles in brilliant colors. Grenin removed a pear-shaped red bottle with a thin and slightly bent neck of a swan.

"Our Master of Alchemy and his apprentices make this little concoction. He's not just talented in the healing arts but also a skilled vintner." He uncorked the delicate bottle with a soft *pop*. The room echoed with the sound of liquid flowing as the munchkin poured into the large tulip-shaped stemless wine glasses. The glass swirled with a red iridescent liquid.

He picked up the glasses and walked toward his Pridyr guest. Ragnus's captain stood and met Grenin halfway and handed one to Ragnus and the other to his guard. She took the last for herself and slid into her seat as the Master Apprentice sat in his. He raised his glass to the Pridyr. They responded in kind, and all drank, the Pridyr more heavily than Grenin.

Ragnus's ears perked up. "Interesting. Cloves and honey," Ragnus said, holding the glass to the candlelight. "Magically infused, I'm guessing?"

"You guessed correctly." Grenin raised his glass and took another sip.

"Our mystics produce similar drinks, but they make most for battle or healing. I don't believe we have any magically infused liquids for recreation." Ragnus chuckled.

"Really?" The Master Apprentice knew a bit about the Pridyr, but he was far from an expert on their ways and customs. The munchkins and humans had infused magic into so many things over the years that it was a foreign concept not to have such readily available.

"Our magical practices have always been more limited, you could say. Reserved for particular things." Ragnus took another sip of the red concoction and smiled at the glass. "I missed the city. On my last visit, I was a bit more distracted. I couldn't appreciate these things then."

The creaks and groans from the chamber doors' hinges announced the entrance of parliament and council members alike. The Pridyr and Grenin stood and greeted those who arrived.

Most members went to the small cabinet and chose their drinks, from colorful bottles of wine to other magically infused alcohols, while some brought water pitchers to the table.

Apprentices of the masters on the Magus Council lined up against the wall. Grenin lowered into his seat as his gaze moved over each student. They mainly ranged from humans and munchkins, but there were two Pridyr in the mix. They approached Ragnus, stood at attention, and saluted him. One Pridyr was from the tundra clans, and the other was from the jungle territories. Ragnus stood and placed his fist over his heart. They stepped back to their places against the wall.

The room rumbled with soft conversation as all the seats between the parliament and council filled. The Grand Magus and the Prime Minister were the only two whose seats remained unfilled, and neither was known to be late.

Grenin stared idly at his wine; some worry was plaguing him about what information Ragnus had brought them.

He thought about how the once cowardly lion had left to return home many years ago. There was no aversion to returning, but it was common for the Pridyr to prefer nature over the city. Most came to the academy and returned to their territories immediately. It was rare to see one of Ragnus's people embrace the city. A few joined the parliament and council, like the two apprentices against the wall. One professor taught magical history and alchemy at the academy. Professor Vrek was a close friend of Grenin's and had studied under him at one point. The memory brought a moment of ease to his thoughts.

The doors swung open, and the Grand Magus entered, his head turned to his right and up as he spoke to the woman with him. He offered her a warm smile and held the door for her. She was of average height for a female human, though only her body could be mistaken for human, as she was a well-known witch.

The dark-haired apprentice closest to the door tapped his staff twice on the floor. "Grand Magus Harvol and Prime Minister Glinda." Those at the table stood at the announcement.

The Grand Magus's colorful robes swirled about him with his steps. Red, blue, and purple cloud-like patterns frame the deep, vibrant orange silk lining. Harvol's amulet, in its golden frame, hung from a chain around his neck. The entire Magus Council and its students wore amulets as a right and as a mark of being part of the council. His salt-and-pepper hair matched his beard, and the wrinkles on his features gave way to the many years he'd seen, both good and bad. He held out his hand. Glinda smiled and took it, and he started walking her to her seat—a sign of respect he had not just for the station but also for the woman who held it.

As she passed by each candle, her strawberry-blond hair shone. Her curled locks looked like a waterfall of pink champagne cascading past her chest. Her skin was that of an Irish cream, well complemented by her sky-blue dress. It was sleeveless, held over her delicate shoulders by a rose-gold spaghetti strap. Shimmers of gold moved through the blue chiffon as her gliding steps took her to the south end of the table.

She stood next to her chair in low conversation with the Grand Magus. They exchanged a few more words before she slid gracefully into her seat with a nod and a polite smile.

The Grand Magus returned the gestures and shuffled to the north chair opposite the Prime Minister. He stood between the chair and the table and gestured for the rest of the congregation to sit. Grand Magus Harvol folded his hands before him and looked over each present. The dark-haired man, who had announced their entrance, caught his eye. The Master of Alchemy's apprentice dipped his head to him. He always carried himself well, and he listened more than he spoke. The Grand Magus smiled and brought his attention back to the table.

"I would like to introduce our old friend, though I believe most of you know and remember him well. General Ragnus of the Celehawk Clan, son of Chieftain Urvan, formally, Ragnus, the Cowardly and Exiled. We welcome you back to the Emerald City." The Magus finished with a respectful bow of his head, which was returned, and those gathered gave their respectful nods and greetings. But the Grand Magus surprised Grenin by announcing Ragnus's former title.

"Your Grace, Prime Minister Glinda has requested the Magus Council for this meeting. I will turn the floor over to her." The Grand Magus bowed his head and sat. "Prime Minister," he said, gesturing for her to begin.

She stood and said, "I apologize for requesting the Magus Council, but the information brought to me involves both the council and the parliament."

A soft rumble of curiosity and worry flooded the air. Glinda raised her hand, and the room calmed.

"Yes, I understand you all recognize the severity of the situation if an envoy requires the attention of both bodies. General Ragnus," she said, her blue eyes falling on him. "Would you be so kind as to relay the information to the parliament and council of what passes?"

"Of course, your grace," he stated as he stood, his seat creaking. Although accustomed to speaking in front of large groups, it was usually out on the field or in a Pridyr meeting hall. His ability to appear calm and collected would make no one wiser about his feelings as he spoke.

"As both the parliament and the council know, the Pridyr clans have taken up the mantle of protectors of the land and its people. One of our many duties is vigilance. The Celehawk Clan has stood watch over the mountains to the west and the Wicked Witch's broken fortress for many years," he said.

"It's an average of five days' travel time between our home plains and the Emerald City. We made it in three." He tensed a bit. "Three days ago, two of our best guardian sergeants saw significant movement within the decaying fortress."

Grenin almost spat out his drink, and the room erupted with panicked whispers. He gathered his composure but couldn't wipe the horrific shock from his expression. It lingered in his eyes.

Glinda stood and cleared her throat. "Please allow our honored guest to finish. We cannot act appropriately in a panic and lack information. There's no need to get worked up yet." She nodded to Ragnus as she lowered into her seat.

"None of her soldiers nor goblins have entered the upper level in years. Not since the day she died. The loyal ones have kept an encampment outside and only enter the rooms on the bottom level." Ragnus clenched his jaw. Some expressions around the room were curious, others concerned.

"My guardians relayed that a sudden storm appeared. The wind and clouds were the most notable at first." The lion's eyes hardened, determined to speak the unpleasant reality. "They saw the shredded tapestries move in the witch's room, and one of her goblins ran into the fortress. Her room ignited with green flashes." His chair groaned as he sat.

A thick silence permeated the air. The Grand Magus had an uneasy feeling and forced himself to speak. "This indeed is troubling." He sighed, his gaze falling on Ragnus. "Thank you for your haste in bringing us this information."

"Of course, Grand Magus Harvol." Ragnus leaned back, took the glass of wine from the table, and downed the rest in a single gulp. He grabbed a fresh glass and poured some water from the pitcher.

Glinda rested her arms on the table. "I'm sure the clans have prepared for such events. What would that comprise, General Ragnus?"

"We'll be bolstering our defenses around the perimeter of the mountains and sending out a call to all the clans. I would rather prepare for a war that never comes than a dragon I didn't believe existed killing me." Reality barreled onto his shoulders.

A member of the parliament chuckled. "And thankful we are no longer troubled by the beasts."

Grenin felt no amusement at the attempted mirth and hardened his expression. "No, we have far worse things to deal with now."

# Chapter 7

It was not the first time Cheshire had maneuvered through the swirling cosmos between realities, a pastime he enjoyed. Traveling in such a method took a lot out of any being, but his kind was rarely affected. Those few who possessed the ability and knowledge could not withstand the drain of the universe for long periods.

The cat's people, the Faelias, were the only known creatures that could, at will, meld into reflective surfaces and slip into the expansive realm between time and space. Ambitious power seekers, some of them being his brethren, destroyed their homes. He escaped many years ago and had yet to cross the path of another Faelia.

Cheshire gave little thought to his people or his homeland. Far more pressing matters guided his thoughts and actions. He passed windows and mirrors showing the past and present of many realities. The future was never attainable since present actions determined future events. Nothing promised what would come, and the future always remained fluid.

"Ah, here we are," he said satisfactorily. He stepped up to a line of large, suspended mirrors gently bobbing like buoys.

Cheshire glanced down at his boots. They looked old and worn compared to the brilliance of the swirling stars and nebulas he stood on, like a dark blemish on a stained-glass masterpiece. He was used to this beauty, but he still took a moment to watch the nimbus below swirl in their hypnotic dance. Breaking from the star-flecked ballet, he lifted his eyes to the mirror the length of his lean body. Its silver frame had intricately laid patterns around the edges of the glass. He turned. More stars and another mirror, this one almost identical, except it was a deep blue.

"The Earth realm never disappoints." He smirked, placed his fingertips on the glass, and brushed them counterclockwise. The surface rippled as if he were disturbing a slumbering pond.

The mirror sparked to life. His image faded into a billowing gray fog that gave way to a scene long since passed. A meek girl of around seventeen sat in a field, her arms wrapped around her knees as she rocked.

Cheshire heard soft rustling sounds and watched the girl turn her head. Her expression changed from strained to anxious, and another figure stepped into view.

"It's time," the gruff male said.

"I'm sorry, Uncle Henry." Her voice shook, holding back tears. "I tried to make it stop."

He lowered his head and sighed. "I know, Dorothy. I'm sorry, as well. There is just nothing more your aunt and I can do. You need to go with Dr. Miller. The program is our only way to eliminate this Oz nonsense once and for all."

The girl said nothing, just offered a simple nod before reluctantly standing. She brushed off the bits of grass clinging to her white dress and turned toward Uncle Henry. His expression showed that he did not want to do this any more than she wanted to go.

"You're having daily episodes, and we've run out of options."

She looked up at him; the tears glistening in the Kansas sun. Uncle Henry pulled her into a deep hug. Holding back the tears became impossible.

"It's going to be okay, Dorothy." He did his best to console his niece, but they both knew that statement was a verbal Band-Aid for what might be on the horizon.

The girl pulled back from her uncle and wiped a tear traveling down her cheek. Uncle Henry wrapped his arm around her again, turned, and disappeared into the rush of returning gray.

Cheshire dramatically spun on his heels and sauntered toward the mirror directly across from the one he had just viewed. His form disappeared into the fog as if on cue, but this scene differed significantly from the previous one.

Alice bolted down the long hallway of a lavish school, her uniform skirt flinging up with each hurried step. Cheshire heard the voices of others behind her, and as she broke out into a full-on sprint, their bodies took shape.

She reached the door at the end of the hall, lined with school lockers, and stopped. Alice tried the handle, but she found it locked. She spun around and faced her pursuers, all teenagers around her age. Cheshire knew she was used to bullying, but this day seemed bad.

Alice pressed her back against the wall and tried to slink around the group, but a larger girl slammed her hand into the lockers, narrowly missing Alice's face. Alice halted her retreat and simply stood with her back against the lockers, looking into the eyes of the four picking on her.

"Oh, what's wrong? Mommy and Auntie are not here to save you? Because they tattled on me to the principal, I have two weeks of detention and grounding. Do I need to teach you to shut your mouth?" the larger girl asked mockingly.

Alice tilted her chin up. "I would think the detention and being grounded would have taught *you* a lesson."

Alice's head whipped to the side with the blunt force of the girl's fist. She turned back and stared at the group, a bruise swelling on her cheek.

"Poor little Alice. Only Auntie and Mommy care. Oh, wait, no... You are quite popular, from what we hear. Chase, any white rabbits recently?" The girl chuckled, and her lackeys joined in. "We'd better be careful, guys, or she might get her army of fluffy critters to save her!"

Alice said nothing, her expression unreadable and neutral. It was hard to tell if anything was getting to her.

The girl moved in closer, bringing her face uncomfortably close to Alice's. Alice did not move.

"Did Mommy and Auntie save you from the big, evil queen? What was it? The Queen of Tarts?" The group burst into another round of mocking laughter.

Alice grabbed the bigger girl by the throat and slammed her against the lockers. She pressed her body in and squeezed her neck. Veins popped out of the other girl's forehead.

Cheshire smirked. "The small girl is far stronger than she looks."

The three girls stepped back with wide eyes as their leader gasped for air. She clawed at Alice's hand, but Alice only squeezed harder.

"I. Don't. Need. Saving," she whispered. She pulled the girl off the lockers and then slammed her back hard. She let her grip fall from her throat. The girl slid down to a seated position, wheezing and coughing.

Alice turned. The other girls gave her a wide berth as she passed and walked down the hall. She never looked back.

The fog blew in behind her, removing the past.

"Interesting . . ." Cheshire mused, turning from the mirror. He stepped to another mirror that had sparked to life. This one hung next to the first.

As he approached, he saw the inside of an office, a nineteen-year-old Dorothy standing timidly in the corner facing out. Her hands were on her blue jeans, folded, and her head was down.

"Now, Dorothy, we've been through this." The male voice was firm, demanding, and held an air of narcissism.

"Yes, Dr. Miller," she said, angling her face to the shadows.

"Look at me." "What are young ladies supposed to do?"

It took her a moment to squeak out the words, but in a strangled breath, she replied, "What they are told." Her expression said she wanted to turn away, but she stayed steadfast in obedience.

"Good girl." The praising tone was short. "Come sit next to me, Dorothy." He tapped the seat of the couch next to him.

She cringed slightly as she walked over and sat beside him, her body stiff. She kept her eyes straight ahead, her hands folded and fidgeting in her lap.

A man in his early forties, Dr. Miller turned to his patient. He narrowed his eyes and looked at her more like a specimen than a human, tapping his pen on his notepad.

"Get me a cup of coffee," he barked. Dorothy stood looking reluctant, but still she complied. She grabbed his coffee cup off his desk and walked back to him. Her steps ceased with the shaking of his head. "No, a fresh cup." He pointed to the coffee maker behind his desk.

She nodded and went to a small wet bar on the other side of the office. The old coffee swirled down the drain slowly, prolonging the time before she had to sit next to the doctor again.

Once she finished pouring a hot cup, she closed the distance between herself and the doctor and handed him the fresh mug of coffee. She stepped back and folded her hands in front of her.

"Good, take a seat in the chair." He gestured to the leather chaise across from him. She sat as told. "I believe we only need to keep you six more months," he said and took a drink.

Dorothy nodded, keeping her head down.

Dr. Miller tapped his pen several times, filling the awkward silence tainting the room.

"I think that's enough for today." He hit a small box on the end table.

A buzz sounded, and Dorothy took half a breath before the nurse swooped in and ushered her out like an unwanted vagrant. As the door slammed, the fog returned.

Cheshire's ears perked as he heard movement. He glanced down the pathway of mirrors, but it was coming from the one behind him, decorated like the one that had shown Alice in the school hallway.

He sauntered over, crossed his arms, and settled his weight on one foot. Another vision of the past swirled into existence.

Alice moved the box set up onto the desk portion of her vanity. She encased the delicate items in protective wrap and slid each one into the box. A light knock came from the door, but Alice didn't respond. Moments went by before a couple of other taps sounded.

"Come in," Alice said. She made no motion to look back.

A woman in her late forties with primarily gray hair entered. The remaining life in her hair mirrored Alice's golden locks. Worn, tired, and worried, she had crisp blue eyes that showed her age.

"Are you sure about this? It's a long way from home."

"Yes."

"Why?"

"There's nothing left for me here."

"What do you mean? You have your aunt and me. Every school within reasonable driving distance accepted you, yet you're taking a gamble on a job in an unfamiliar city."

"It's an opportunity I can't pass up."

"That might go nowhere, and then where will you be? Stuck in a city, on the streets. I'm not sure if you should take this big step; your aunt and I can help you if you get into trouble."

Alice finished wrapping a small bottle with the words *drink me* on the label. A flash of hope flickered in the older woman's eyes but vanished as Alice finished protecting the minor item and placed it safely inside the box.

"I won't need your help. I know I might fail. That doesn't mean I won't take it, Mom." She closed the lid and turned.

Her mother sighed and gave her a resigned nod as she enveloped her daughter in a hug, only half reciprocated. "I'll leave you to it then." She kissed her forehead and closed the door behind her.

As Alice resumed packing, a flash at her neck caught Cheshire's attention, and the cat's famous grin crept back onto his lips.

"We haven't forgotten. Fantastic." He chuckled as the fog rolled in over the scene, returning the past to nothing but a memory.

The surrounding cosmos and nebulas dancing like Earth's aurora borealis dimmed. Darkness gripped the atmosphere, and the stars flickered timidly. A foreboding air settled in the time between realms.

Further down the line of mirrors, a frame sparked with small green electric currents. Its once plain silver border blackened and moved like melted metal until its surface curved like gnarled, dead tree limbs.

"Now, this is new," Cheshire mused. The scene revealed it was not Earth or Wonderland, but the magic within told him that wherever this was, it was not the past but the present.

An old, bent figure with messy black hair and gray skin gasped and leaned heavily onto a crystal ball with the same green electricity that ran through the mirror's new frame. He heard a male voice, though it was hard to determine what it said. The woman placed her fingertips on the ball's surface. It rippled, and her fingers disappeared within.

Cheshire's grin intensified, and a soft chuckle sounded in his throat.

"Fantastic . . ."

# **Chapter 8**

Liquid glass crept up the witch's fingertips and spread over her arm. The sensation sent a chill through her body, and pieces of her felt incorporeal, as if death were calling her back to oblivion. But she felt too much to die. Within moments, her stone-cold reflection encased her arm; the mirrored surface seized her like silver slithering molasses.

"Let me educate you." The deep, melodic voice cast a ripple over the moving glass.

Something pulled the witch into the darkness of the crystal ball's liquid form. She braced and closed her eyes, but that was her only reaction. Opening her eyes, she stood within her ball's black dome and looked out at her crumbling throne.

"So, is this my new prison? Conscious oblivion? I would have much preferred you'd left me dead." The red shape paced about on the other side of the glass surface. The witch followed it with narrowed eyes, but with the only light coming in from her throne room, she couldn't gather more than the black ground she stood on.

"Prison?" The voice let forth a mocking laugh. "That all depends on you, my dear."

The void shifted before the witch could lash a retort, and black fog swirled at her feet. As it filled the space, she clenched her jaw. She did not like being played with.

"Much has happened since your demise. How are you to finish what you started without knowing?" The voice moved through the fog, and the black mass dissipated, leaving her in the middle of a bustling street.

The witch scanned her new surroundings. Emerald City's main street ran in front of the Myst Library. People zipped by at an inhuman pace as more details solidified.

She saw a slightly familiar figure walking next to a munchkin. As the two got closer, time slowed and then froze.

All time and space stood in limbo, and the witch fixed her eyes on the Scarecrow. Moments passed before she circled him and his munchkin companion, hate seething behind her gaze.

"These are mere reflections," the voice began, but a snarl from the witch interrupted it.

"I get how visions of the past work. You said you didn't like your time wasted, and neither do I. Show me what needs to be seen."

The melodic chuckle was the overture before the space about her erupted with sound, and time moved at an average pace. The Scarecrow and the Munchkin brushed past and turned to the library's monstrous white marble steps. Her deadly gaze studied Scarecrow's face as she ascended next to him.

"What was the name of that Earther philosopher again? We were discussing him last week." Scarecrow snapped his fingers and closed his eyes. His brow furrowed.

"Socrates?"

"Ah, yes! I was contemplating his death," the Scarecrow said as he climbed the stairs, crowned on each side with giant statues representing the people of the prides.

The female lion to his left sat casually with one leg propped on the step. One paw rested on her leg, and the other held a delicate yet dangerous-looking spear. Leather armor covered her lithe form, and her expression was ever vigilant. The breathtaking statue to the right was of a large male humanoid lion wearing heavy robes and holding a book to his chest, with his arm reaching toward the street behind them.

"That's a rather dismal thing to be contemplating on such a beautiful day, don't you think?" the middle-aged munchkin said.

"Ah, yes, it is, but I'm confused. Why did they sentence him to death for bringing wisdom? Such a horrid way to go, too." He lifted his head to the carved figures at the top of the building—a peaceful scene of men, women, munchkins, and Pridyr people mingling in social situations.

"Not all Earthers are like Dorothy," the munchkin said, stopping just before the large wooden doors trimmed with gold. "There are many who fear knowledge for the power it has and can be... extraordinary." He smiled.

Scarecrow nodded, grabbed the gold handle of the door, and pulled it open. He held it for the Magus Apprentice to walk through first and followed. The witch gracefully slipped in before the door shut with a quiet thump.

The Scarecrow seemed slightly taken aback. Flickering candles hovering just above their heads filled the large domed entryway. Books zipped from one side to another and coasted to a stop on the tables. The books would flip open, and people would read the magically requested page.

A soft, throaty chuckle escaped the apprentice magus. "Young scholar, this cannot be your first venture to our magnificent library. Surely, mere ponds haven't distracted you in your recent quest for knowledge."

"I wish I could say you were incorrect, but I believe I have gotten myself distracted with ponds and fell short of the lake," he said, looking at the beautifully carved green marble dome ceiling—a three-dimensional masterpiece.

Though standing directly behind the two, the witch rarely broke her heated gaze from the Scarecrow. She held her gaze on the Scarecrow, ignoring words and feelings, until she turned to the Apprentice Magus.

"Grenin," she snarled. Time slowed once more until all figures stood still. The witch whipped to the front of the two.

"Ah, you remember the name?" the melodic voice echoed off the walls of the memory.

"Of course I do. I remember everything," she whispered, venom laced the witch's lips. She circled the two, her steps graceful and deadly. Each tap of her heel mimicked a ticking clock, a heartbeat strained.

"I'm ready to see more." She took her original place behind them, her hands clasped behind her back, her chin tilted upward. The Scarecrow and Grenin burst back into their conversation, unknowingly showing their old enemy everything she needed to know.

Deep within the Myst Library, the witch skirted around a long table, following her old foes. Her fingertips brushed over the wood surface as she focused on the two forms, Scarecrow settling into one of the bench seats, and Grenin standing at his side.

The Scarecrow sat before an enormous pile of books; the long wooden table dwarfed the size of the stack. His gaze moved over the others seated further down. They read through different pages and different bindings, from history to fantasy. He looked lost.

The Scarecrow jumped when Grenin touched his shoulder.

"Don't let it intimidate you." The munchkin laughed. "It looks far worse than it is. My first visit here, as a naïve young academy student, left me feeling like I had been thrown into battle without a sword."

Grenin gave Scarecrow a reassuring squeeze on his shoulder and folded his hands in front of him.

"Was it that obvious?" Scarecrow asked with a sheepish grin.

"Just a little, but nothing to distract us." He gestured to the books on the table. "This is a history lesson for today. You have several more days to prepare for your induction into the academy."

Scarecrow nodded, pulling the closest book to him.

"History of Magic in Zemra," Scarecrow read the gold writing on the worn brown leather. His head tilted. "What is Zemra?"

"Zemra was before the Emerald City. It was when the only structures and cities of the land were small towns that traded with each other. It was primarily munchkins and the people of the prides. There were some humans, but few. Before the Emerald City, the Great and Powerful Oz, and Dorothy, people knew the land as Zerma."

"Stop!" The harsh feminine voice pierced through the past, and time halted again. The witch stepped away from the table and glared at the ceiling. "I do not understand the point of showing me this. I couldn't care less if the useless bag of hay attended the academy. How is this to help me?"

"To know your enemy's capabilities is a gift few receive. Do not let your anger blind you to the knowledge that will help you. The Scarecrow is not the buffoon he once was. Do not underestimate him, plus..." the deep voice chuckled softly, "I thought you would want to see an old friend."

Time sped up to a normal pace. The witch stood with her hands clasped behind her. Whoever he was, he was not wrong.

Her haste had cost her greatly before, and she would not allow it to happen again.

"Good afternoon, darlings," the tender voice came from behind Grenin.

The witch's grip on her hands intensified. She turned to see Glinda striding up in a flowing yellow gown. Her hair had lightened to a strawberry blond and cascaded down her shoulders.

"I apologize for my tardiness, Grenin. Grand Magus Harvol sends his regards and thanks you for taking our dear friend under your tutelage." She smiled, taking his small hand in both of hers. "Though your choice to remove yourself from the consideration for Grand Magus does still baffle me."

"I have my reasons. Grand Magus Harvol is a far better choice than I. I'm perfectly content with Master Apprentice." He offered a warm smile.

"It is not my path." "Only you can do what's right for you, and I will always support it." She smiled in return. "I have to check Scarecrow's progress and see if you need anything. Oh, and there is one other thing — some council business. Master Apprentice Grenin, could we speak privately for one moment? It won't take long, and I'd like to get this out of the way so we can focus on Scarecrow's studies."

"Of course." Grenin gestured for Glinda to lead the way.

The two reached the door at the end of the aisle. Glinda unlocked one room and opened the door. Before either could move through, the witch slipped in and stood in the corner on the right; her hands still folded behind her.

Glinda's calm demeanor changed with the click of the door.

"Are you certain you made that potion correctly?"

Grenin looked bewildered. "Your Grace, the application and delivery were flawless within the concoction. We tested everything, and it worked as intended. No one ever questioned my alchemy before, but I understand the severe consequences if this potion fails."

"Glinda, I promise you, she's dead. We saw it for ourselves, remember?" He squeezed her hands. "Can you have a bit more faith in me, dear? It's also been two years since the day she was killed. Her fortress has fallen into ruins, and most of her people have either died or scattered across the land. Even her Gragskals retreated to their original home in the mountain caves."

"Thank the land; those creatures are gone. They are rather dangerous." Glinda sighed, some relief in her breath.

"What brought this on? We have barely spoken about that day since. Something had to have sparked this." Grenin peered up at her, his brow furrowing.

She stared at the floor. "I... had a dream. Far too vivid." Her eyes finally came up and met his. "It was a warning."

"What was this warning?" Concern clung to his words.

"Dark shadows danced in a green flame at the base of the Great Spire. When I moved closer, I saw the shadows dancing around a faded gray blanket, and on top lay the once silver, now emerald, slippers worn by Dorothy Gale of Kansas." As Glinda finished, her eyes seemed distant and hollow. Her gaze dropped to the floor. "There was more, but that's the most I remember."

"We shall take all warnings seriously and make the appropriate preparations." He gently tugged her hand toward him and softly kissed her fingers. An empathetic smile crossed his lips. "It was still just a dream. We will speak to the Grand Magus tomorrow about it, yes? In the meantime, would you accompany me this afternoon and into the evening, my lady?"

Glinda's face softened into a cheerful demeanor. She bent and kissed the Master Apprentice's cheek. "Of course."

The munchkin opened the door for Glinda. They stepped through, leaving the witch alone in the corner.

Her expression hardened. With the realization that there were more people responsible for her demise, she dug her nails so deeply into her palms that blood trickled.

"What... potion...?" she said through her gritted teeth.

"The two-part potion that drained your life," the voice said. "Glinda, using her magic and the distraction of Dorothy and her brood coming to claim your head, disguised herself as one of your own. That drink you had before they were at your gates was more than just wine."

She shrieked, seething with hate. Too weak to do much more, she leaned on the wall for support, burying her agonized expression into the arm bracing herself up.

"Now, now, my gray beauty. There's more to see and so much more to do. Save your strength."

The witch took a deep breath and pushed away from the wall. She was about to move to the door, but a flash of red in the gloss of the wooden table caught her eye. Her eyes narrowed as she stepped closer to the delicate, shifting blur.

She glanced around to find the reflection's source but could not identify it. Frustrated, she whipped around and headed to the door, tilting her head up. "I'm ready to continue."

The dense fog billowed from the ground, enveloping her. Once it had dissipated, she stood in the Spectral Woods, her feet planted firmly on a dirt path outside a log cabin. The yellow brick road, the only safe path through the dark forest, lay in the distance. She recognized the cabin, and her gaze focused on it.

"The Tin Man," she growled, striding forward. She took hold of the brass knob on the front door. She threw the door open to a rather ornate home. The wood inside was a rich cherry, and the furniture was classy and simple. Before a fireplace, a red and black rug lay under the carved coffee table. A low flame flickered, giving the house a warm and inviting glow.

The carvings and ornate detail on the frames around the windows, the heavy blankets draped on the couch, and the two chairs fueled her anger, and she dug her nails into her palms.

"What is wrong, my dear?" The mocking tone did not help her mood. "Is it hard to see your enemies prosper so much?"

She inhaled, forcing herself to calm down. This was important. She needed to push back the rage, and though difficult, she relaxed her shoulders.

"This is an empty cabin."

"The door on the right, darling."

The witch set her jaw. She hated being addressed in such a manner. Instead of spitting something back, she crossed the room and heard tapping and clicking from behind the door. Pushing it open, she saw Tin Man sitting at a desk and what looked like gears from a broken clock spread in front of him.

Upon moving closer, she realized it was the body of a metal sparrow sporting all colors of different metals, ranging from bronze to chrome. Tin Man hovered over his work, both palms on the desk. Frustration froze on his lips as his index finger tapped the tabletop.

"I know I connected the right gear," he said to the motionless creature. He nipped his lower lip.

Tin Man pushed away from the desk and walked over to the small window. His hand came to his chin, a pensive expression lingering on his metal features.

"Our old mechanical friend here had left the Emerald City first, shortly after Dorothy returned to Kansas. The newfound metaphorical heart had developed a passion in him to create and tinker that he had not had before." The voice chimed in as the witch watched Tin Man work. "In his human days, he had never known compassion, but that's what drove him to be in his current state. His lack of empathy toward others created his life, but the events since Dorothy and Scarecrow had brought him to a new mindset." The voice paused before letting out a chuckle. "Becoming passionate about evolving oneself and what is around them can present a rather dangerous foe. His drive to create could offer unwanted barriers."

Tin Man glanced back at the still form on his desk and sighed.

He walked to the built-in shelves on the workshop walls and moved his index finger past the different gadgets and tools. A replica of his right arm was among the parts and pieces of various metals and wood: three barrels and a stock sitting next to a few triggers alluded to the project's intent.

A dull thud from the living room caused Tin Man and the witch to turn toward the sound, though the only one to move toward the door was Tin Man. The witch's glare fixed on his metal features, studying every change from the last time she saw him.

He looked less mechanical and closer to a man, but one could not completely mask the small bolts and gears. He was still a metal man.

After he passed by her, she stepped into his wake and followed him to the main room. Ragnus stood by the fireplace, wiping his bloody hands on a rag.

"I take it the hunt went well, then?" Tin Man asked and smiled.

"That it did. I've already prepared the stag and will light the pit outside momentarily." He slid the cloth into the bag beside the chair. "Did you figure out the problem with your little friend?"

"Unfortunately, no, but these things take time." He huffed. "You're going back, eh?"

"It's time. I've run long enough from my past." Ragnus walked by, giving a nod, but looked unconvinced by his own words.

Both stepped out of the front door. Plenty of wood was piled inside the stone circle to build a sizable cooking fire. The lion sat on one of the carved log benches next to the fire pit and lit the fire.

"What about you, Tin Man?" He grabbed another wood log and flipped it onto the pile as the flame climbed.

"What do you mean?" he asked, sitting beside his friend.

"Your past."

"My past, like yours, has led me to sit next to you at this fire. I didn't run from mine but was careless with it." He gazed deeply into the flames. "It's rather funny to think about." His laugh rang with a hint of irony. "I was more metal as flesh and blood than now."

"How is that, Tin Man?"

"Flint," he replied.

"Flint?"

"Nicolas Chopper was what I was called lifetimes ago, but now, just Flint."

Ragnus gave him a warm smile, accompanied by a nod. He pushed up with his massive paws and walked over to the spit with a stag on it. "You still didn't answer my question." The lion picked up the spit and placed it in the holders over the fire.

"I wanted a heart. I wanted to know what it was to feel... love and be loved, and now," his hand dropped to the tunic on his newly forged chest. He had fashioned parts to look more human — his frame and muscle definition — but he was still bronze and chrome. "The want to create has always been unknown to me. I was a walking emotional chaos and destruction to myself and those around me." He smiled. "I'm a different man."

"I never would have known. Your concern for all of us proved otherwise." Ragnus spun the stag slowly and deliberately.

"Just like you, I've learned from my past and seen what I'm capable of." He folded his hands as he leaned closer to the building flames and rested his elbows on his knees. "Forward," he said, nodding once.

"Forward," Ragnus replied.

The witch stood in the doorway, observing every detail, listening to every word spoken. She would remember everything. The flames slowed down and turned into a vibrant statue.

She went back into the cabin and rested her hand on the windowsill. Energy seeped from her again. Breathing became more difficult, and her heart rate climbed. Bracing both her palms on the sill, she looked through the window at the two frozen figures by the silent fire.

The witch saw something out of the corner of her eye. Red again, but it was the reflection of the glass. The red mist waltzed like a ribbon in the wind.

"What of the girl?"

"That is beyond our capabilities, but I know she lives. Come," the voice beckoned. "There's more to see."

# **Chapter 9**

As Grand Magus Harvol completed his conversation with his dark-haired apprentice, the Master Apprentice kept his gaze upon him. The older munchkin's features were unreadable. The Grand Magus's eyes held the same concern they showed throughout the meeting.

"Everything alright, Grand Magus?" Grenin slid from his seat and approached.

"Yes, just troubling times overall, it seems." His gaze veered to the green amulet hanging from his neck. The gold that framed the green gem and the chain looked brighter than usual, and the gem boasted a more vibrant hue.

"Have you replaced your amulet, Master Harvol?"

The Grand Magus seemed fixated on the green jewel. "Hmm?" He raised his head and offered a small smile. "Oh, no. No, I'm just inspecting the job Apprentice Zellik did on it. I had set it on my desk when Zellik came in to talk about a class at the academy. He tripped and pushed into the bust on my desk. It toppled over and cracked the emerald. Overcome with shame, the young man offered to repair the gem and restore the magical bindings." "The bust was of my master, who originally gave me the amulet."

"We live in a world that offers us strange opportunities and sometimes humor." The corner of Grenin's mouth quirked up.

A low, yet booming rumble behind Grenin paused their conversation. Ragnus stepped up, clearing his throat, with his captain and guard at his sides.

"I apologize, but because of this matter, I think we should begin the journey back to our lands at dawn," Ragnus said.

"Of course." The Grand Magus dipped his head in a respectful bow. "I hope the next time we see each other; it's under far better circumstances." He looked at Grenin. "I'll be in my chambers near the main spire. Come see me when you've finished."

The aged Magus shuffled around the table and out the door, Apprentice Zellik in his wake. The only individuals remaining other than Grenin and the Pridyr were two parliament members speaking with Glinda at the far end of the table.

With a curious expression, the Master Apprentice tilted his head up at Ragnus. "That name, Cowardly…" he paused. "You still carry that scar. Your deeds for the Land of Oz and what you did here in the Emerald City would have long banished that from your name."

Ragnus huffed a soft chuckle. "Our people do not ignore their past or where we came from. It brought me where I am today, and to forget one's mistakes is to stunt growth."

Grenin was surprised, but he nodded. "That is a fantastic outlook. I wish more would adopt such a philosophy."

"Most Pridyr have some unsavory titles attached to their names. The ones that don't are young and have not experienced life yet."

"When time permits, I would love to learn more about your culture. I wish the Pridyr and the Emerald City had started their relationship sooner."

"Yes, I do as well." The lion looked around the room and dropped his voice. "What is happening, Grenin? Our mystics are on edge. They have been on alert for months."

"Have you felt any tremors?" The Master Apprentice fixed the cuffs of his shirt, unease billowing in the back of his throat.

"A few here and there, not much to speak of other than that. Why do you ask?"

"The city is the center, and you are farther away." Your mystics are not incorrect in feeling the strange shifts. Ripples in the metaphysical, you could say. It is something the council has been investigating. At first, we thought it was just natural occurrences within the different magical fields, but this news from the mountains is... troubling, to put it lightly. It leads me to believe we might face worse scenarios."

"You don't think she'd be able to come back?" Ragnus asked, concern pulling at his tone.

"It would take a substantial amount of magical ability and manipulation to return the dead, which is an area I'd rather avoid."

"We may not get that luxury." He sighed, running his paw-like hand through his lush salt-and-pepper mane. The toll of the clan wars, protecting the Land of Oz's borders, and the physical and mental wounds showed.

"That is a reality I've not wanted to accept, but with this information, the days of fantasy are over, I'm afraid." Grenin hadn't wanted to accept what the tremors and weather patterns had alluded to, but now he had no choice.

The Pridyr General studied the munchkin's face before folding his arms over his chest.

"You're not telling me everything."

"I'm not telling you everything, no. As usual, governing bodies keep some things quiet." Admitting deceit to a Pridyr wouldn't go without consequence.

"How knowledgeable are you about atmospheric rips?" Ragnus's captain tensed her shoulders, but if the general noticed, he didn't show it.

"My chosen is a mystic. She passed this knowledge on to me. I know it's a forbidden magic within my people." Ragnus tilted his head. "Why do you ask?"

"Not everything that slips through the cracks is as meek as Dorothy. One of the primary jobs of the Magus Council is to shield our world from threats, but we cannot always detect them." Grenin plucked his empty glass from the table, headed to the cabinet, and grabbed the same bottle.

"Magical atmospheric rips are not entirely uncommon and usually produce some effect. Most of the time, it's an individual falling from one world to another. That's how the few Earthers we have are here today. That's how Dorothy came to us." Grenin popped the cork and began refilling his glass.

"I thought a tornado carried Dorothy here," Ragnus said.

"Natural disasters are merely a tool used. Either wielded with purpose or completely by accident. There was a tear in the realm, and the tornado was the effect. That was no ordinary twister." Grenin chuckled as he corked the bottle and slid it back into the cabinet.

"I'm not catching the connection between the information being withheld and these magical rips."

"Not all things that come through these tears are like Dorothy, and sometimes we don't have the luxury of being forthcoming with information." Grenin returned to the table and saw the recognition in Ragnus's eyes. The lion nodded.

"Can you tell me where these anomalies are coming from?"

Grenin investigated his glass and swirled the liquid.

"I can give you my speculation," he said, taking a long sip. "The spires are more than what they appear, and I fear our time is running out."

"The emerald spires? Is that so?"

Grenin noticed the confusion clinging to his old friend's expression. He deserved more than a cryptic answer.

"There was a great evil many years ago, long before the Emerald City. The first council built the spires to shield our world, warding it from any who would seek to harm the Land of Oz." Grenin's throat tightened. "Nothing lasts forever."

"Was the witch one of these great evils?"

"No, this was worse than her," Grenin stated, meeting the Pridyr General's gaze.

"I see," he sighed. "I will relay all that transpired to our chieftain, and we will deliver the message to the rest of the clans to prepare for war."

"Good, we'll send you reinforcements within a day or two." Grenin sipped his wine and gave Ragnus a nod.

"Grenin, have you heard anything from Flint recently?"

"The last I heard, he was still at his cabin tinkering and perfecting a few projects, but this was months ago. Knowing him, I guess he's most likely doing the same thing." He hadn't seen Tin Man for almost six months, but most knew how and where to find him.

"And Scarecrow?"

"He's Lucian now. He changed his name just after you returned home, but he's gone to Munchkin City to work with the magical professors there." Grenin let out a long sigh. "But now I must send for him to return early after what you've brought to light. I need him here."

"He's a good man to have around and at your back. I miss him and Flint." There was sadness that hovered in his tone. Grenin could relate. He tapped his glass with the ring on his index finger.

"Some paths cross multiple times, General."

Ragnus turned and halted. He dipped his head toward Grenin. "Could the witch cheat death with her powers? Even after all these years?"

Grenin slowly swirled his wine and inhaled. "Yes, it is possible. She was, and always has been, a formidable foe, and you should take none of the information lightly."

"I was worried you would say that, but I'd rather not underestimate an enemy."

"Wise in your years, General Ragnus," Grenin said, lifting a glass to the Pridyr. Ragnus smiled.

"Appreciated, always, Master Apprentice." He brought his fist to his heart and bowed his head. His captain and guard responded in kind, following their general's gesture of respect. The three Pridyr headed to the door and saluted the Prime Minister. The door shut in their wake.

Grenin slid back into his seat, sipping his wine. The spark of life in the witch's fortress, the sudden storm, and the physical and magical tremors suggested a looming possibility he did not want to revisit. He glanced at Glinda as she finished her conversation with the two parliament members, but he was not hearing or seeing anything.

He finished his second glass and placed his hands in his lap. His intuition continued to pull at his senses. These weren't all coincidences, and he couldn't ignore them.

He looked towards the spires within the citadel and shook his head. "No, one thing at a time now. One thing at a time."


Glinda politely bid the two men farewell. The door shut with a soft click behind them. She turned toward Grenin and smiled.

The wine glass sat empty and lifeless on the table, and he stared at it with a troubled expression. She cleared her throat rather dramatically.

The munchkin chuckled, stood, and met her halfway.

"Yes, I'm troubled," Grenin said with a smirk.

"I don't even need to ask anymore, do I? Are you able to read minds now?"

"Just yours, dear." He gestured toward the door. "I'm not sure about you, but I've had enough of meeting chambers and classrooms."

Glinda walked with him to the door. She smiled as she stepped through, and they walked down the long hall toward the foyer. As they neared the entrance, Grenin reflected on the corridor. This wing of the citadel comprised formal meeting and banquet rooms that catered to the parliament, the council, and their guests. Many important decisions made in these halls shaped today's world.

"I'm guessing we may need to postpone our dinner plans for the evening?" she said.

"Let's not be too hasty yet. My classes are over for the day, but the Grand Magus wants to see me when I'm done here."

"Ah, but do you think your meeting with the Grand Magus will last only a few minutes?"

"Fair point, but let's see if we might have luck on our side tonight, yes?"

Glinda smiled. "Optimistic, I like that."

"With the uncertainty at our fingertips, I might as well stay positive where I can." He chuckled.

The two maneuvered around people, waiting to meet someone from the council or parliament in the foyer. The closer they got to her office on the south side of the citadel, the sparser the people became. Guards permitted few people past the first two offices, and even fewer past the offices near her chambers at the wing's end.

Glinda brought her fingertips together, recited an incantation, then pulled them apart. A thin silver wand with iridescent etchings on the handle materialized and hovered before her. She plucked it from the air and pointed the tip at the door handle. Violet wisps flowed forth, grasped the knob, and swirled about the lock in a counterclockwise fashion. Runes, which matched the color of the wisps, lit up on the wood. The latch unlocked, and the door opened.

Grenin entered behind her, turning to wave his hand over the lock, putting the wards back in place as the door shut. The oil paintings on each wall had vibrant colors that shifted as he walked past. The carved frames matched the chair's design, which was deep cherry wood accented with silver.

Glinda glided over to her chair, grabbed another she had, and pulled it over next to hers, the Master Apprentice taking a seat. She placed her wand on her desk, settled into the dark lavender cushion on her chair, and noticed his concerned expression.

"Talk to me, Glinda. I can feel you holding everything in." He reached forward and cupped his wife's hand in his.

Her gaze fell to her lap. She didn't voice what was on her mind for fear of giving it more power than it already had. She let out a long breath before meeting his eyes again.

"It's him. I know it is." Her throat tightened, and her shoulders tensed. Everything calm and collected left her.

"Now, let's not jump to that just yet, okay? That's extreme."

"What else could it be? The incident at the witch's fortress . . ."

"We should handle this as a separate issue for now. We know nothing yet. Once Ragnus puts his defenses into motion, we will have more information. If we split our focus or concerns, we could build an army for a shadow at our front just to be stabbed in the back."

She squeezed his hand. "Right," she huffed out. Nothing good ever came from panicking, and rash decisions could prove fatal.

"The council will make the defense preparations and send what we can to help Ragnus. Once we know more, we can address the other issue. I would not so callously throw away the possibility of some involvement from him, but let's make sure." He brushed his thumb over her cheek and cupped her chin.

His touch sparked some life back into her eyes. She closed them and leaned into his hand. "Of course," she whispered.

"We've fought demons before. This will be no different. Remember, it's how we met." He chuckled.

Glinda half-smiled and opened her eyes. "Yes, but when do we get to stop fighting demons?"

"We don't. It's simply not in our nature." He kissed her cheek and folded his hands in his lap.

His words brought clarity. He wasn't wrong. Their lives weren't destined for quiet, and they wouldn't have desired that.

"I'm going to call a meeting, and we'll discuss the next steps. There are just too many things that could happen if we wait. I'm guessing under the circumstances, the council will meet at a moment's notice, correct?" Glinda picked up the wand from her desk. She murmured under her breath, and the wand hovered above her palm. Wisps encased her wand, and she blew into it. The wand disappeared.

"Yes, and I will bring that to the Grand Magus when I talk with him. I'm positive he already has that on his mind. The council and the parliament should stay in close contact."

"What else do you have to finish up?" she asked, shuffling the papers on her desk.

"I must send a courier to the Munchkin City to request Lucian's return. Then I'll be meeting with the Grand Magus." Grenin slid off his chair, adjusted the lapel on his jacket, and smoothed out the wrinkles on the front of it.

"That's enough time for me to arrange for the parliament to meet." She stood, papers in hand.

"Late dinner then." He took her hand and kissed it, giving her a wink.

Glinda laughed. "I'll send a message and let you know when we're done. Knowing how long the Grand Magus keeps you, I might wait for a message."

"Yes, well, remember who waited on whom last time; how many hours was it?"

"Listen, I have no control over some tantrums thrown over property disputes." She scoffed, but the grin did not leave her lips.

"I will prepare the Grand Magus for a meeting with parliament tomorrow. Morning, I'm assuming?"

"Yes, please. I feel we've already lost days since Ragnus brought us this news. I hate we must disrupt Lucian's progress."

"He's been a wonderful student and a surprisingly quick learner. Consider this hands-on training. I don't see this delaying his graduation or induction into the council apprenticeship."

"Will you be sending for Flint as well?" she asked.

"I would prefer not to hinder his tinkering. He has been working on a few projects for the parliament and the council. I know he's working on a venture to bolster our defenses, so I will not send for him."

"You know, he may not wait for a delivered message."

"Yes, our demons never cease." He smirked.

Glinda shook her head but couldn't help grinning back. "I think the Grand Magus is expecting you, isn't he, dear?"

He chuckled. "Okay, okay, I'm leaving. I'll see you at dinner."

"Late dinner."

"Late dinner." Grenin pointed his index and middle finger at the lock. He made a swiping motion to the left, then right. The lock slid to the side, and the door creaked open.

# Chapter 10

Grenin rested his elbows on his knees and covered his face with his hands. The deep sigh rushing through his fingers turned into an annoyed grunt. He'd been in the Grand Magus's chambers for a couple of hours, debating the best steps to take, and the conversation always came back to the main spire in the courtyard.

"We can't just ignore that he could be the source of these odd occurrences," Grenin grumbled into his palms.

"You're jumping too quickly to that," Master Harvol said again. He looked just as exhausted, leaning into the back of his green velvet chair, hands folded on his desk, and staring at the ceiling as if the answer was in the grains of wood.

Grenin pushed himself back with another frustrated sigh. He had to address things one at a time.

"Okay, not jumping to that. We still have a potentially devastating problem with what Ragnus brought to us. You and I both lived through the days of her and her sister terrorizing our people. We know only some of what they were capable of, and the stories allude to far worse." Grenin wished he had some of that wine. Whenever he finally got to dinner, he would not be skimping on anything tonight.

"At least we have to deal with only one now."

"I'm not sure that's a comfort. And how do we know that the Wicked Witch of the East won't return either?"

A choke escaped him, and Grenin saw a spark of dread flood his pupils.

"You said you were going to send for Lucian?" the older munchkin inquired.

"I already have. He'll get the message by morning."

"How did you send it so fast? You didn't send one of the squires, did you?"

"Of course not. They wouldn't have been able to get it there for two days." Grenin placed his palms on his pant legs, the weight of everything pushing down on him. "I summoned Amon, one of his crows, to deliver the message."

"I thought they only spoke to him."

"Amon is the only one who will answer me, and that was after work and practice on my behalf. Lucian's magic is still new and chaotic. It's close to what the Pridyr mystics do with their spirit totems."

"Yes, those magics are still quite foreign to us here."

Grenin clasped his fingers together. His mind came back to the subject that kept plaguing him. He could not shake himself, the dread climbing to the back of his throat. He couldn't let the matter rest.

"And what if he has something to do with all this?" Grenin asked, looking up from his hands.

"We'll do what we've done for years."

"Build another spire?" Grenin groaned and slid from his chair. "How many spires will we build until we figure out another way?"

"It worked, and it's what we planned from the beginning. I don't see the point in deviating from what we laid down years ago." The Grand Magus reached around a cluster of metal and crystal relics and grabbed a pewter goblet off his desk. He took a sip of the liquid inside. Even from the other side of the desk, Grenin could tell it was the concoction he drank to ease aging joints.

"Death and change are the only two things promised in this life." "We cannot expect the same method to work as things around us evolve, magic included. Do you not think a more secure method could be implemented?" Grenin's frustrations were peaking, but he was not one to allow his emotions to envelop his actions so quickly.

"Yes, we can improve, but... one thing at a time, Master Apprentice."

The mantra taught to every student who graced the academy echoed in his mind, and Grenin nodded. He did not like sweeping the looming issue under the rug. The recurring tremors and the strange storm flux might connect to the witch's fortress. There was no simple answer. They had to deal with what was directly in front of them.

"Right. I'll relay the message to the council about the meeting time in the morning. I'll also find out from Glinda when we will send the reinforcements to Ragnus." Grenin walked to the door that mirrored Glinda's. He waved his hand over the lock. Etchings within the wood sparked to life, casting an emerald hue onto the room. The door was unlatched and pushed open.

"Good evening, Master Apprentice."

"Rest well, Master Harvol," Grenin said as he departed.

The council wing was empty. His black dress shoes clicked on the marble floor as he passed each master's office, including his own. Candle flames and moonlight lit the foyer ahead.

The massive windows of the citadel's large entry allowed the light from the courtyard and city park to flood in, giving the foyer an enchanting atmosphere. Rarely was there anyone in the building past sunset, let alone late into the evening, so few got to appreciate the view.

Grenin welcomed the sight and pushed the doors open. He headed down the steps and toward the blue brick road to his right, his mind still on the unsettling conversation with Master Harvol.

He glanced down at the Academy District, where the green bricks led, before approaching his destination.

People sold, traded, and practiced every manner of legal magic there, in the Divination District, also known as the Magic District, which had blue brick paving. Towering wooden cabins were mixed in with older brick and cobblestone structures along the street. It looked like an old fairy tale town and held the same atmosphere. Each sparkling blue and purple hue of lamplight illuminating the road made travelers aware that magic never slept here, and it brought a moment of peace to Grenin as he entered the district.

The shops on the street had been closed for an hour, so traffic was sparse. The clanking of his shoes echoed as he walked, and his thoughts returned to the discussion with the Grand Magus. Something about it was still tugging at his mind.

He made it a point not to jump at shadows, but some shadows were far more ominous than others, so he shouldn't toss them away carelessly. Granted, a lot was happening, for many reasons, but brushing off an ever-looming presence made Grenin reevaluate the situation.

It troubled him that the Grand Magus was not more concerned with the subject, but the munchkin never steered the council wrong. A few times, Grenin did not understand his reasoning until more came to light, but he wasn't sure if he could blindly put faith in his old friend's actions or lack thereof.

The news from Ragnus was far more pressing than some quakes, which could be a natural shift in the land. He knew in his gut that wasn't true, but out of respect for the Grand Magus's decision, he tried to keep his focus on the west.

He stopped and peered back at the citadel. Even in the distance, the shadows of the spires were massive and spread out all along the city. Clouds rolled in again, yet the moon was still visible, appearing as a ghostly face veiled by an uncertain gathering storm.

Grenin grimaced at the haunting green glow the spires had cast upon the thickening cloud cover. He wanted to trust the Grand Magus fully, but the few times he ignored that voice... that nagging pull in his stomach, things went wrong.

The right thing can be such an evil task.

He needed to get to Glinda.

He quickened his pace down the serene path, and the end of the Divination District came into view. It was the city's downtown area, better known as Sorcerer's Village, and Grenin's destination. Filled with restaurants, stores, and many galas, Sorcerer's Village was where most went for entertainment. Every evening offered some event.

The soft glow from inside a large two-story pub illuminated the cobblestones. The wooden sign hovering over the door of his favorite restaurant read *Night Grove Chalet.* Its words pulsed with a rose gold shine that showed they were glowing of their own volition.

Grenin pushed open the door, hoping for some respite from the events.

The warm ambiance of the candlelight and fireplace next to the front door washed over him. A tall woman with blond hair down to her shoulders in a sleek purple dress approached him with a smile on her lips.

"Master Apprentice, welcome back. Prime Minister Glinda is already here. Let me show you to your seat." She gestured toward the massive bow windows at the back of the restaurant.

"Thank you, Lissa." Grenin followed her and relaxed his shoulders, probably for the first time that day, but the atmosphere here always helped improve his mood.

They maneuvered through the quaint pub in front of the restaurant. The dark finish on the wood of the cabin-like structure would have made it feel more like a home, except for the extravagant additions. All along the walls, brass sconces clung. Magically suspended flames flickered over purple candlesticks that would never melt.

A mixture of long wooden tables and smaller round ones filled the middle. Purple velvet drapes, tied back with gold cords, separated the booths against the wall. Behind each booth, charming paintings of places all over the Land of Oz hung, and each one would change depending on the season.

Tonight, the paintings showed stormy weather, some covered in snow, but he noticed the paintings that showed the Spectral Woods were darker than normal. The black trees, void of leaves, contrasted with the brilliant snow. He must have stared at it longer than he thought; Lissa waited patiently at the top of the steps.

"I apologize," he said as he closed the gap between them.

"It's alright," she said, walking down the steps to the section overlooking downtown's beautiful lake.

"Lissa, the paintings show snow, but we are at least three months off from the first flake."

"We are just as baffled. It started a few weeks ago, but it was subtle. I believe the strange weather we are having is throwing them off."

Glinda looked even more radiant than the last time they spoke. She had pinned up much of her hair, with two strawberry-blond curled locks dangling on each cheek, framing her delicate features.

Her shoulders were bare, but chiffon sleeves flowed down to her wrists. The jade-green silk of her dress caught much of the light.

Grenin sat across from her, next to the massive windows that arched up to the ceiling. The glow from the spires and candles bathed the restaurant in a soft green, but Grenin only noticed her.

Lissa smiled before wishing them a good evening, and Grenin forced his focus to leave Glinda for a moment so as not to be impolite and nodded.

Glinda laughed softly. "What? Do I have something on my face?"

"No." He leaned forward and took her hand. "Being with you here is a welcome reprieve from everything. I'm going to enjoy it." His suit was well-tailored, but sitting across from such a woman, he felt he was in a beggar's clothing.

"I wish I could have made myself a bit more presentable." He laughed, running his fingers down his lapel.

"I would say you're dressed better than when we first met, and you caught my attention then, didn't you?"

"Fair enough." The light harp music played in the background as he stared into her blue eyes, the jade dress making them almost turquoise, and the stress melted from his limbs. He smiled, huffing a laugh in a way that asked how he could have been so lucky as to have found her.

"You're doing it again," she whispered.

"Oh, apologies. I seem to have lost myself."

A Munchkin server arrived with wine glasses in one hand and a bottle of the Master of Alchemy's latest concoction.

"Trelen! I'm glad we caught you on a night you're here." Grenin reached over, took the glasses from his student's hands, and placed them on the table. The young munchkin smiled and put the bottle next to the glasses.

"Evening, Professor Grenin." He turned to Glinda and bowed his head slightly. "Your grace. If you need anything this evening, let me know. I'm assuming the usual lamb and mint pies?"

"Yes, please. It's gotten rather chilly outside, hasn't it?" Grenin asked.

"Strangely so," Glinda said. "I had to bring my cloak."

"Our Master of Weather has found it strange, but he says it's nothing more than natural causes." Grenin offered as he reached forward and plucked the bottle and one glass from the table.

"Oh, Professor, allow me," Trelen said, but Grenin waved him away.

"I see how hard you work at the academy. I can pour our wine. It's a busy night." Grenin gestured toward the filled seats. Trelen gave him a thankful nod and shuffled off to another table.

Grenin finished pouring a glass and set it in front of Glinda. "The weather is just another reason for the pulling at my gut," he said, pouring his glass and setting down the bottle. "Speaking of which, I brought up some of my concerns to the Grand Magus."

"And?"

"You will not like it."

"I still want to know," she said before taking a long sip. Glinda was not one for intoxication, but she might need more wine than usual tonight.

Grenin took in the iridescent liquid in his glass, the Master of Alchemy's seasonal wine for the snowy months. In a subconscious or maybe fully conscious attempt at avoiding the subject, he sipped slowly.

He dropped his voice so that only she could hear him. With the other chatter, music, and their table being placed farthest away, she would be the only one able to hear. "He is concerned about the mountains in the west."

"Tell me the part I will not like first because, so far, we agree."

He sighed and took another sip. "I don't like his blowing off my concerns about the spires."

Her face instantly broke into a worried expression. She dropped her gaze into her glass and looked out over the lake. The green-painted storm brewing overhead reflected off the serene water.

"Why would he blow that off?" she whispered.

"One thing at a time is what he said."

Silence stretched between them. Grenin's mind fought over the dilemma that had plagued him since he left the citadel.

"I worry the Grand Magus may not be thinking everything through," he said, returning his attention to Glinda.

Her expression held slight shock. It was understandable. His doubting Magus Harvol privately was one thing, but to speak it aloud was a recognition of action needing to be made.

"I agree that this should not be discarded so callously, but..." she paused with concern. "I've seen that look before. What do you plan on doing?"

"The matter needs to be investigated. There are too many coincidences for my liking, and the more I think about the growing tremors and strange weather patterns, and now the news from the west?" He shook his head and stared at the hypnotic, swirling liquid. "He doesn't seem concerned about the spires and what they hold."

Grenin reached out and took Glinda's hand. "I can't risk the safety of the entire land and everyone here. Sometimes... the right thing can be such an evil task."

The war raging inside built in his gaze, and she squeezed his hand. Going against the Grand Magus was treason, and they both knew it. However, the possibility of their losing everything they had built was far too great, and drastic actions needed to be taken, including making himself a villain to the council if he had to.

"If the parliament sees how he is on the subject, they will panic, and there will be a division among us. That is the last thing we need right now," Glinda said, leaning back in her chair.

"I'm aware, and that is why I will do what I can to see if anything is being kept from us. I'll have one of my apprentices investigate the matter subtly."

Grenin noticed Trelen navigating his way to them and placed a polite smile on his face. A purple light burst out next to him and formed a small table. Seconds later, their lamb-mint pies popped into existence. Trelen took both and placed one in front of Glinda and then Grenin. He bowed, wished them a pleasant meal, and then headed to another table.

"It will be okay, Glinda." He did not know if he was saying it more for his comfort or hers, but her shoulders relaxed.

"I just hope the meeting tomorrow morning doesn't turn sour. People filled the parliament to witness the destructive capabilities of. . ." She picked up her fork and shook her head.

"I know, and we will endure now as we endured then, yes? We knew this could become a problem again, and now it's on our doorstep. What we do now will paint the future for everyone. We cannot panic," he said, grabbing his fork. The pie smelled divine, but the subject messed with his appetite. Once he took a bite, the gravy, lamb, potatoes, and mint jelly gave him some of his warmth back.

"I put my trust in you as I always have." She broke the top crust of the pie.

The atmosphere, company, and food relieved some of their stress, and their conversation turned to more pleasant subjects: music, entertainment, and upcoming events at the academy.

They finished their meal, paid the bill, and left, feeling better than when they had entered, but the glow from the spires was a constant reminder. They walked along the blue and purple-lit path. Weeping willows lined the banks, flicking their limbs in the occasional evening breeze. The air had a crisp feel, and the smell of rain permeated the air. The rumbling thunder rolled over the poppy fields surrounding the city gates.

Glinda slipped her hand into Grenin's as they walked, keeping her cloak tight around her. The night fell colder with each passing hour, and they would have to go home soon. She admired the trees and tiny insects, like magical fireflies, each a different color, painting the leaves in a mystical rainbow of illumination.

"Are you sure you don't regret this?" Grenin's question yanked her from her thoughts.

"Regret what?"

"This." He gestured between them.

"Why would I ever regret that?"

"I know how badly you wanted children, and I feel I've done you a disservice."

She stopped and drew him closer. She bent toward him, kissed him softly, and pulled away to look him in the eyes.

"I'd be missing everything if you were not in my life. No, I regret nothing between us, and I never will." She made to stand, but he pulled her back and kissed her again.

He planted another kiss on her cheek, and they continued down the path.

The nightly fireworks began. Created by magic, they exploded silently, and the live music played in the large pavilion flooded the air.

As they approached the music, Grenin glanced at Glinda, thinking of the first day they had met in Munchkin City so many years prior. Thankful for every moment, good and bad, his face broke into a smile.

# Chapter 11

Lucian woke to a frantic tapping on his door. He had been staying at the small tavern in the older part of Munchkin City. He liked the old wood cabin, and the family that ran it was a cheerful brood, always welcoming the weary traveler with a bottle of ale and warm stew.

No one at the inn should be up at this hour. Even the patrons with too much ale had passed out either on a tavern bench or in their rooms.

The tapping came again, accompanied by a soft caw on the other side of the door. The noise finally registered. It was one of his crows. He forced himself out of bed. In his groggy state, he shuffled to the door, tripping over one of his boots.

The years had changed him, but for the better, in his opinion. The Scarecrow had replaced his coarse old straw with sweet meadow hay. Some friends within the academy gladly offered to freshen his burlap skin to something more human-like.

The magic available and the student's abilities surprised him. Until his time in the city, he did not know such options existed. When he finished, his midnight blue stitching, soft, long grass, and black leaves that formed his shoulder-length hair were the only parts that revealed his true nature. A braided strand of hair adorned with black crow feathers and magically rune-carved silver beads rested over his left eye. He plucked the leaves from trees within the Spectral Woods, and they exuded a "positive power," as the magic students called it. Not everything within the forest was negative or evil.

As he stumbled across the room, he stayed light on his feet. He opened the door to his crow perched on a nearby sconce, making as little noise as possible. "Amon."

The bird landed on his shoulder and began twittering and clicking. He glanced down the end of the hallway and noticed the open window before shutting the door behind him. Once the information came to Lucian, he leaned against the wall and slid down, his hand going to his head. He looked at his bare chest. An amulet with a swirling deep blue iris behind the silhouette of a crow hung there, and he just stared. Over and over, he heard, "Movement in the western mountains." The message Ragnus had traveled from the plains to relay to the city made him anxious.

Amon dropped from his shoulder and perched on his knee. The crow pulled at his pant leg, and Lucian offered the bird an apologetic smile. He stood and grabbed a strawberry from the table, pulled a few small pieces off, and fed them to him as Amon moved to perch back onto his shoulder.

"I'm sorry to ask you to hurry back, but I need you to tell Grenin that I'll be traveling by sunrise. I will inform the Munchkin City Council representative of what you told me. Return to me when you are done. I should be almost back by then."

The crow squawked and fluttered over to the windowsill. Lucian grabbed his purple silk poet shirt and slid it on before flipping the window latch and pushing it open. Amon flew into the early morning chill.

Lucian closed the window and started throwing things into his large brown satchel—two books and his personal effects. He tied the satchel shut, let the flap fall over the opening, and then latched the flap to the bag. He tossed the bag onto the chair, picked up his boots, sat on his bed, and slid one on.

Lucian stared at the dying embers in the fireplace as he slid on the second boot, the early-morning message making him queasy. Lingering too long could prove an issue, so his movements were swift. He scanned the small tavern room. Satisfied that he had gathered all his belongings, he grabbed the brass key and shut the door, careful to make little noise when he locked it.

Nothing but closed and sleeping doors greeted him in the hall. He watched his footsteps on the wooden flooring. On the staircase, something dark flickered in the corner of his eye. He stopped and watched for a few moments. Lucian gathered it was a natural shadow in the hallway's lamplight and went to the inn's entrance.

He left a note with his room key on the front desk announcing his departure before heading to the front door of the tavern.

The chill hit him far worse when he stepped fully into it. Lucian gripped his satchel, swung it over his shoulder, and headed for the headmistress's cottage behind the school. It was a considerably extensive structure for a city of this size, but with the growth of the Emerald City, prosperity came to the land. Something he had been thankful for.

He followed the small red brick road around the school to her dwelling. Lucian sighed, not wanting to wake her up at this hour, but he knocked softly on the door. After a few moments, someone inside shuffled. Lucian waited, shifting his weight, the severity of the news sinking in more and more.

The door opened, and an older munchkin with long braided silver hair and a lush red robe opened it. She squinted and tilted her head, then motioned impatiently for him to come in.

"Headmistress Virta." He nodded and ducked through the door. Once inside, he still hunched over a bit. He was thankful her magical light fixtures were on the walls.

"Lucian, what are you doing here so early? We don't even have class today," she said, shutting the door. "I'll get some hot tea for you. It's rather cold out." She walked to the kitchen.

Lucian followed. "Grenin sent a message. He sent Amon." The headmistress stopped cold and turned.

"What's wrong?" She asked, her tone tight.

"Ragnus came to the Emerald City. There's been movement in the witch's castle in the western mountains. They've requested my return under the circumstances."

"I don't disagree," she said, grabbing a teapot, filling it with water, and setting it on the stove. She snapped her fingers, and the burners lit. "Do you have enough rations for two days?"

"I can manage." He adjusted the bag on his shoulder.

"I would prefer you did better than just manage. I'm giving you some things to take with you." She rifled through cabinets, some filled with foods, teas, and other more magical items.

"That... that really won't be necessary. I don't want to. . ." He paused as she turned and looked at him.

"I'm giving you this stuff to take, and you will take it. Along with some of this tea, I'm making. It will help in keeping you moving and warm."

Defeated, Lucian nodded but smirked. Headmistress Virta had been a fantastic teacher for many years and was the mother of seven. Two of her children sat on the council; her oldest was the Master of Alchemy. Scarecrow knew better than to tell a concerned mother not to worry. He always appreciated her kindness and accepted every jar of magical stuff and bag of food she pushed into his hands.

The pouch, packed to the brim, was not too heavy, something he was thankful for since he would lug it with him for two days. He set it on the ground at his feet. Typically, someone would have offered an invitation to sit, but they didn't have time.

The teapot whistled, and Virta grabbed it. She poured the hot water into a cup she'd prepared with magical herbs, honey, and tea leaves grown and harvested by the tundra Pridyr clans. They called this mixture snow leaf, and the tea leaves had magical properties.

Lucian only had tea twice, as it was challenging to get. It had a smooth flavor and could warm someone out of frostbite.

She slid the cup into his hand, and he drank. A hint of mint, berries, and honey filled his mouth. He closed his eyes as warmth flushed through him. If he was not fully awake before, he was now. He gave a contented sigh and returned the empty cup to her.

"Thank you," he said and smiled.

"Travel safe, Lucian. Please tell Grenin I'll be making appropriate preparations here, and I'll relay what you've told me to the mayor." She took his hand in hers; concern was plain on her aged face.

"I will, I promise. I'll return once things have settled." He squeezed her hand and moved toward the door.

When he opened the door, he turned back, and the headmistress was making her tea. Neither of them were getting back to sleep soon. He smiled again and quietly shut the door behind him.

He walked up the path to the main road, the yellow and red bricks mixing with blues and greens. Lucian stepped off the multicolor mix of bricks and onto the main yellow one leading to the Emerald City. Something pulled at his mind, strong enough that it caused his steps to cease.

Next to the yellow brick road was a monument—a remembrance of a fateful day preserved by the city. A house that, despite having crash-landed, remained intact for its age. It seemed like a lifetime had passed since Dorothy's Kansas house had fallen on the Wicked Witch of the East, but the structure still stood.

Only the pieces of the porch showed signs of damage. Special curators preserved the location weekly to ensure that no animals or other unsavory creatures from the forest took up residence inside.

Lucian placed his hand on the fence and surveyed the sight. Despite the longing he felt for his old friends, he was awash in a sense of dread. This location had been such a place of positivity and associated with the freeing of Munchkin City, but all he felt was anguish.

A light flickered below the porch. It started as a singular green flash but quickly covered the soil like electric glitter.

He fixated on the softly pulsating light. He dropped his hand from the fence and gripped the strap of his satchel. A piercing wind burst from the house, blowing the shutters and door open with a hiss. He turned away from the icy wind. The gust lasted only a few seconds, and the house turned silent again.

Something pulled at his mind, dark. A guttural voice unlike any he had ever heard. An ethereal echo spoke directly into his ear.

*They . . . belong . . . to us. . . .*

Lucian spun, wondering if he had heard the words spoken or if they had been projected directly into his mind. He backed away from the house and hurriedly started his two-day journey to the Emerald City.

The words did not leave him as he put more distance between himself and Dorothy's old house, but they became fainter.

*They... belong... to us...*
*They... belong... to us...*
*They... belong... to us...*

The whispers finally ceased as he left Munchkin City, but the words kept repeating in his mind.

# Chapter 12

The seventh bell tolled, echoing through the citadel, marking the time for many important meetings to begin. Still, the meeting in the main council chambers was the focus of the Magus Council and Emerald Parliament.

The Magus Council chamber in the northern wing resembled the one where the members had met the day before, but someone had decorated the walls with stained glass windows that had sparkling magical lights behind them. These glass art pieces showed many magical elements—fire, wind, water, soil, rock, soul, and spiritual energies. The colors bathed the room in a warm and welcoming feel. They put wine, water, and a couple of bottles of unknown liquid in the middle of the table.

The double doors flew open, and the rest of the council and parliament entered.

Everyone walked around the table to their respective seats, an arrangement that mirrored that of other meeting chambers. Glinda pushed her glass aside and sat. Her purple silk covered everything except her shoulders and neck. Her slender fingers intertwined, and her gaze met the Grand Magus's.

He tucked his colorful robes of dark blues and greens with teal accents under him and settled into his seat. He accepted a glass of wine that Grenin had poured for him. The master apprentice sipped at his glass.

Grand Magus Harvol stood, placed his hands firmly on the table, and sighed.

"The information brought to us by General Ragnus is grave and should not be taken lightly," he said, and a few murmurs of agreement circulated the room.

"Grand Magus, what will the council's path be in this trying time?" Glinda asked.

"We've decided to send some of our own to aid General Ragnus, not just to look deeper into this and find information, but on the chance that she has returned, they will need magical support."

"What of the Pridyr mystics?" a parliament member asked.

"Though powerful, their magic is different, literally. I would rather err on the side of caution and send some of our own to help. I would feel responsible if the clans faced more than they could handle, and we didn't send aid."

The parliament member nodded. Others simply listened.

The room was tense. The pregnant pauses between each statement made Grenin feel like he was swimming through emotional rapids.

Grenin stood. "I know I have clarified that Flint, or Tin Man as some of you still know him, was not to be disturbed. After much contemplation of this issue's severity, we must send him with our counsel to aid General Ragnus."

Glinda's eyes widened momentarily, but he had reasons for changing his mind. She would not question his tactics. There was always a method to his madness.

"What is the reasoning for this, Master-Apprentice?" another parliament member asked.

"We all know what the witch and her minions are capable of. We watched her and her late sister terrorize many villages and cities. They kidnapped and used everyone and everything they could for their magic. Not all those goblins were goblins once."

A few gasps from Parliament told him not everyone was knowledgeable about the genuine horror. He politely raised his hand to calm the room.

"The council is more than aware of the magic she and her people possess. Flint has been working furiously to help our defense of the land over the past few years. I know he's ready to put some of his inventions to work."

Those present calmed slightly. Well, as calmly as one can, knowing a great evil may have resurfaced. Grenin nodded to the Grand Magus as he sat. He glanced at Glinda. Behind her was a window showing the towering spires. Usually, it flicked between emerald green and jade, but a shadow quickly passed over the spires, and he squinted. He shook his head and hoped this was just a potent batch of winter plum wine.

"I'd like to turn the floor over to our prime minister." The Grand Magus gestured to Glinda and sat.

With her hands clasped in front of her, she rose. "There's something we must address before leaving this meeting today. The weather shifts and tremors are not natural causes, and neither our council nor students of magic are responsible. I'm concerned, as is the rest of the parliament, that these issues have not been addressed."

Much agreeing chatter circulated through parliament and the council, but some raised rather loud concerns. All fell silent as the Grand Magus stood once more.

"I understand your concerns, Prime Minister, but I assure you the council is aware of these odd shifts and is looking into them. Also, there has been no confirmation that they aren't just natural causes. We have since paused our pursuit of knowledge with that subject because of what General Ragnus brought us yesterday."

"Yes, but what of the days before? What did they accomplish or discover? The Emerald Parliament has given us nothing but silence when we have asked you or the council for information about either of these issues."

"I understand this, Prime Minister, but as you know, sometimes the council, because of magical investigations such as these, prefers not to come forward until we have a better answer than 'we think.' We want to bring what we know. As of right now, we have found no source."

Grenin remained seated while agitated conversations swept through the room. As the distressed chatter hit a crescendo, he stood, and the meeting chambers silenced. With his eyes still cast down, he passed behind each occupant's seat.

"The council does its best to bring information that isn't just to pacify the Emerald Parliament and the citizens of our fair city, but considering these rather odd events happening so closely, I believe it may be folly for us to turn our attention to the west completely." He stopped when he reached the middle and looked at the council member sitting there.

"Balanor, would you be so kind as to pass me that blue bottle?" The man grabbed the one with the pear-shaped bottom and handed it to Grenin.

The munchkin started walking back to his seat as he took the bottle and refilled the glass in his hand. "That is why, out of respect for our Grand Magus's wishes and to ease our parliament brethren, I'd like to volunteer my services and investigate this matter."

The members consented, but the Grand Magus's expression didn't change.

"No." The Grand Magus's answer came down like a sledgehammer. All attention turned back to him.

There was no question. They needed to take more extreme measures to protect the land, and one word forced the Master Apprentice into an unfavorable position. The parliament and the council in the Land of Oz had never experienced this kind of divide. There had always been bickering and disagreements, but the finality of the Grand Magus's statement today was the first time that Master Harvol was not open to debate.

"Very well, Grand Magus," Grenin said as he sat, his focus returning to the liquid in his glass. He slid the bottle back onto the table in front of him.

"Grand Magus Harvol, everyone who sits at this table knows the energies and magics within the spire could very well cause these odd shifts, and now with the witch," Glinda said.

"The witch is more than capable of rising on her own with no involvement from the spires." He looked about the room and placed his palms firmly on the table. "With all due respect to the parliament and you, Prime Minister, we must handle one thing at a time."

"I think you're focusing on the wrong issue first," Glinda said civilly.

"I understand that, and from what I can see, the parliament agrees with you, but a threat that's more than a change in weather patterns and the land shaking occasionally has become apparent. We need to focus on the most prominent issue at our door."

Over his wineglass, Grenin saw a flicker in the Grand Magus's amulet.

The movement was subtle, but a glance around the table assured him he was the only one who saw it. He squinted to see if another shadow would cross it, but everything was normal.

"What if the incidents connect?" Glinda asked.

"A dangerous assumption, and one that has no backing. A distraction that could cause a bleeding wound to our side." Master Harvol countered.

"I'm not trying to discredit the concern to the west," Glinda said. "But we all know what will happen if the spires fall."

"We also know what will happen if the witch gains power again," said the Grand Magus with a tone of seriousness and a hint of terror.

There was no talking to him. He was not entirely wrong, so Glinda and the parliament remained politely seated. Still, no one seemed comfortable ignoring the possibility that the spires could cause these magical interruptions.

"Then, Grand Magus, the parliament shall respect the council's wishes and support in sending aid to General Ragnus." She leaned back in her chair.

She sensed the parliament's strain. Although they would not speak out openly at such a meeting, there would be unrest in their meeting later that afternoon.

"We have settled it. Grenin, I need you to choose those who will go west. Please send a message to Flint, preparing him for his journey." The Grand Magus stepped around his chair and gestured for the council to follow him.

Grenin was the last to stand. He downed the rest of his wine and glanced up at Glinda. The doubt in her eyes matched his.

He slid the glass onto the table and gave the parliament a forced half-smile before slipping through the door.


It would be an understatement to say that Grenin was displeased with the meeting. His jaw tightened, and he stood at the window, his hands folded behind his back.

"Master Grenin," a soft female voice jolted him out of his thoughts. Standing next to him was a woman of average human height with a troubled expression.

"Ah, yes, Umiko." He turned toward her and bowed his head. "The last conversation we had early this morning?"

"Yes?" she said, her fingers fidgeting.

"We must speak further about that part of your training. Do you have a few moments?" Grenin inquired with a smile.

"I-I have no more classes for today, Master Grenin."

"Excellent, follow me." He gestured with his hand.

Down the hallway, the two went to a meditation room. The room had an entire wall filled with concoctions from the Master of Alchemy, with no tables or chairs. The style of the decor was the same as that of the other rooms throughout the citadel, but the hanging artwork was a mix of colorful sculptures built directly into the wooden wall and more stained glass. They all showed images of magic, swirling colors, and flickering lights. Some moved as they walked over the large purple and black rug on the wood floor. Soft purple, blue, and green cushions lying about the room and the free-floating lights gave the entire area a mystical feel.

Grenin headed for a beautiful silver, purple, and black tapestry on the back wall. He waved his hand over it, and the cloth flipped up, revealing a small door.

Umiko looked back and stopped her fidgeting to secure the entrance before she followed him through the secret door. The tapestry fell back into place behind them.

Grenin snapped his fingers, producing a sparkling blue light at his fingertips that helped light their way in the short hallway.

Once they reached the door, he snuffed out the light and waved his hand counterclockwise before flicking his fingers. He unlatched the door with his push, and it creaked open.

As Umiko crossed the threshold and slid the door shut, her hands stopped fidgeting, and she took on a calmer demeanor that alluded to her fidgeting being more of an act to mislead others.

"Things must be severe if we are to speak here, Master Grenin," she said, sitting on one of the large, round blue cushions. The same soft lights glinted in her amber-colored, almond-shaped eyes. Her shoulder-length black hair reflected the blue lights, giving her an ethereal glow. Her lavender robes hugged her lithe form as she adjusted her position on the cushion.

"It's unfortunate, but you're correct." He leaned down and opened a cabinet in the far corner. Grenin pulled out two small bottles and uncorked both, then slipped one into her hand and flopped down onto a silver cushion beside her. The thick red liquid shimmered as it moved, and he wasted no time taking his first sip. His face scrunched. "Oh, this one is strong."

Umiko took a sip as well and coughed. She cracked an embarrassed smile and held the bottle on her lap between her palms.

"You weren't kidding. Does this one have any effect? Other than intoxication?" she snickered.

"Not so much intoxication, more mental clarity among other magical enhancements. Primarily, it keeps your aura neutral for twenty-four hours."

"What?"

"It will help you with the task I have for you." He gulped down more of the red liquid.

"It tastes of night cherries," she said before taking another sip and squinting. "But why would I need it?"

"The Grand Magus has given me the job of picking out the council members who will travel to Flint's cabin and then to the west."

"He trusts you. We know this. That's an important task."

Grenin nodded, his gaze downward.

"Umiko, I know you've noticed the strange weather patterns, the tremors, the magical shifts. What is your take on it?"

She was hesitant in responding.

"I, uh..." She leaned forward on her cushion, set the bottle at her feet, and placed her elbows on her knees. "Something isn't right. I've felt the shift in the magical frequencies, and... it's dark. I fear for the land if my gut is correct."

He let out a long sigh. He was happy to see his student in tune with her ability, but that solidified his concerns.

"How many others feel this?"

"A few. Though we don't speak about it around Zellik."

Curiously, the munchkin eyed her, perplexed. "Why is that?"

"Do you remember Christof?"

"Of course. He recently dropped out of an apprenticeship and returned to the academy to study. Why?"

"What about Loren?"

"Yes. Wasn't she also returned to the academy?"

Grenin turned toward her. "A few apprentices have recently returned to the academy."

Umiko nodded, grabbing the bottle. She took a long swig before nestling the glass into the rug.

Grenin sat back, stunned. It was not uncommon for an apprentice to decide to change the course of their studies or show that they weren't ready, but there had been an influx of such situations as of late.

"They spoke out about their feelings on the matter, and each time, it was in front of Zellik. He promptly reported the incident to the Grand Magus. The next day, the apprentices had disappeared from the citadel and the apprentice chambers." She looked at Grenin with unease.

"Now that you mention it, I haven't even seen them at the academy. I assumed they weren't taking my courses and had different schedules." Grenin's brow furrowed.

"No one has seen them. That's the issue; everyone who has noticed is too scared to say anything. Even some of the council members."

"Why has no one said anything to me, Umiko?" The concern was deep in his features, making him look more his age as the stress wore on him.

"We felt you might also be too close to the Grand Magus. Many of us don't know what to do, Master Grenin." She looked down into her hands, her shoulders slumping.

Grenin reached over and encased her hands in his as a worried father would. "Look at me, Umiko."

She lifted her head, tears gathering in her eyes. One slipped down her cheek.

"What are we going to do? So many strange things have been happening, and it seems to be gaining speed."

"Listen, the Prime Minister and I are fully aware something is off. The entire parliament is on edge because of it, and the dismissive attitude of the Grand Magus is something we cannot ignore. You and the others are not alone. I need to know who else has been in the shadows on this."

Her brow furrowed, and her eyes met her lap once more. "Councilman Balanor, Councilwoman Verria, Councilman Arken, and there are some apprentices spread among the masters who whisper the same concerns, though all of your apprentices feel the same as I do."

"I understand why none of you came to me, but I wish you had. Your task is ready, and then you'll go west with the group. I will send the names you mentioned and some apprentices."

"But isn't that dangerous? What if the witch truly has returned? How can we face her?" Umiko grabbed the bottle and studied it in her fingers, an attempt to distract even slightly from the situation.

"I have confidence in your abilities. You should as well. Nowhere is safe anymore. If the spires were to fall, it would be far more dangerous here than with Flint and General Ragnus. If you reveal your true feelings, I want you safely away from Zellik and the Grand Magus." Grenin tensed his jaw and decided not to continue his thought.

She nodded, taking another drink. "What task did you need from me?" She set the empty bottle on the rug.

Grenin pulled a small blue stone from his inner jacket pocket. "Do you know what this is?"

"A stone of insight." She looked at it in awe. "Only masters may possess and use them. I've only studied them. They are powerful little creations."

"Your studies serve you well. Are you aware of what its purpose is?"

"Yes, you set them in a place, and they gather all information provided within that area. An enchantment activates the moment you set it down."

"Do you know this enchantment?"

She looked like a child who had gotten their hand caught in the cookie jar.

"Yes, I may have been reading some books beyond my teachings in class."

Grenin laughed and shook his head. "Have you put it into practice?"

"I won't get into details, but yes, I've had to use a stone of insight recently, and I could make it work properly."

Umiko was always ambitious in knowledge and could be a loose cannon, but a friendly spirit lived beyond her more chaotic demeanor.

"I would do this myself, except the Grand Magus is becoming wary of my prodding. I need you to slip this into his office. You're one of my students closest to finishing and becoming a council member. It would make more sense for you to request an audience with him than for others. Plus, with your particular... skill set, you're the best for the task."

"You mean being a thief and sometimes a scoundrel."

"Eh, let's not get into specifics, shall we?" He chuckled, and Umiko's strained features finally broke into a soft smile.

She tilted her head as she looked at the stone, and he held it out to her.

"Umiko, I would not ask you to do this unless the entire land and its people were in danger. I do not want to do this either. Grand Magus Harvol is not just our leader but also an old friend of mine. It hurts my heart to do such a thing, but I don't believe he is thinking clearly. I fear there may be more going on."

A long, strained silence followed. He gauged she was allowing everything to sink in. She took the stone from him and turned it over with her fingers.

"I will do this for the good of the land and its people, Master Grenin. However, it is against everything we both believe in. This is treason."

"Perhaps that's true, but we might lose everything if we don't act now. The storm gathers. I'd rather cast myself out for treason than sit idly."

Thunder shook the citadel's foundation, and they looked at the ceiling. Unease sank into the serene atmosphere.

"When do we leave?"

"This afternoon. Make sure this is in his office before you and the others depart. I will retrieve it in the morning. I have a meeting with him so that it won't be anything spontaneous or out of the ordinary."

"Won't we be traveling into the evening? Through the Spectral Woods? Isn't that dangerous?"

"Although the Grand Magus focuses on the west, his concerns are valid. We cannot waste any more time. You should reach Flint's cabin before true night sets in."

Umiko stood, placing the stone into a small coin satchel attached to her hip by a white ribbon. "I will have this done, and myself prepared to leave by the afternoon."

"I will send for the others. Meet in the meditation room when you get the summons to depart. I must prepare the rest to leave; only a few hours remain."

She nodded, but her hands fidgeted again. She crossed the room and exited the small door before Grenin could gather their empty bottles. He heard the door shut, and the severity of the situation settled into his mind. Things would never be the same.

# Chapter 13

It was fifteen minutes from the bus stop to Dorothy's third-floor studio apartment. It wasn't a terrible spot, but it would not be luxurious either. Her neighbors were starving artist types and small families, so it was not bad, just struggling.

She stepped in, turned on the light, and set her keys, apron, and purse on the small table next to the front door. Her full-size bed sat against the wall, giving the tiny space an open center. The kitchen and bathroom were directly next to each other, and her television, no larger than a computer monitor, sat on the bar connecting the kitchen to the rest of the room. The place was not much, but it was hers and away from everyone.

She walked over to the bed and fell flat on her stomach, her face buried in the one pillow she owned. She embraced it like a friend she hadn't seen in years and inhaled a breath of relief.

Dorothy made it a point not to think of what had happened earlier. She'd had another episode on her way to work, which set up the rest of the day as stressful chaos. She needed peace of mind since, most of the time, she was in a constant state of stress and worry. Just as she drifted from the waking world, a familiar face flashed in her mind. A pair of kind blue eyes peered at her, but they were not as soft and pleasant as she remembered. They showed pain and tears.

Glinda had reached out to her, begging for help. Dorothy's brow furrowed as the disturbing vision continued. Green electricity shot across her mind's eye, burning green streaks into her inward vision.

Something invisible yet dark stood between Dorothy and the Good Witch, peering at her, but then she saw the old Wicked Witch step from a swirling oblivion next to Glinda. A bright red blur followed the Wicked Witch, and a dominant black aura figure hovered at the edge of her sight.

Another green flash erased the scene but brought her yet another horrific vision. Dorothy froze. A massive black oak's trunk pinned a man who resembled Scarecrow against it. Two monstrous winged monkeys loomed over his pinned form.

Green sparks shot through her vision again. A bloodied battlefield and the Cowardly Lion limping and dragging a wounded Pridyr with him replaced the Scarecrow. This spun into the Tin Man sitting in front of a log cabin, a small gathering around his fire pit, with everyone present turning their faces to the sky as a violent storm rolled in.

That is when she heard that cackle of laughter that had haunted her dreams almost nightly through her childhood and still found her many years later. Dorothy knew that laugh all too well, and there was no question. This was no dream; it was a warning.

Her eyes flew wide. Sweat soaked her pillow, and her grip on the thing turned her knuckles white. She pushed up from the bed, her breathing labored. Her gaze moved to the sliding glass door of the tiny balcony. The sun had long since set.

Dorothy slid off the bed and stumbled over to the bathroom, shaking, lost somewhere between the waking world and a living nightmare. She flipped the light on and leaned her shoulder against the doorframe. She could not bring herself to look at her reflection, and her stomach dropped from fear of what she would find if she did.

Long moments passed, and she slowed her breathing. She finally looked in the mirror only when the remnants of her nightmare lifted.

Her hair stuck to her head, sweat dried, and her bloodshot eyes showed she had been crying. Given what she remembered, she didn't doubt she had been.

With the intake of a deep, shuddering breath to calm herself, she turned away.

The cackle echoed through her mind, and no matter what she did, she could not shake the sound or the queasy feeling clawing at her gut. The laughter faded slightly, and a voice she knew all too well spoke one sentence.

"You didn't think this was the end, did you?"

Before she could retreat from her reflection, the glass fogged over from the other side of the mirror. Black clouds with streaks of brilliant green electricity closed in, removing everything but Dorothy's terrified expression. Her mind screamed to run, but her body would not listen.

That horrid laughter surrounded her, and it grew to an octave she was sure would cause the neighbors to call the police.

Her wide-eyed reflection suddenly shifted and gave way to hauntingly familiar eyes, and before she could mentally process what she was seeing, the bathroom mirror exploded.

Dorothy turned her face away in time and dropped to her knees. Glittering shrapnel hit more of the shower curtain and toilet than her body. She scampered out of the bathroom and into the tiny entryway, and she collapsed, her hands still clutching the sides of her head. Huddled on the floor, panting, she stared at the bathroom.

She thought she heard her name from one neighbor outside her door, but it wasn't easy to make out anything over the cackle.


The emergency services came and went, leaving Dorothy alone, sitting on her bed with an empty cup of tea, just staring at the glass-glittered carpet.

The firefighters found no explanation for the mirror's destruction, and after seeing the medication from her doctor on the bathroom floor, they asked if she had done it. She didn't go into detail, but she tried to convince them it wasn't her. After a few exchanged words, the men insisted she call her doctor. Reluctantly, she complied. Her doctor sent for her aunt, whom she now waited for.

A rap on the door pulled her from her thoughts. She let the blanket slip back onto the bed and opened the door.

"Aunt Em."

The woman pushed through the door and hugged her. "What have you done this time, Dorothy? How bad is the damage?" Her voice shook with concern.

"I'm not sure what happened, but it's just a shattered mirror, nothing else." She sighed and wiggled out of her aunt's embrace.

"Have you been taking the new prescription?"

"Yes," she huffed, flopping back onto the bed. She grabbed the blanket and wrapped it around herself. Aunt Em hobbled over to the mirror. She stopped just outside the door.

"Do you have a vacuum?"

"In the hall closet," she said, pointing toward the front door.

The vacuum was strategically placed in front of the box containing folded clothes. Aunt Em pulled the vacuum from the closet and began cleaning the mess.

Dorothy stared at the carpet, lost in her thoughts. The only thing she heard was that laugh. Images flashed through her head, each moment replaying vividly and gruesomely as if she were watching it happen all over again. The sound of someone clearing their throat snapped her back to her aunt standing over her.

"Your uncle and I have been doing better at the farm financially, so we wanted to set you up for a few days in a pleasant hotel just outside the city. I talked with Dr. Boyde, and he already contacted your employer, who put you on medical leave. We all feel some time away from the city, and a break from your daily routine would do you some good."

Dorothy blinked in response. She didn't know how she should feel about a forced leave of absence; they hadn't even consulted her. However, the evening's events showed her she needed a break. Something was causing these episodes to get worse. Maybe it was just stress.

"Let me pack a few things." She moved about her apartment like a ghost, grasping for past comforts, plucking necessities, and tossing them on her bed. She bent down on one knee and pulled a duffel bag from under her bed. Her aunt shuffled about the room as Dorothy placed her clothes, toiletries, and medication in her bag.

"I think that's everything," the older woman said, turning off the light in the bathroom.

Dorothy glanced at the dark room, and her skin crawled. She wanted to run toward the door. Instead, she slipped the duffle bag strap over her shoulder and grabbed her purse and keys from the entry table.

"I'm ready. Let's go, Aunt Em."

The windows shook as they walked down the long hallway to the stairs on the other side.

"Boy, these storms are getting worse this fall, aren't they?"

Dorothy looked out the window next to her apartment door, streaks of water forming gentle patterns on the glass, the rain making pinging noises on the roof. "I have a feeling it's only just begun," she said with a timid shake in her voice. Her aunt continued marching down the hall, and Dorothy pulled the strap in toward herself, hoping a tighter grip would comfort her.

"We were going to have you return to the farm, but Dr. Boyde said it might only inflame your condition."

*Inflame her condition.* The words stung, and she forced back tears. A broken woman and a burden were all she had become.

With her shoulders slumped, Dorothy followed her aunt to the old pickup truck. They made it moments before the parking meter expired.

"I think you'll like this hotel. It's just twenty minutes from the city in a quiet suburban town." Aunt Em paused for a moment, but Dorothy remained silent. "We put a little extra funds in your account as well. You must do everything you can to...".

"What if it's not just stress, Aunt Em?"

"Then we address it as we get more information. Worrying about things we don't know about is pointless. One thing at a time." She gave Dorothy a single nod.

They didn't speak again until they arrived at the hotel. Aunt Em walked her to her room on the second floor and wished her niece well. She hugged her and left her in a lovely room.

There was one bed, a bathroom, and a television — all she needed for a few days. She noticed some pretty ponds and parks surrounding the property, and she'd brought a couple of books she'd been meaning to read, but all she wanted to do was crawl into the freshly made bed and forget the day ever happened.

Dorothy hoped this much-needed time off and her new prescription would silence the dreams, even for a short time. She slipped into a deep sleep, her body relaxing for the first time in days.

# Chapter 14

Grenin opened the large doors to the parliament's main chambers. Glinda looked up from the oval table, and the rest of the parliament stared at Grenin with wide eyes.

"Prime Minister, please forgive this interruption, but I must speak with the parliament immediately." He folded his hands in front of him.

"Of course, Master Apprentice, please." She gestured for him to sit at the table, but he turned and waved his hand over the door handles in an intricate pattern that would not be easily replicated, locking the doors magically.

"Apologies to the Prime Minister and the parliament. Please remain calm. To prevent interruptions or eavesdropping is my intent. I want to address the meeting earlier with the council. I'm here to listen to the parliament and its concerns, along with openly apologizing for certain behaviors of the council and its members."

A few looked uncomfortable with his presence, but most of the parliament knew Grenin.

"I think you already know the parliament's stance on the conversation earlier. We are concerned the Grand Magus is not taking everything seriously," a middle-aged woman said from across the table.

"Rightly so, and I have found that the parliament is not the only one that holds the same concerns."

"I have since spoken to a few members of the council and my apprentices. Not all of us will look the other way, and I wanted to assure the parliament of this so as not to split ourselves in this trying time. We must stay united, or we will lose everything we've worked to build."

An older gentleman next to him clasped his hands. "But how can we do such a thing if our trust in the Grand Magus is waning? It's obvious that this news from the West clouds his mind."

"That is why I'm here. We must maintain unity and do our best to support the council's decision." Grenin sighed and placed his palms on the table's glossy surface. "And do our best not to break the council's trust in the process or create more turmoil."

"Someone should remove him from his position!" a young man shouted.

Chaotic yelling and shocked gasps erupted before Glinda tapped on the table, returning the room to silence.

"The Grand Magus is a wise leader, and it's because of him, Grenin, me, and a couple of others on the council that the spires exist. We are the ones who put the securities in place, and Dorothy brought us peace." Her name hung in the air. It was apparent they missed her.

It was quiet until a voice broke through the room's stillness. "Do we have any information about Dorothy?"

Glinda and Grenin exchanged looks. "As most of you know, the ability to move between worlds is a chaotic magic that has yet to be harnessed," she said. "It happens sporadically, and the only thing to understand about it is that it happens with an intense emotional reaction. We briefly opened a vision portal many years back and saw her... struggling, but safe."

"If the witch has returned, Dorothy is not safe if she comes here." Grenin pushed back from the table. "She may not be safe on Earth either, but at least harder to get a hold of."

"The witch is vengeful," the older gentleman said.

"She is, but the rules of magic do not bend for anyone," Glinda interjected. "It would take an immense surge of emotion and power for her to pull Dorothy back, let alone find her. For now, we must keep our focus here. It is more prevalent. But I do not think we have considered Dorothy's safety as well. She is another concern, but we must deal with what is staring us in the face right now." She exchanged another worried look with Grenin.

"But the witch has powerful emotions, which will lead to powerful magic. Wouldn't such a thing come easier for her?" An older Munchkin woman said.

"Unhinged emotion and chaos do not constitute practiced magic. She is highly emotional, yes, which makes her current abilities dangerous. It's something else to create such a tear in realms to connect them briefly. We won't ignore the possibility, although her ability to make that connection is currently beyond her focus." He let the idea simmer in his mind before continuing.

"I've taken some precautions that I will keep to myself for my protection and all of yours. I'm looking into these strange occurrences plaguing us for the past few months."

"But didn't the Grand Magus say no?" the young man asked.

"He did, yes, and I have already assigned the council members who will travel with Flint to aid General Ragnus, and they will leave within the hour. I completed my task." The nods he received from the parliament showed they had an understanding.

"I think I can speak for the parliament. Thank you for putting our minds at ease, Master Apprentice." Glinda smiled. "The strain between the two bodies would have guaranteed our weakness against anything thrown at us."

Satisfied with the conversation, Grenin gave a respectful bow. "Speaking to our prime minister and the Emerald Parliament is a pleasure. Once I receive more information, I will call a meeting. In the meantime, please note any oddities you see and bring them to me or one of my apprentices."

"Of course, Master Grenin," Glinda replied with a bow of the head.

"I will see myself out now. Good afternoon, Prime Minister. Ladies and gentlemen of the parliament, be well."

Grenin repeated the hand motions, except backward. The door's lock was unlatched, and he disappeared into the hallway.


Umiko rapped on the door. She heard scuffling coming from within and the latch coming undone.

The Grand Magus leaned against the door as he opened it, a smile coming to his aged face. "Ah, Umiko, what a lovely surprise. What brings you to see me so close to your departure?" He sounded shaky and strained, but his lean appearance surprised her.

"Grand Magus Harvol, are you... okay? You look tired." It was the politest way she could put it, and she did well to mask her shock.

"Ah, yes, just trying times, you know." He hobbled back to his desk. She slipped in and shut the door. With his back turned, she dipped into the coin purse at her hip and cradled the stone behind her back.

"Yes, that they are. Um . . . how did you know I was leaving?" She shifted from leg to leg and rolled her shoulders.

"I received the list of those going west from Master Grenin two hours ago. He's also meeting with the parliament to relay the information to them." He lowered into his chair with a groan.

"You do not look well. Can I get you anything, Grand Magus?"

"You are too kind. If you could grab that tin jug and pour some of that into a glass for me, I'd be most appreciative."

"Of course."

She stepped to the vanity and moved her hands to the front as she whispered the incantation under her breath. The stone nestled perfectly among all the other trinkets and gems decorating the wooden surface.

Umiko took the jug and poured it with barely a ripple. From the citrus smell, she thought it was a medicine to ease one's physical pain.

"This cold weather is not kind to someone my age." He rattled out a chuckle before hacking into his hand.

"You seemed fine this morning, Grand Magus. A sickness coming on this rapidly is of no concern to you?"

"Oh, it is, child, but time is not allowing me to focus solely on my health. This will pass. The occurrences to the west may not."

She nodded and set the glass on his desk. A shadow crossed the emerald amulet around his neck as she leaned down. Umiko blinked, and it glistened in its normal hue. She believed it was a trick of the light but still knew better than to dismiss it. She smiled and walked to the other side of his desk.

"I apologize for coming to you this late, but as this is my first assignment, I wanted to know if there was any wisdom or insight I could gather before leaving."

"You are a wise woman beyond your years. I know you were too young to remember the witch and the darkness that plagued our land before she came to power, but never underestimate either."

"Either?"

"Yes. Not everyone who seems like a foe is evil, and not every hand offered is help. Know who you can trust and whom to keep an eye on."

She furrowed her brow and nodded. It was not what she had expected, but it was insightful. For a moment, she saw the munchkin she knew and smiled.

"Thank you, Grand Magus. I hope our return is with good news," she said, bowing her head.

"We all do, dear." The old munchkin strained as he leaned over, opening a drawer near his feet. He pulled out a small item and offered it to her. A charm dangling from a silver chain. "Take this. It's reminding you of why we do what we do."

Umiko took the necklace and laid it in her palm. The charm was a pair of emerald shoes.

"Dorothy's slippers!"

"Yes, a symbol of protection and hope. May it help you in the most trying of times, Umiko."

"Thank you, Grand Magus." A tug at the back of her throat caused her to choke a bit. Something was not right with Grand Magus Harvol, but the glimmer of what he was came through at that moment, and she glanced at where she hid the stone.

It tugged at her heart, but this had to be done. Determined, she slipped the necklace on, bowed, and headed for the door.

As she left the Grand Magus, her moral compass screamed at her.

"No. Some evils are necessary. I commune with the higher magics to forgive me."

# Chapter 15

Flint squinted his metal eye as a dark, oily fluid shot into his face. He had been attempting to reconstruct his arm for hours, but he kept experiencing issues with one of the fluid lines.

He grunted as he grabbed a dirty rag with his still-attached hand and wiped what he could from his face.

Flint returned to tinkering, using different tools to dig deeper and move the wires and tubes about.

A twitch of life came to the fingers as he probed the inner forearm with a sharp tool designed for delicate adjustments. He shook his head and sat back on his work stool.

A light tapping brought his steely gray gaze to the window. A small clockwork bird sat on the windowsill, and Flint popped the window open enough for the little metal creature to hop down onto his work desk.

As the small creature hopped around, clicking and chittering, he couldn't help but admire his work. The bird was the size of a sparrow, made of bronze, iron, and copper. Rotating gears clicked on its breast, and each metal feather was a shade of brown or gray.

"You're back early." Flint smiled and offered his index finger to the little critter.

The bird skittered from his desk onto Tin Man's hand. It chirped and whirred, its wings flapping.

Flint listened carefully, his metal brow raising as the creature's tale climaxed. If a metal bird could look frazzled, his best guess was that this was what it would look like.

Tin Man stood and looked out the window, his hand lowering the bird back to the desk, and he braced his weight on his good arm. He leaned his head out the open window.

He encountered an uncanny silence, and the sun started falling toward the horizon. The surrounding trees cast a shadow onto his cabin, and the scene was serene.

"What disturbance, my friend? It looks as calm as any other sunset." The nervous bird's feet made a *clack-clack-clack* noise as it paced. "I fear you may need a tune-up. How long has it been?"

The bird looked at the disassembled arm on the table and rapidly shook its head.

Flint chuckled and shut the window. He took his seat, his good hand reaching for his other arm, but he froze when a slight tremor vibrated the floor.

He looked over at the bird flapping its wings. The little creature took flight and found a dark spot in the rafters above.

A thunderous groan sounded outside, and he grabbed his arm from the table. He placed the shoulder under his attached limb, flicked a switch just above the forearm of the detached appendage, and a spinning Gatling gun popped up.

Flint ran outside, his arm aimed at whatever might be out front of his cabin. Instead of seeing some strange beings or assailants, he saw thick clouds rolling in from the east.

He chuckled, spinning the gun back into place, ensuring it was dormant again. He flung the arm over his shoulder, and it slumped to rest.

"Is the Master of Weather drunk again? I don't believe the rainy season is supposed to be here for a couple of months."

The metal bird twittered and sputtered a rapid response. It hopped around frantically on the carved awning over the door.

"So that's where you've been. Grenin is sending members of the council and his apprentices here. . . ." Flint glanced up at the odd weather pattern and pursed his lips. "And we are to travel west to Ragnus?"

The day he hoped would always be a worry of the future was at his doorstep. The bird's mention of the armory and other experiments he had been tinkering with also raised a red flag.

"Did he explain any reason?"

The bird clicked and twittered.

"Then I shall ask when they arrive." He sighed and held out his hand for the bird, and they returned to the cabin's warmth.

Tin Man walked to his workroom, and another tremor shook the foundation as he settled into his work.

Flint felt the electric energy charge in the air, his metal skin tingling, the magic more prevalent in the Spectral Woods than anywhere else in Oz. The news and the change in the atmosphere put a sense of urgency in his motions. He grabbed his arm and attached it to his right shoulder. He would only have some of its functions, but primary usage was all he needed for now.

Once he reattached his arm, he flexed his hand and tested its grip and dexterity. Satisfied, he walked to a storage trunk against the wall next to his desk. He flipped open the lid, grabbed a large traveling sack, and threw a few devices inside. Some looked like they could be deadly, but all were strange and mechanical.

"We will prepare for our journey now," Flint began, but a far more violent tremor almost shook him from his feet.

The bird on his shoulder looked at the metal man with uncertainty.

"It's fine, little friend." He threw the sack over his shoulder and left his workroom, shutting the door behind him. He laid the pouch next to the front door and headed for the kitchen to prepare for his guests. The clouds reached their looming grasp to snuff out the setting sun, and his bird's information said they would arrive somewhere around supper.

The bird never left Flint's shoulder as he hustled about preparing some venison from last night's hunt and warm accommodations for the evening, spreading blankets and pillows around the glowing fire. It had been some time since he had seen anyone other than his creations and those who inhabited the forest.

Occasionally, he would receive a weary traveler from the yellow brick road, but even travelers had ceased their journeys. He had heard Lucian had recently passed by, but knew he wouldn't have had time to stop for even a few moments to visit. It is unfortunate, but that is the path of the avid student.

Flint smiled at the thought of how far Lucian had come since Dorothy had found him in the cornfield. Not just Lucian but Ragnus and himself as well. The entire land and its people had flourished because of Dorothy and her actions.

He glanced out the kitchen window as he rotated his index finger. A sharp blade flipped out, and the finger shifted to the palm of his hand, melding into his smooth metal skin. After he finished slicing carrots and celery for a stew, he moved them to the side.

Flint studied the gathering storm with more scrutiny. "Nothing lasts forever, and change is inevitable, but what would the next shift be?"

The little news he'd gotten from his friend that clung to his shoulder was enough to make him suspicious of the entire situation. He hoped Grenin's decisions were those of a man being overly cautious, but the munchkin wasn't one to jump at shadows. The whole thing bothered him.

A flame flickered in the distance, easily seen with the cloud covering the light from the rising moon.

Flint ran his blade over a clean kitchen rag on the wood counter. The index finger in his palm replaced the blade.

He reached for the elegantly carved axe on the wall next to the doorframe, his most practiced and preferred weapon. The silver bit of the axe shone with the rest of the metal mixed with an obsidian stone. His hand gripped the handle made from black trees in the Spectral Woods. The weapon had an intimidatingly dark look. A hum resonated as Flint gave the axe a well-practiced spin in his palm, and a wave of blue fire ignited from the silver bit as he walked out of the cabin.

Though he lived in one of the more mundane areas of the Spectral Woods, it was still an enchanted forest, so he should approach all things within the trees with caution and always have a way to defend himself.

He kept the axe low, but his grip on the handle was tight and ready. Flint stood next to the fire pit, with the wood already in place, heating stones, and a sizable black cauldron set on top, ready to be lit.

The bird on his shoulder clicked and whirled as the flame in the forest split into four. Flint tilted his head down to listen and nodded.

"Yes, I believe it is the council as well, but let's make sure before we get too excited, yeah?" He smiled at the little bird and returned to the approaching lights.

As the figure passed through the dense trees, he saw their robes, which were only worn by the Magus Council. The grip on his axe loosened, and he spun it around before slipping the handle into his belt. The blue flame snuffed out, but the sheen from the polished metal and gloss finish of the wood caught the light of the torches as they broke through the tree line.

Umiko lowered her hood to her shoulders, and her face brightened. "Flint!" she yelled out, ran, and hugged him.

"How is Grenin's troublemaker?" he chuckled.

"Well, I'm here, so that could be good or bad." She stepped back as the others filed in around the dormant fire pit. Everyone greeted the Tin Man, mostly with handshakes, but those who knew him well wrapped him in a warm hug.

"I hope you can fill me in. I'm still lost on what's happening," he stated, opening the door. He held it for his guests, and they dropped their bags near his front door. They had laid out blankets and pillows for all of them. Though the group was not huge, it filled the cabin.

He propped open the door and walked back to the fire pit. He pulled the axe from his belt and, in one smooth move, ignited the flame and struck the wood. It burst into a roaring bonfire, heating the stones to a glowing orange-red.

As he turned, he saw Umiko carrying out the bowl of potatoes he'd laid out. "Thank you, but you didn't have to." She shook her head.

"You're kind enough to house us for the evening. It's the least we could do." The council members followed her with items and dropped them into the cauldron. Balanor emerged with bowls and utensils, including a ladle and a wooden spoon, and set them on a small wooden table next to the fire pit.

Flint slid the axe into his belt with a grin and nodded. The council and parliament members came out, the apprentices following right behind, bringing the last of the ingredients. They sat beside the blazing fire. Tin Man grabbed the long wooden spoon, dipped it into the broth, and stirred.

Everyone was in good spirits despite the bleak reason for their travels and the worsening chill.

"Please tell me the Master of Weather is drunk again," Flint said as he gestured toward the clouds.

"I wish that were the case," Balanor said, sitting between Flint and Umiko. "We'd already checked into that when the weather patterns first started, but he's making his rounds to all the farms, preparing them for the next rainy season. We would probably have more answers about the weather patterns if he were in the city, but the only word we received back was that these were not his doing, and the source was a magical influence."

Flint paused in his stirring, and those around the fire quieted.

A loud snap from the growing flames broke the silence, and he stirred the stew again while the others made small talk among themselves. They avoided the subject that brought them to his doorstep, and he was happy to accommodate, sidestepping that business until his guests had eaten.

Flint dipped the spoon in and filled each wooden bowl to the brim. Everyone near the fire received a bowl and spoons.

The air turned frigid as the evening set in. Steam from the stew wrapped itself in the air, dancing with the flames in a hypnotic display. Travel-worn and worrying about what would come, they ate in a trance.

The fire was enormous enough to warm them. They sat in a circle, a couple eating greedily, and the stew brought some life back into them.

Umiko looked over at Flint, who had taken a seat next to her. He didn't need the same nutrients, having a primarily mechanical system now, but he was a gracious host and ensured his guests had everything they needed.

"Well, now's as good a time as any," Umiko said.

The sudden bluntness surprised him.

"I'm sorry, what?"

"The reason we are here and why we all are traveling to the western plains," she said, shoveling another spoonful of stew into her mouth.

Seeing almost everyone was about to be finished, he nodded and focused on her. "I did find it strange that the brief word I received was only moments before you were here."

"Master Grenin apologizes, but the nature of the matter is rather... dire." She finished the last couple of bites and set the spoon in the bowl on the bench.

Flint folded his arms over his chest and leaned back. "Just tell me why the Emerald City suddenly needs my experiments."

"General Ragnus came to the city requesting an audience with the council and the parliament."

"What did he say?"

"There's been movement in the witch's throne room."

She barely got the words out before Flint hacked a cough. "And we know it wasn't just a goblin or one of her soldiers, correct?"

"Correct." Umiko nodded. "And some of us think something worse might be related to the weather patterns and tremors. We are headed to help General Ragnus bolster defenses. That's why Grenin requested your presence with us and to help the Celehawk Clan."

Flint's gaze moved from her to the fire, his lips pursed. "This is bleak news, but it could be worse."

It was deep into the evening. They would have to travel before dawn to make it to the west in decent time, so their time for sleep was drawing short.

"We should get some rest," he suggested.

He stood and attempted to gather the empty bowls, but they insisted on helping clean. Within a few minutes, the fire was smoldering, and everyone moved back into the warm cabin.

Next to Flint's workroom at the back was a staircase leading to the loft above. After making sure all were comfortable, he climbed the stairs, wary of the information brought to him. If Grenin and members of both the council and parliament were concerned about the witch, it was nothing to take lightly.

There was not just the danger to the west; they'd also have to travel through the Spectral Woods and off the main roads. So many things . . .

He shook his head before sitting at a small desk. He had never needed much as he went to sleep, so the mattress on the floor had always been enough.

It would be nice to see Ragnus again, but it would not be the reunion he had imagined under the circumstances.

Flint huffed and turned away from the ominous storm out his window. Just as he did, a flash of light streaked across the sky, lighting up the cabin. Thunder growled overhead.

The light tapping of rain streaked across the windows as he lay down. The morning was not far, and even he needed his rest.

He could work with what he had, although he would have appreciated more information. Flint knew Ragnus would have more for them when they arrived, so worrying over things he could not control was useless.


The early morning sun would have customarily been peeking over the horizon, but the black clouds overhead prevented natural light from shining on the sleeping Emerald City.

Grenin slipped out of his house onto the red brick road in the residential district. His breath was present in the chilled air, and the rumbling above muffled his steps. Tiny droplets hit the cobblestones and bricks lining the road and walkways.

As he approached the city's center, his eyes fell upon the slumbering Myst Library, hugged between the yellow and green brick roads. The buildings lining the green brick road comprised scholarly shops, small eateries, and schools for young children, all leading up to the Oz Academy at the end of the road. A longing nostalgia—a subconscious yearning for simpler times—pulled at him, his eyes lingering down the green brick road, memories racing through his mind. He forced himself to refocus, returning his attention to the task.

He stepped onto the yellow and followed it to the citadel steps. He rushed up the stairs and through the large glass doors. The warmth from inside washed over him, and he shook off his long black coat and pulled the blue-striped scarf from his neck. He draped both over his arm and headed to the Grand Magus's office.

Though the air was warm, the hall chilled his soul. He stopped and looked up and down the corridor. He felt eyes on him, but even with a magical inspection, he found himself alone.

His shoes shuffled on the carpeted floor as he approached the Grand Magus's door. The muffled murmurs coming from the other side ceased when he rapped.

Grand Magus Harvol cleared his throat. "Come in," he said, sounding worn.

Grenin motioned over the lock as the door closed. When he turned, he almost dropped his coat and scarf on the rug.

"M-master Harvol, you look ill. Are you okay?" Grand Magus looked weak, reclining in his chair, practically wheezing. He coughed and waved a dismissive hand.

"This damned weather, Grenin. My body doesn't handle the cold as it once did. I fear I may have caught something from being in the rain." He placed his elbows on the desk and leaned on them.

"Should I call for a mender?" Grenin was ready to leave and wake one of their healers, but a raised hand from the Grand Magus stopped him.

"We don't have time to trouble them, and I don't have time to be troubled by them." He hacked out a cough and settled back. "What is the final report on those we sent west?"

"Allow me to at least get you some water, Master? Please? Ease my mind a bit."

The old Magus's eyes sparked with a familiar fire. He chuckled and nodded. "If it will get you to give me the report, bring me the entire jug."

Grenin half-smiled and walked to the vanity with the water jug and an empty glass next to it. As he poured, he saw the stone behind the brass frame of the mirror, but it would not be easy to take it without being seen.

The Master Apprentice kept his peripheral vision. He placed the jug directly next to the stone, and as he moved his hand back, he caught the shiny object with his fingertips. He curled the stone into his palm with his best sleight of hand. Something he learned from Umiko. A survival skill, she called it, which always warranted a look from him.

"What is that?" Master Harvol said. Grenin froze, a glass of water in his left hand and his right in his pants pocket. The stone caught the lip of the pocket and slipped in.

"I'm sorry. What is what, Grand Magus?" He turned and faced the other munchkin.

"I thought I saw you move something on the vanity." He started hacking again.

"Ah, yes, sorry." Grenin picked up a small coin-like item beside where he had plucked the stone. "Caught my eye. I don't remember this being here."

The Master Apprentice placed the glass and the strange brass coin on the desk. He held his breath, asking the celestial bodies and elements of magic that his ruse worked.

Master Harvol's face broke into a weary grin, and Grenin's shoulders relaxed. He exhaled and covered his relief with an expression of interest.

"What is that coin? It doesn't look like the currency we use here."

"A traveler gave it to me many years ago. He told me He is from a distant land."

"Do you think he's one like Dorothy?" Grenin draped his coat and scarf onto the chair.

"It's possible, but many places in our land are still forgotten. We rarely travel to the Pridyr territories; some less-than-savory places are on the borders." The older magus drank a few large gulps, which seemed to bring some life back into him.

"We are rather preoccupied here, I think."

"The Emerald City has always been a haven for everyone in the Land of Oz. That's why many stayed. It's peaceful here, and we must keep it that way." He cleared his throat before gesturing for Grenin to continue. "Please go ahead with your report."

"Ah, yes." Grenin nodded, gathering his thoughts. "Balanor, Verria, Turl, and Norra volunteered with my apprentices, Umiko, Lorinna, Alleren, and Tristan. A healthy representation of both the Emerald Parliament and the Magus Council. They were to meet Flint at his cabin last night and travel to the Celehawk territories this morning. I would guess they are already on the road since Umiko told me they would leave before dawn."

The Grand Magus nodded. "Please let me know as soon as you find out more information," he said, placing the empty glass on his desk.

"I will, Grand Magus. Is there anything else you need from me today?" Grenin asked as he scooped up his coat and scarf.

"Did I hear you canceled all classes for the next two days?"

"I did. Under the circumstances, I figured for the safety of our students and professors, it might be prudent of us to allow a couple of unplanned vacation days." Grenin offered a warm grin to his old friend.

"An appropriate response, Master Apprentice. I know we both have a grueling day ahead. Shall we get it over with?" He strained as he pushed from his chair, cracks and groans audible as he moved.

Grenin walked over to help him, but the Grand Magus shooed him away. "Oh, stop it. It's just a cold. I'll be fine," he said, hobbling to the door. He raised his hand and swiped it to the right. The door unlatched and slowly creaked open.

"Get some rest, Master." Grenin stepped out and heard a cough and a chuckle as the door thudded closed.

The Master Apprentice brushed the palm of his hand over his pocket and sighed a breath of relief when he felt the stone.

His feet could not carry him fast enough toward the massive glass doors. He pushed one open, and raindrops hit his skin. The sun should have been waking up the city; instead, the hovering gray mass had kept most inside, and those outside walked at a feverish pace.

Grenin pulled on his jacket and draped his scarf over his shoulders as he ran down the steps. He headed for the Myst Library. It was time to get some answers.

# Chapter 16

The billowing fog dissipated, and the witch stood on the outskirts of the plains, just inside the Spectral Woods. It had been many years since she had seen her mountainside from this view, but the large creature standing next to an old, gnarled oak tree caught her interest.

At the edge of the trees, the Cowardly Lion lingered. The Plains of Pri'doth never looked as beautiful as they do now. The tall grass waved in the breeze as if welcoming him home. His gaze dragged up from the land to catch the setting sun that sank below the snow-brushed mountain peaks to the west. It had been ages since he had left his people. A mishap that earned him his name, but he returned, redeemed by those who did not know his past. He wondered if his people would welcome him home with the same enthusiasm he experienced within the Emerald City. Either way, it was time for him to come home and face what he had run from for so long.

Self-exiled to the Spectral Woods, then spending a year within the city walls had taken him far from his roots, but here he stood, many years later, and a different Pridyr.

He let out a long breath, filled with thought and doubt, but the lure of his home was too strong to ignore. He had left the Emerald City with his newly gained outlook and attempted to take his place amongst his people once more.

His eyes dipped to the tree he stood next to before returning to the tall grass. Gathering his nerves, he lifted his head and left the trees, pushing through the fields toward the small town of the Plains Tribe. The town was a mere speck deep in the distance, closer to the hills and mountains. With each step, the urge to turn and return to his dark sanctuary grew, but he denied himself instant gratification. He refused to feed his fear any longer.

The moon lit his path by the time he reached the edge of the village. He could see the large fire in the middle of the town still blazing as it did every night from his youth, and nostalgia sent his heart skipping in anticipation.

The Cowardly Lion stopped just outside the entrance. A tall wooden fence surrounded the village, each end spiked, intending to spear anything that crossed over. Two Pridyr guards stood above in a lookout tower, peering down at him.

"Well, I'll be damned," one stated as they watched the form become clearer as he stepped up to the large wooden doors.

The lion was still. He stared at the gate, pushing back the past that nipped at his thoughts. His eyes closed, and he took a deep breath.

"Ragnus the Cowardly, son of Chieftain Urvan, self-exiled, shamed of the Celehawk Clan Army, requests an audience with Chief Urvan and his Chosen Lurisa."

The looks the two guards exchanged were unreadable from the Cowardly Lion's position, but he could tell his declaration of his proper name and intent had startled them. He watched as one descended the ladder and could hear his leather armor moving at a pace that was probably chafing his fur. Seconds later, one side of the large gate opened, and the one guard standing barely visible behind it.

Ragnus hesitated as his gaze lingered over the watchtower, bringing it down to the gate. He felt his knees buckle, but he urged himself forward. His fear would not own him.

As he passed through the gate, he dipped his head in thanks to the guard, whom he suspected might put his wrists in shackles. The guard made no such move. Instead, he respectfully stepped aside, securing the gate firmly behind them.

He did not know what to expect—much had transpired since he'd last walked through the town's trade pavilion. Many street occupants turned as they saw Ragnus head for the Chieftain's Hall at the end of the road. The color-streaked canopies overhead rustled softly as the crisp new night air rushed through, bringing some chill from the mountains.

Ragnus approached the massive fire pit just outside the city's great hall. It lit the entire pavilion, casting a daunting shadow on the rune-carved doors before him. He watched the flames flicker and sway, but he focused solely on where opening this door would lead.

He stepped past the flames, determined to close the distance between the fire and the entrance to the great hall. Reluctantly, he pushed the pads of his imposing paws up against the aged wood. Creaking from the old structure announced his entrance, and all talk ceased once the realization of who had just entered set in.

There were three long oak tables, each with a mix of Pridyr from different tribes. Almost all nursed some manner of drink in their hand, from drinking horns to steins, which took pause when the door settled shut and Ragnus, the disgraced son of the Plains' chieftain, stood just inside the hall, his paw-like hands clasped respectfully in front of him.

The group made no motion, and all was silent for a long moment, save for a few creaks as some patrons adjusted to view the enormous form at the entrance.

Ragnus forced his gaze to meet his father's. The older lion sat at an ornate wooden table before the chieftain and his chosen. They both rested on opulent thrones that were hand-carved and covered with luxurious furs. His mother Lurisa's expression was between shock and relief, but his father's hardened features were hard to read.

The chieftain's mane was now primarily gray, along with his muzzle. The aged chieftain showed his years, but it never shamed him. He rose from his throne, placing his stein on the table with barely a tap, still studying the face of the son who had left so long ago.

The sound of the table scraping on the floor echoed through the tense air, but the only thing the occupants focused on was Chieftain Urvan as he descended the three small steps leading to his throne.

The chieftain moved as if he were wading through a dense swamp, each foot dragging, his leather armor and fur cloak the only things making noise.

Ragnus noticed that the closer his father got, the more his hardened expression revealed to be broken but relieved. The former Cowardly Lion did not know what to expect but would accept anything his father would give. He had finished running, even if it meant a trial or, worse, death. The lion braced himself as his father's massive paw moved upward, expecting entirely to be knocked out.

He felt the impact, but no pain, no darkness; instead, he felt as if his ribs might pop as his father wrapped his arms around his son, pulling him in.

"Word travels faster than you do, it seems," his father spoke into his ear before releasing him and placing his paw on Ragnus's arm.

"I stayed after Dorothy left," Ragnus stated, still concerned and waiting for something to happen, possibly, but when he saw the rest of the hall and its patrons, his shoulders relaxed slightly.

Chief Urvan placed his palm on Rangus's back and guided him toward the stairs, where they stood and turned to face those gathered. He reached back, plucked his stein from the table, and raised it.

"Today marks a genuine reason to celebrate, my friends. Ragnus is home!" he shouted into the hall, and then people immediately yelled, cheered, and pushed steins and drinking horns into the air.

The hall erupted into conversation once more than Chief Urvan walked his son over to his mother, who was still standing and speechless.

Ragnus skirted around the table and stood before his mother. He held back, pushing down the swell of emotion pulling at his throat. He could put only one thing into words that finally made it past his lips.

"I'm sorry" The lion almost broke, and she pulled him into another tight embrace. She hugged him close, closing her eyes and taking a deep, shuddering breath.

"Never again," she whispered. "Do you understand me?"

"Never again," Ragnus replied, looking back slightly at his mother's aged features. She had gray and white streaks through her once-golden fur.

"Touching moment, don't you think, my gray beauty?" The voice echoed over the hall, and all action and noise ceased.

The witch stepped out of a darkened corner, her eyes on the lion with every step.

"What am I to learn from this? The lion's courage has returned?" She walked up to the two Pridyr suspended in their perfect moment.

"Did not you recognize the location of their village?" The melodic question hung in the air as the witch circled Ragnus and his mother, her hands clasped behind her back.

"They live on the plains on the outskirts of my fortress. This is something I already knew." She clenched her teeth but kept her anger at bay.

"This moment led to a great unification among the Pridyr tribes. They pose a threat, especially since their strength and numbers have grown. The Emerald City openly welcomes them, and they will resist you greatly."

Looking into the lion's large green orbs, the witch narrowed her eyes, and her nostrils flared. She was about to advance further onto the peaceful scene, but in Lurisa's stein, a strange red blur appeared. The witch's slender nose wrinkled as she attempted to get a better look.

As more of the image took shape, though still a blur, she saw a hunched form. The fog returned and thickened in the Pridyrs' great hall, snuffing out the image and leaving her in a blanket of gray.

The witch waited for some change in the scene, for things to take shape and form in front of her once more, but all that welcomed her was the thick mass.

Anger brewed and climbed up her limbs like a creeping, poisonous spider ready to strike the back of her throat. She let out a long exhale, attempting to suppress her rage.

There was no voice, there was no direction; there was her and the fog. A screech broke from her lips, her eyes shooting daggers skyward.

"You toy with me as if I were mere food!" Her words turned muffled as if something encased her. Silence was her answer, and she screamed again. This time, the sound did not travel beyond her nose.

"We must come to an understanding. Then I'll be more willing to let you go."

"What understanding is this?" she said through gritted teeth.

"You do what I need to retake what is mine, and you return to power," the voice chuckled, "As I stated before, I'll even throw in the girl to show you I can be a giving master."

"I have no master, nor will I ever bow to one," she spat. The fog to her right swirled as if someone had walked by. Her eyes narrowed at the spot.

"I don't need you to bow, my gray gem. I need you to cooperate." The voice moved melodically around her, but she had yet to see an owner. She doubted she would. She just wanted to be released.

"Your 'gifts' are mere distractions to acceptance of slavery. A will that is not my own is not one I wish to submit."

"Ah, my dear, what if our wills are on parallel paths?"

"Continue."

"Without me, you would still be dead, and if you refuse, well," the voice chuckled. "You'll either return to that state or remain here. Now, I would prefer a powerful beauty helping guide the hand of destruction rather than falling to it. If you accept my offer, I believe we will have far more benefits."

She balled her hands into fists. "Which is what exactly? You have not been forthcoming with that detail."

"You help your sister make our two worlds one and help me retake the lands that belong to me. In return, you shall receive all the power you once had and more. Also," the fog on her left became denser. "I promised you vengeance, not just to one, but to the many responsible for your fall."

The fog formed a perfect replica of Dorothy, an image the witch scorned with an intense glare. She turned away and looked up. She saw her broken throne and the torn tapestries fluttering in the wind.

"I already have a sister! She died because of that brat!"

"I see you need more... incentive," the voice jeered as another form took shape. Though it came not from fog, it had an ethereal presence.

The witch froze, stunned to be face to face with the Wicked Witch of the East. A face she had not looked upon in years. She choked.

"I think of myself as generous. I brought you back. I can do the same for her," the voice said.

The witch could not take her eyes off the specter wandering, lost in another realm.

"I'll leave you to consider my offer," the last word echoed around the witch.

The gray-skinned older woman looked from her sister's ghostly features to the throne room outside her crystal ball. She had no choice but to regain her power and carry out the deserved vengeance against her foes.

On the opposite side of her and the apparition, the fog solidified into a mirror and hovered at eye level. The most prominent thing in the glass was the red shape.

The mirror stretched to full body length, its surface rippling like water. She watched the frameshift from gray fog to ornate gold and found the mirror placed next to her as if it had always been there.

The witch glanced back at her wandering sister before stepping into the mirror. She tilted her head, looking harder at the red form in the liquid glass, trying to make some sense of it all. The ripples stilled, the red mist took shape, and she smiled.

"This is the fate of the great Queen of Hearts." The woman stared at her reflection in a full-length mirror on the wall of her throne room.

Behind her reflection, the heart-carved dark wooden throne stood firm, even after all these years. It was the only thing in her room that had not been spoiled.

Dull blue eyes and the wrinkle-caked features of a ninety-year-old gazed back. Her once vibrant red hair had turned gray and straw-like. It dragged lifelessly on the ground, no care or love given to her locks for many ages.

"My kingdom..." Her voice quivered. "And you left me to my shame," she said. A solitary tear escaped the corner of her eye and streaked down her worn face.

Memories of her youth wrapped her in a false utopia, but loneliness had stolen those comforts. The sapphire sparkle in her eyes vanished, and she used every ounce of effort to walk from her throne to the mirror, but she would not give up the daily ritual.

She sneered at the memory of the young girl who stole her kingdom and beauty. Only a promise kept her moving daily, but hope was fading, and the vow seemed lost to the winds.

She cast down her eyes and could no longer see what the Queen of Hearts had become. She was greeted by the sight of her twisted and wrinkled hands.

A deep-seated rage swelled in her chest, and unable to contain the pain within, she let out a scream and slammed her hand into the wall.

"Your promise!" she cried. "My beauty! My power! I gave you my will, and you gave me a promise!"

Her outburst took its toll, and she rested her palms on the smooth glass surface of the mirror and placed her forehead against her reflection. Two women locked in a desperate embrace for an answer; another tear graced her old skin, and she squeezed her eyes shut.

"Your... promise..." she whispered to the mirror. "You have abandoned me...."

A gentle breeze kissed the tear from her cheek, and she opened her eyes wide. The breeze was familiar, and her heart tightened. She stood silently, waiting for another ghostly embrace.

"I never truly left you, my red vision. I would not abandon one of my chosen." The deep, melodic voice played like a symphony through the vacant room, and the queen's heart jumped into her throat. Years of solitude melted away with the presence.

"It's been so long," the Queen of Hearts' voice quivered. Relief and anger mixed with infatuation.

"A necessary absence, I'm afraid, darling."

She spun, frantically searching for the owner of the voice that haunted her, but the man's physical presence had always remained aloof.

"You're back then? What has caused such an absence? It has been lonely and desperate without your encouragement, my love."

"Time will reveal the answer."

"Things have deteriorated," the old queen said, looking about the crumbling throne room. She brought her crippled hands into view and turned back toward the mirror. "Myself included. I ..." she said, another tear rolling down her cheek.

The voice's haunting chuckle reverberated through the throne room and deep into the queen's tarnished heart.

"You mock me!" she screamed into the ceiling, the anger causing her to shake so violently that it forced her hands back to the mirror. She braced herself again. She put all her energy into the tears streaming down her cheeks. "Why must you return, if only to mock me?"

"I do not intend to mock, darling. You standalone no longer."

The old queen pushed away from the mirror. She stared hard at herself. Black streaks covered the length of her face. "I am no longer fit for your eyes," she whispered.

As the queen investigated the glass, a spark of green flickered on the other side. The image was clouded, but she noticed subtle movement.

The fear in her gut subsided, and curiosity took over. She stared at her reflection. "What have you done?" She asked, directing the words at the voice that held her heart captive.

"Building, darling. It takes time to create doorways."

"This has taken you from me?"

"This brings you to me, and in return..." The voice paused as a green spark came out of the glass. The image on the other side took shape: "It brings my beautiful vision to fruition."

"Your promise."

"My promise."

The surface of the glass liquefied, and the green electric currents enveloped the entire mirror.

"You must use all that remains."

"My soul is all that remains. Is my love and will not enough?"

The stone floor beneath the queen's feet pulsed. The liquefied glass rippled as the shaking became more violent. She tried to understand better what was on the other side, but the form continued to evade her. She whipped around, almost losing her balance, and braced herself on the wall. When she turned back to the mirror, she could only see her visage surrounded by dark gray swirls and flashes that mimicked lightning.

"Step through, my queen. Your enemies have taken advantage of your mental state and your self-made prison."

She hesitated, but the mention of those who brought her downfall dissolved any doubt. She gripped the gold frame for balance and slid her aged form past the quivering surface and into the opaque mist.

"I want my beauty and power restored," she said, glancing back at the settling ripples and her broken throne. "And I want Alice."

"My promise awaits, darling."

It was difficult for the old queen to maneuver her way into the mirror and find her footing. The fog dissipated, and as she slowly turned, buildings took shape. She was standing in front of a large obsidian marble fountain in the center of what looked like a market.

Life erupted around her, swarming her senses, like wasps picking at her ears. She grasped the stone structure for support.

The older woman gathered herself and stood as straight as possible, still hunched. She caught her reflection in the obsidian and trailed her gaze upward until it landed on the carving of a familiar face. Heat flamed in her cheeks, and she felt them redden. She was staring up at Alice.

Having been in solitude for so long, the commotion of the busy marketplace drove her to recoil. "What is this place?" the Queen screeched, her hands gripping her straw-like hair. Her eyes darted about, looking for anything to be familiar.

"The Night Market, my queen. They built it some time ago to... undermine you. Those who resisted you built this as their sanctuary. What I present to you is a vision of the past, shortly after its establishment."

"Would you like to see who is responsible?" the voice asked.

The question gave the red crone new life. She steadied her stance and focused on those around her.

"Show me."

"The tavern behind the statue." As the voice spoke, the details of the market distorted and took bodily form. She hobbled to the tavern door, which creaked open before she reached for the handle.

Two flamingo mallets stumbled out and tripped. They hit the cobbled street, laughed, and pushed each other, obviously intoxicated. Her face twisted in disgust and anger; she made her way into the tavern, then stopped immediately.

The White Rabbit sat at a table, laughing and conversing with the White Knight. Over in a dark corner, a tall, slim figure wearing a black fedora with a teal and green plume leaned against the wall. He had his arms folded across his chest. His fur was primarily gray, with black and white accents around his face and indigo eyes. She sneered.

"Cheshire..."

"He's been extremely active in your absence. He has a monopoly on everything magical and unsavory. A friend to no one but a necessity for everyone. There's nothing he can't get his hands on, but the White Rabbit, now... that one stings a little, doesn't it, darling?"

The queen stepped closer, reaching the round table where the two sat. She pulled out an empty chair and lowered her aching limbs onto it.

"So, she was outplayed?" asked the knight.

"Absolutely. I knew the moment I met that little girl that this was the change we'd all been looking for. It was only a matter of time," the White Rabbit stated before taking a drink from his mug. "How have things been out in the fields?"

"Other than the White and Red queens constantly bickering over silly things, it's been quiet." The knight cleared his throat as if to say more but stayed silent.

"And the Jabberwocky?" the White Rabbit inquired, glancing at the knight's tense expression.

"Still in captivity. After everything, the red and white army swore to lay down their swords, share the fields, and focus their resources and efforts to keep it... contained." The White Knight took a long gulp of his drink.

"Good, that's the last thing our world needs. That and the Queen of Hearts," the rabbit said into his drink.

The queen flinched and narrowed her gaze at him.

Movement slowed, the sound ceased, and the queen was as still as the past.

"That... and the Queen of Hearts," the voice echoed in a sultry tone. "You chose your allies and subjects poorly, my dear."

"You mock me, yet again," the queen said, broken yet unwavering.

"Dear, you should not ignore the truth in my words. Not if you want to win."

Green flashed over the bottles lining the shelves behind the bar. Within each, she saw the same green electrical current. She used the chair to brace her weight as she stood, every creak of her bones reminding her of her frailty.

The queen shuffled to the bar and leaned over it to look closer. The light moved from bottle to bottle, sometimes occupying more than one.

"My red vision," the voice began. Startled, her gaze leaped to the ceiling.

"Yes."

"Step through the door, please."

The only tangible thing around her was the tavern door. Everything else was dense fog. The door opened for her, and she stepped through. Her eyes strained against the sudden brightness, but once they focused, the scene created more seething anger within.

# Chapter 17

The White Rabbit stared into the rippling puddle, pushed and prodded by the soft wind blowing through Merchant's Square in the Night Market. Years... nothing but a number and memories now. He couldn't help but notice the white mixed in his gray fur—the only true sign that much time had passed since the queen's fall and Alice returned to her realm.

His chest heaved with a deep sigh as he wondered what had happened to that girl.

Rapid footsteps caused his ears to twitch, and the owner of the footsteps splashed into his rippled reflection.

"Dad, are you okay? You've got that lost look again."

The rabbit cleared his throat, offered a half-weary grin, and gestured for them to continue through the main plaza.

"Ah, yes, just reminiscing," he chuckled as he looped his arm around his son's shoulders.

"Alice?"

"That would be her, yes." His eyes kept a thoughtful look; her yellow locks bounced through his mind.

"What do you think happened to her?"

The White Rabbit tilted his head skyward. The festive flags over the Merchant's Square blew gently, and the stars winked in the clear night sky.

"I'm not sure, but a legend like that does not die easily. I'm betting she's doing what she does best."

"What's that?"

"Succeeding." He gave his son's shoulders an affectionate squeeze.

"And thanks to her, we have the life we have now. Not just for our family but for Wonderland. We were fortunate the day she followed me down that old hole."

The two walked through the heart of Merchant's Square, filled with bustling excitement at almost every moment of the day. Even in the early morning, festive noises came from the tavern behind the large fountain.

They continued amidst the shouts for fresh fruit, meats, and other items. Wooden signs boasting the vendors' wares hung from colorful awnings. The rabbit brushed by a stand with sugar dates, figs, and other handmade candies. As they passed, he gave the merchant a smile and a dip of the head. The merchant reached over his wares, grabbed the rabbit's hand, and shook it vigorously.

The White Rabbit removed the young blond girl from his thoughts. He stopped and returned the handshake, and his smile broadened.

"Deller, how are you this evening?"

"Mayor, sir, we are happy to see you and your son this weekend! A real treat. We haven't seen you for some time. Here, please take some of these." The merchant grabbed something from under his table.

The White Rabbit waited patiently, a smile still warming his face.

"Dad?" His son gestured to a booth closer to the fountain.

"Go on, son. I'll only be a moment," the White Rabbit said, watching his son move through the light crowd to a booth holding small trinkets and statues.

Deller mumbled to himself, rummaging and searching for something. Only a moment passed before the older man popped his head up, a bag grasped in his hand.

"Here you are." He placed the bag into the White Rabbit's hand. "Exotic candies from all over Wonderland. Look, I could even get my hands on some honey hearts."

The White Rabbit almost dropped the bag. "Wait, you... how? Those only grow around the queen's old castle, and no one's ventured there for years."

"I know someone." Deller smiled. "I promise they are safe. There's a grove of trees further back from the main court. They're untainted."

The mayor looked at the large assortment of sweet delicacies and the tiny, candied fruit. He dipped his fur-covered hand into the bag and pulled a honey heart out to inspect it. He remembered them from when he had been a steward for the Queen of Hearts in his youth. They looked harmless, but before he shared the treat with his son, he would test it himself.

Nostalgia coated his tongue with a sugary snap, and he sighed. They were as he remembered, and the smile returned to his face.

"Deller, you certainly have a knack for finding rare and exotic treats. I would think that would branch into other useful areas as well." He chuckled, rolling the bag closed.

"Ah, you're too kind, Mayor. I'm just an old man who likes the better things in life." He grabbed his oversized belly and shook it, and they laughed.

"Let me pick up some sugar dates as well. My wife deserves a surprise for dealing with the twins all week." He looked up to check on his son, who was conversing deeply with the traveling merchants.

"No charge, Mayor White," Deller said, handing him the second bag.

"What kind of rabbit would I be not to support my people and city?" he asked. "You've always been hospitable. Please, how much for the dates?"

Deller laughed hard before stating the going price for high-end sugar dates. The mayor placed the money in his hand and squeezed it.

"You're a good man. It's always a pleasure. Don't you ever change." The White Rabbit nodded at the merchant and walked toward the wood carver's booth.

"I've been this way for over fifty years. I'm not changing now!" Deller called after him and returned to call out his product to the growing crowd at the night market.

The White Rabbit's gaze slowly passed over the tables, which led to his son. He stood before a beautiful black marble fountain just outside the tavern. It was at the heart of everything, just like the little girl the fountain gave tribute to.

The mayor's grin formed into a smile that sang of fond memories. Lost in his thoughts, he dropped his gaze to the water. The light reflected on the rippling surface. His reflection danced, brightened by every hue from the lights, but he was seeing beyond. He lifted his eyes to the girl who sat atop the mushroom. One delicate foot hung down, almost touching the detailed carved flowers, pouring water into the large petal base.

He missed the day that marked the beginning for everyone. He missed it, not in mourning but as one would miss a friend.

"Dad!"

The rabbit's attention snapped to his son, wildly waving him over. He cleared his throat and blinked a few times, considering how long he had been lost in his mind. He walked over to the booth where his son was.

"What is it, Tovar?"

His son held up a beautifully carved hand mirror. The mayor paused in his steps. Something curious about the item intrigued him, so he plucked it from his son's hand and turned it over.

Someone made the frame and handle from mahogany and carved them like braided tree roots. Where the handle began was a familiar symbol he had not seen in years, and only a few would recognize it.

"What does that symbol mean?" his son asked.

"Where did you get this?" the rabbit asked the grinning merchant with large, mechanical-like glasses that whirled and spun with gears and smaller focus lenses, resting on a tattered brown gambler's hat with a red plume. His clothes were a chaotic mash—a red vest, brown pants, and an oversized flowing shirt that was probably white at one point.

He puffed on a wooden pipe, and the smoke trailed from the corner of his smirking mouth. He reached back to a thick trench coat with many pockets hanging on the wall. The man dropped his hand into a large pocket and pulled out a small device that moved and clicked. He turned it counterclockwise before placing it back.

"I acquire many wares over my travels, Mayor White. I have a knack for finding the unique." Turning his head to the side, he gave the rabbit a sly look. "You know this, yet you ask. I wonder if something of mine has finally taken our beloved mayor's fancy."

"It just might have. How much for it?"

"I couldn't charge you, sir." He took a long inhale from his pipe and stood respectfully. "For everything you've done for Wonderland, I owe you."

The rabbit let out a long sigh. "Now, Veil, you know I am going to pay you. Just give me the price, or I'll make one up. I promise I will overcharge myself, so you better tell me." He held up a small pouch.

Veil laughed and offered his hand. "Do you have low-court currency or high court?"

"Both," the mayor said, opening the strings of the pouch.

"Hmm... low court would be one gold and two silvers."

"Are you sure? I don't mind—"

Veil held up his hand. "I'll be needing that currency for my next travels."

"I see," the White Rabbit said, pulling out the coins. He placed them in Veil's dirty hand and noticed the blood-soaked bandage wrapping his palm.

"Not all my dealings are this easy. There are some rougher areas of Wonderland. Thankfully, fewer nowadays." He glanced at the fountain.

The White Rabbit smiled briefly before looking at the mirror in his hand, contemplating where he had seen it before.

The mayor and his son bid Veil farewell and continued toward the tavern at the top of the square.

"Dad?" Tov said.

"This," he pointed to the symbol, "is Alice's symbol."

His son reached over, gently took the mirror, and looked closer at the marking. It was a lily with a braided stem lying open on a star.

"That, son, was once a sign of hope. It still is, but those were much darker times when that symbol was more well-known."

"I've seen this before," Tov began and stopped.

"Where?"

"I-in your office."

"Oh, is that right?" he asked, taking on the whole dad posture as his arms folded over his chest.

"I'm in trouble, aren't I?"

"Let's have that chat when we get home, yes? No need to make your grounding a public scene."

The younger rabbit's shoulders slumped, and he groaned.

Mayor White handed the mirror back to his son.

"Really?"

"Of course. In the darkest times, we need to remember what's important." He pointed at the mirror. "Look."

Tov brought the mirror up. His reflection was that of a slightly awkward adolescent rabbit, but one growing into an adult body. His big green eyes stared back at him for a long moment.

"The light within can shine brighter than whatever darkness life throws at us." Tov's father slipped behind him, and he met his gaze in the mirror. "And no matter what, you're never truly alone."

The mayor's index finger pointed to the symbol. "And if you ever need something to cling to or guide you, remember the lily from the star. It helped many of us, including your old man." He patted his son's shoulder. "Now, how about a hot peach honey brew?"

The wind kicked up, and Tov's fur stood on end. "It got cold rather quickly, didn't it?" He walked toward the tavern but stopped short when he realized his dad had stayed planted close to the fountain. Tov followed his father's gaze and was shocked by the ominous black clouds above them.

They rushed into the tavern. Warmth and laughter washed over them, which only slightly calmed Tov's senses. They sat at one of the long tables in front of the bar.

"It's the Fluffy Mayor and little Fluffy!" came a cheerful voice.

"Yes! Yes!" A hefty mass of a man plopped next to the White Rabbit, smiling. The bench groaned and creaked under the weight.

"The Tweedle brothers," the mayor chuckled. "Still pushing drinks around the tavern, are you?"

"Of course! Would you see us anywhere else?" Tweedle Dee asked.

"There's no better place to be! This is the center of Wonderland now, and you know how much we adore the masses!" Tweedle Dum added. "Will it be the usual for Mayor Fluffy and Little Fluffy?"

The White Rabbit looked over at his son, who had his hand firmly placed over his face. He chuckled again and nodded to the robust brothers. Tweedle Dum popped up from the bench and shuffled over to the bar. He placed the drink orders as Tweedle Dee grabbed a rag from his waistband and wiped the spot next to the two rabbits.

"It's been a while since we've seen you two here."

"There's been some unrest with the less savory types in the town. It's kept me preoccupied."

"Where's Cheshire?" Tweedle Dee prodded with a sarcastic grin.

"Last time I spoke with him, he was on his way to keep tabs on someone, and since then, he has disappeared." The White Rabbit sighed, folding his hands on the table.

"You couldn't have expected any less from him," Tweedle Dum said from behind his brother, sliding two wooden steins onto the table. They stopped directly in front of the mayor and his son. Both took hold of their respective drinks.

"I knew what was involved and what could happen, but Cheshire's interest is not solely his own, though it is his major drive," the mayor said, taking a long drink of the toasty, rich nectar. The peach and honey brew had a kick of cinnamon and nutmeg, which warmed his limbs. He looked over his stein at Tov, gulping down the drink and letting forth a long, satisfied sigh.

The Tweedle brothers exchanged looks before smiling at the rabbits.

"Let us know if you need anything else," Tweedle Dee said, turning to the table behind them.

"Interesting. It got busy," the other Tweedle brother said as he looked at many from the streets piling in.

The mayor moved to the entrance, and Tov on his heels. They walked out and into the Night Market's main square. The White Rabbit lifted his head to the storm above. Something in the air made his nose twitch.

The market awnings flipped and waved in the wind. The usually loud, bustling hub had an eerie heaviness, and the merchants and their customers sounded like they were talking through pillows. Dread crept over the once-happy Merchant's Square.

# Chapter 18

"Judgment!" three voices exclaimed at once. The shouts echoed across the table, the dense fog dissipating. The sounds of clinking dishes and chatter filled the queen's ears as she watched the scene take shape.

The March Hare stood on his chair in a velvet maroon suit with navy blue accents, lifting a matching top hat high over his head as if offering to some invisible entities above. The Dormouse sat in a teapot on the seat across from him. His button-up green vest made the small creature look like a bank teller who most likely enjoyed fight clubs after work. The mouse clapped his little paws and pointed to the hat in the Hare's hand.

"Yes! Judgment must be called for!" the little creature yelled before picking up a tiny blue teacup.

The Hare placed the top hat on his head again, his ears moving to give way to the object of everyone's concern.

"I will run across this table myself and kick it clean from your head, Hare!" the Hatter threatened as he calmly sat in his chair at the head of the table. "It is unbecoming of your demeanor." He took a sip. "And it is just downright hideous."

The Hatter placed his cup on the table and leaned back, his right hand resting on his cane. The bright blue gemstone handle sparkled under his grip.

He stood and put the cane between his legs as he reached up and grabbed the lapel of his suit. His aquamarine hair spilled over his shoulders from under his purple top hat. He cleared his throat, turning his blue eyes on the Hare.

"Hideous? How do you find such a lovely hat hideous? It mirrors your own!" cried the Hare.

"Oh, so you admit to mocking my own?" The Hatter removed his cane from between his legs, spun it a few times, and planted the bottom on the lawn. "Then yes, I call judgment as well! Double judgment!"

"Judgment!" screamed the Dormouse.

All three fixed their gazes on a green-feathered flamingo sitting on the Hatter's right, with a gold monocle placed over his left eye, and his orange beak turned upward. He reached up with his wings and pulled at his blue suit jacket. He made a "hurmph" noise in his throat and surveyed those who called for judgment.

"I, Sir William, Duke of Grell, find judgment that," the flamingo stared at the Hare for some time as the others leaned slightly forward, "the hat complements the Hare."

The Hare puffed out his chest, and the Dormouse clapped excitedly, but the two stopped when Sir William, Duke of Grell, cleared his throat obnoxiously loudly.

"I find the judgment's resemblance to our host uncanny, mocking, and deserving of fire." Slamming his wing onto the table. The dishes shook and clattered. The Hatter tapped his cane on the table victoriously, shot it forward, and knocked the hat off the Hare's head.

The Hare toppled over his chair, which fell on top of him.

Dishes too close to the table's edge smashed to the ground. The Hare rolled onto his side, avoiding one of the dishes, to have a teacup hit him as he pushed himself up.

"Oof," he grunted, grabbing the table for support. He stood and rubbed the bump forming behind his left ear. His face twisted with annoyance, but his expression turned to shock when the front gate swung open.

"Good afternoon, everyone!" the White Rabbit declared as he burst into the yard with Cheshire not far behind.

The cat gave a dramatic dip of its head and followed it with a theatrical bow. The Hatter's eyes narrowed at Cheshire. He shrugged and returned Cheshire's flamboyant bow.

"Welcome, friends; please have a seat. The March Hare was just about to retrieve more tea and cakes for losing a judgment," the Hatter said, giving the hare a sarcastic smirk.

The Hare's shoulders slumped, and he dragged each step until he disappeared into the Hatter's house.

The decrepit Queen of Hearts scowled as she sat on the chair just outside the front door. She dug her hands into the chair arms, leaving claw marks and the tips of her fingernails behind. Her burning gaze pierced through each guest with violent desire.

The White Rabbit took the Hatter's hand and shook it firmly. He sat beside him, and Cheshire went to the other side and whispered into the Hatter's ear. It was strange, but the Queen of Hearts heard the conversation as though she were standing beside them.

"I found her," the cat whispered.

"And?"

"No one else has attempted contact. The queen has no power left, but I cannot turn down consistent work. If you keep paying me to be vigilant, I would be a fool to say no."

"It would be better if I didn't have to pay you to care, but her safety means more." He pulled a sack from his belt and slapped it into the cat's hand. "Just keep me and the White Rabbit informed, yeah?"

Cheshire responded with another bow before turning and heading to the gate, which opened with no physical manipulation that the queen could see.

While William of Grell and the Dormouse conversed over a tea flavor, the March Hare returned, balancing teapots and small cakes on plates.

As the Hare reached the table, the queen stood, her eyes wet. She expected such from the Hatter, but to have one of her most trusted servants betray her was more than she could take.

Fog rolled in, leaving her in a gray sea, but green electrical currents sparked to life within the thick mass.

"You never had the rabbit, my dear. He served you, yes, but he was not loyal."

The voice brought no comfort, but it rarely did. "The Hatter is right, however. My power has left me."

"This is not the end, my queen. Step through and reclaim what is yours," the voice echoed as the fog before her formed an impressive archway. She forced herself to walk through and enter the green storm.


The witch stood in the oblivion of her glass orb, looking at her broken obsidian throne and the torn tapestries hanging lifelessly on the stone walls. The fog swirled about her.

Muffled footsteps came from the other side of the fog wall. She squinted and pushed forward, but more fog billowed up, making it impossible to see anything except the specter of her sister wandering.

She had tried to talk to her. The Wicked Witch of the West did everything to get her sister to acknowledge her, but as she knew, the strange entity's proposal was her sister's only chance of survival.

The reward of taking such a deal and her ambition were too great. Few received a second chance, and she was not one to squander an opportunity.

"Have you considered my offer?"

"I have," she said, her eyes still locked on her sister's apparition.

A melodic chuckle echoed about her—the only thing not muffled. "And?"

"I accept your offer, though begrudgingly. I'm no fool."

"A wise witch. Your failure before will be but a lesson. Our stories will read far differently in this next chapter," the voice said directly in her ear, soft and promising. Her nostrils flared.

"What's different this time?"

"You're not alone," the voice said as the Queen of Hearts stepped through the form of the Wicked Witch of the East.

Rage caught in the witch's throat as her sister disappeared, but she pushed it back and focused on her new ally. A withered smile broke on the old queen's lips.

"The two of you, my dark champions, will combine our worlds as one and rule together. This is only the beginning. Take your sister's hand, my gray beauty. Use your remaining strength to make us one, and we will complete what began years ago."

"The girls..." the queen whispered, offering her frail hand to the witch.

The Wicked Witch hesitated, but her instinct told her to grasp the opportunity presented.

"The girls," she said, taking the queen's hand.

As the two women gripped tightly, the fog burst into a whirl of life. The force almost knocked them off their feet, but they held steadfast and closed their eyes.

"Give yourself willingly," the voice commanded.

"I give myself willingly."

"My essence, my being, to make us one."

"My essence, my being, to make us one," they recited.

The witch's deepest part screamed as if her soul was being siphoned from her body. Her concentration waned, and her eyes fluttered open. The fog had dissipated, replaced by something that filled her with awe and uncertainty.

A brilliant mixture of vibrant colors and swirling nebulas spun around them. She was standing on the stars, and she caught herself being sucked into the sight below.

When she looked at the queen, whose hand she still grasped, she saw the old woman was having just as much trouble pulling away from the allure at their feet.

"Stay with me."

The magic between the two women pulsed, green electric currents and red mist enveloping their forms.

Something fell behind the queen, and the witch realized she was looking through the mirror into the castle. The heart throne stood strong as the stones crumbled around it.

Curious, the witch looked up. A similar scene played through her crystal ball. Her fortress was shattering, but her obsidian throne remained amongst the debris.

The Queen of Hearts said, "Let's finish what we started, sister."

Red mist-like fingers materialized at the mirror and grabbed the green current from the witch's crystal ball.

The two energies danced and encased them entirely in their colorful ballet. As the mirror and crystal ball moved toward each other, the celestial body shrank.

When the mirror and crystal ball's surfaces neared, the women fell back into their worlds.

Their red and green magic held onto the foundations of the fortress and castle and thrust them together. The blinding flash of light disoriented the witch. The light subsided, and she waited a few moments before opening her eyes.

Two thrones sat beside each other, a crystal ball next to hers and a mirror by the heart-shaped throne on the wall.

Her strength was gone, but her eyes scanned for the queen.

The old queen lay on the steps leading to the thrones, her breathing labored. She was alive but in the same weakened state.

The witch mustered enough energy to pull herself over to the queen and place her hand on the queen's shoulder. "The voice..."

"He promised..."

The queen passed out, and darkness crept in before the witch could respond. The doors to the throne room flew open, and footsteps rushed toward her.

# Chapter 19

Grenin made sure the Stone of Insight was secure in his pocket by running his hand down his vest. He put his hands behind his back and rocked on the balls of his feet, the leather of his dress shoes squeaking.

Sliding the stone from its hidden spot, he gave it a scan. Footsteps sounded on the floor behind him, and he slipped the item back into place. He spun around and gave the approaching munchkin a polite nod.

"Grenin, sir, the room is ready." The council squire gestured to one of the larger meeting rooms.

"Squire Hylen, thank you for your help." Grenin picked up his jacket and scarf from the table and followed the squire past the massive bookcases to the room.

"Of course, Master Apprentice. It was no trouble." Hylen opened the door and secured it behind him as the older munchkin entered.

Little fluttering yellow lights that mimicked a candle flame sparked to life. They gave him plenty of light to work by, and he did not want to attract attention through the one small window. With the academy on holiday and in the early morning hours, he didn't expect anyone to be around except the library's squires and ambitious students.

Grenin peeked out the window to see if Hylen had gone, and for other lingering eyes. Satisfied that he was alone, he turned his attention to the task.

The Master Apprentice pulled the stone from his pocket and laid it on the round meeting table.

Eyes closed, palms placed together, he took a long, focused breath. He waved his right hand over the stone, then his left. He chanted a soft incantation, and wisps of smoke lifted from the surface, making the small object appear as if it were sitting in a fire.

His brow creased as his chanting intensified. With every accented phrase, small cracks forged, and smoke rolled from the newly formed crevasses. The object twitched, moved, and contorted.

He raised his hands, and the smoke climbed with the gesture. He slammed his hands down, stopping just over the rock, the movement driving the spell home—the stone split.

Grenin whipped his hand back, nearly toppling over the chair, and took a few moments to steady his breath. He slumped into the chair and glared at the stone cut down the middle after casting the intricate spell. A stone in only two pieces meant only two things to be seen.

He gathered himself and surveyed the stones closely. He made sure no smaller pieces had broken off to take into consideration. That the stone had split directly down the center worried him.

Both pieces of information held within must be dire. When he felt his energy return, the Master-Apprentice wasted no time picking up the piece on the left and turning it about with his fingertips.

Grenin pushed back into the chair, cupped the left half in his palm, and pulled it to his lips. He spoke into his hand, preparing himself to see the horrible truth.

The words released the spell, and he opened his hand. Only a pile of glittering blue dust remained where the stone once was. He blew it across the table. Each glowing particle sparked to life and swirled into a vibrant blue tornado.

The sand settled and displayed a scene of distorted shapes and bodies. Within the eerie, ethereal glow, voices echoed.

Master Harvol's apprentice walked in, and the conversation seemed like regular council business.

Zellik left Master Harvol alone, but they could hear other voices.

Grenin brought his face closer as the Grand Magus grabbed a pile of papers and sat. He flipped through each page, stopping occasionally to put his quill into the inkwell and write a few things on the parchment.

What bothered Grenin the most was that Master Harvol could not hear, or he ignored the voices.

Something sparked brightly at chest level with the Grand Magus, and upon closer inspection, Grenin could make out the amulet around his neck. Shadows flicked and darted within, a pulsing black, sometimes completely snuffing out the emerald.

It gave the master apprentice a queasy stomach. The shadows and the intensity of the voices seemed to coexist; the darker the amulet got. Taunting jeers and demonic laughter were all a bit too much, even for the seasoned council member.

Sweat formed at Grenin's hairline as the Grand Magus went about his daily work, unable or unwilling to acknowledge whatever was happening around him.

The voices reached their peak. His heart pounded as he strained to hear even one viable word.

Then, all was quiet. The shadows receded, leaving the emerald amulet sparkling.

A screeching cackle erupted from the image, throwing Grenin back into his seat. He never took his eyes off the vision. Not until an abrasive pounding on the door to the meeting room interrupted him.

The scene disappeared, telling Grenin that's all the information it contained.

The pounding came again, Hylen's muffled voice from the other side.

Grenin scooped up the other half of the stone and placed it into his pocket. He snatched his coat and scarf and rushed over to the door. The munchkin glanced at the residue and blew the fragments onto the floor. He grabbed the door handle and swung it open to an exasperated Hylen, his eyes frantic.

"It's the Grand Magus. He needs you now." Hylen's voice was shaky, which made Grenin more concerned. The squire did not rattle easily.

Grenin was already outside the door, pulling on his coat, with Hylen following behind. They went to the main staircase at the back of the library. The Master Apprentice moved through the few people climbing up the double staircase.

"What is happening? Why did the Grand Magus look so ill?" the squire asked.

"Let's just say the storms aren't another one of the Master of Weather's drunk nights in the wine cellar." He shoved the large wooden doors open, and they rushed to the Emerald City's Citadel.

The weather had not kept the Emerald City indoors. The people were in a twisted dance of chaos and happiness down the colorful streets. Many inhabitants within the Land of Oz and their day-to-day hustle remained uninterrupted. Munchkins weaved in and out of the much taller forms. No one noticed the two sprinting across Gale Park. Grenin and Hylen zig-zagged through people as they climbed the stairs and entered the entrance hall.

"Did he specify where he would be?"

"No, he was rushed and made little sense when he asked me to deliver the summons, sir." Hylen stopped and laced his fingers together. "He said he would have someone here waiting for us to arrive."

"Gentlemen!" a voice rang out over the hum of the sizeable crowd inside. They turned toward the entry to the Magus Council's corridor.

"Fen." Grenin was relieved to see the other Magus Apprentice and rushed to him. He leaned in and lowered his tone so only Fen could hear. "What is going on?"

"Possibly nothing, but he doesn't look well," Fen said as he turned down the corridor.

Grenin sighed. "This is something I don't want to be right about."

"Right about what, sir?" Hylen asked.

"Nothing. Where is he?"

"The Grand Magus is at the main spire." Fen looked as if speaking the last two words was difficult, and he swallowed hard.

"Not the one at the end of the yellow brick road..." Fen glanced over his shoulder, but no words followed. "Right. I hoped that was the punchline to a horrid joke, not reality. We'll call it wishful thinking."

"I fear we are beyond wishful thinking," Fen said, turning another corner and gesturing for the other two munchkins to enter the final hallway that led to the Great Spire in the center of the courtyard. It was the heart of the citadel and the highest tower.

When they opened the massive glass doors and stepped outside, Master Harvol stood on the yellow brick road. He never turned to greet them, eyes fixed on the emerald spear that pierced the clouded heavens.

Other towers surrounded the spire, all reaching skyward. The emerald green was a sharp contrast against the dark clouds. A thunderstorm vibrated the ground they stood on, and the three exchanged worried glances.

Others on the Magus Council filled the courtyard and paced about with their heads dipped as they muttered incantations. The tower that had become the symbol of hope and guidance was now a lurking, ominous presence.

"Grand Magus Harvol," Grenin began as he approached, but choked when the older munchkin turned. The man's silver hair, which had once been like silk, was disheveled. Dark circles cradled his tired blue eyes, and the smile plastered onto his face was one of a man who had seen his damnation.

"Ah, Master Apprentice Grenin." The old man rested heavily on his white oak cane, and his usual vibrant robes had faded to mere pastels.

"Master." Grenin said, hurrying to offer the Grand Magus his arm.

"Always respectful, you've remained. I admire that." He nodded and tapped the offered arm gently. He turned back toward the spire.

Unsure that the older man had finally outlived his sanity or had tampered with the wrong magic, Grenin took a shoulder-wide stance beside his master. His hands folded in front of him as he matched the Grand Magus's gaze upward.

"What has transpired to cause such a gathering at one of the most powerful places in the city?" Grenin inquired, keeping his gaze skyward, looking for any clue that might allude to what was happening.

"Why did you stop?" Grand Magus Harvol asked, leaning on his cane.

Grenin let out a long, drawn-out sigh and tightly clasped his hands. "I didn't want or need it. Plus, far more capable men and women are better suited for your position, Grand Master." He dipped his gaze to the well-respected munchkin. "Are you ever going to let this go?"

"You deserve it more than anyone here, and many would agree." His face softened, but a tense expression returned seconds later.

"Rillan will make an excellent Grand Magus once you retire."

"You're twice his age and more than that in knowledge and talent. Master Rillan even agrees."

"I do not. Master Rillan will do wonderfully, and I will be there when needed." He nodded, satisfied, but then concern flooded him. The Grand Magus seemed unaware of his frail state and continued the conversation as if they were having tea.

They observed the clouds above the spire squeezing out all that was left of the sun.

"I failed you," the Grand Magus said, blunt and unforgiving. "Us. I failed us."

Grenin steadied the older munchkin before folding his arms over his chest. His heart dropped, and dread crept up his spine.

"How did one of the most accomplished and wisest men in all the Emerald City fail anyone?" Grenin watched a single tear slip down the Grand Magus's wrinkled cheek. "Master," he began, but stopped, for once not quite knowing how to proceed.

"I let the wrong one in." Grand Magus's blue eyes looked gray, and his hair became more straw-like.

"For the love of the land, what's happening to you?" Grenin said, taking the Grand Magus by the arm.

Grenin looked at the growing, frantic movements of the present council members, their eyes bouncing between him and the spires. The Grand Magus dropped to his knees, his cane falling to the grass. His amulet pulsed with an unholy green light as shadows flicked within.

The Master Apprentice laid Harvol's head in his lap, and the ground trembled.

"Master, what's happening?"

"For years, we have been watchful... mindful of the past..." He took in a deep, raspy breath. "We will continue to protect the future, though the times will be difficult." He grabbed the amulet around his neck, the shadows inside moving violently within the light.

"When this breaks, you must take it with you. The effect will be over, but you will need this. I let the wrong one in..."

A silent scream erupted from the Grand Magus, his eyes and mouth illuminated by a blinding green light. Grenin scrambled away and covered his face with his arm. The ground shook so hard that the members of the council tripped over each other as they ran for the citadel.

When the light dimmed, Grenin looked at where the Grand Magus lay, his dulled robes covered in falling green dust from the shaking spire. With each grief-driven step, he looked in horror at his dead master and friend, seeing the broken amulet.

He reached down and removed the amulet, placing it in his pocket, and looked up at the spire. The same green light and shadows that moved within the amulet slinked up the spire.

Panic gripped his throat. He knew that what they had protected the land against for so long would be unleashed in a matter of moments.

Grenin rushed toward the vaults within the central council's quarters. They built them close in case this day came.

He darted through the frenzied crowd of magus and other citadel occupants. Reality sank in, and terror gripped his gut. He ran through the long halls and instructed the panicked council and parliament members to evacuate the citadel.

Grenin threw open the doors to the main meeting chamber and ran to the tapestry on the back wall, glancing at the seat his friend had occupied just two days before. He shook the thought away and placed two fingers over his amulet. It illuminated a brilliant indigo. Magic burst forward, taking the shape of tiny stars that splashed over the fabric. The stars swirled together and formed a delicate hand that mimicked Grenin's.

He gestured in a circular motion and ended with half a triangle. The hand faded into blue smoke that dissipated shortly after. The tapestry lifted sideways. He heard a clink and pop from the metal vault, and the heavy door creaked open.

Grenin grasped an item that shifted and moved in his hand. When he brought the item into the light, it had shrunk significantly in his palm. He quickly slipped it into his breast pocket and buttoned it.

He turned to leave the chambers when another tremor rumbled through the citadel, this one far more violent than the last. The munchkin had only moments to get out.

# Chapter 20

The White Rabbit looked down the aisle leading to Merchant's Square. The air filled with the deafening crack of thunder, drowning out the few startled screams. A flash of green choked the playful colors of the Night Market.

"Mayor, I believe now would be a time to seek shelter," Veil shouted over the growing rumbles. "I don't think we have much time."

The mayor nodded, unable to peel his eyes away from the strange green cloud cover. Was it descending?

"Dad!" Tov clutched the mirror handle with both hands and brought it to his chest.

The White Rabbit spun and closed the distance between him and his son. Veil had already grabbed some more valuable trinkets and shoved them into his leather traveling bag. He plucked his coat from the wall and took off toward the tavern. Mayor White looked back to see if Deller was leaving the square but found the candy merchant's booth empty.

He took a visual sweep of the market. Most had either disappeared or were making their way indoors. Satisfied, he took his son by the shoulders, doing his best to remain centered. They had just made it past the fountain when the ground jolted so hard they toppled over.

The mayor could stop his fall, but his son slammed his knee onto the cobblestoned road. Despite the sudden tumble, Tov held onto the mirror.

The White Rabbit forced himself up as the earth beneath him violently shifted and moved. Another sharp jolt caused him to careen forward, and he braced himself on the fountain.

Tov moved and stepped forward, but his foot didn't find any ground. He looked down and froze. A dark abyss stared up at him—the road split, giving way to large cracks that led to nowhere.

He fell into the claws of nothingness waiting for him, but the jerk on his arm snapped him back. He stopped falling and dangled over the black void. The young rabbit slipped the mirror into his belt and clasped his father's forearm with his other hand, trying to climb out with his legs as the ground continued its violent dance.

Calm was no longer anywhere on the mayor's face; the sight of his son dangling over the maw of death gripped his chest as he desperately pulled to get him away.

Dark vines shot up and out of the chasm, over the entire square. Tov put his knee on the still-intact ground, but a vine lashed around his ankle, yanking him back down and loosening his grip on his father's hand.

The White Rabbit shouted as he clutched his son's arm with both hands.

"Dad..."

Mayor White looked into his son's tear-filled eyes, knowing what was to come. The storm cracked another fierce bolt, and the thunder played its dark symphony.

"What would she have done, Dad?"

"Survive." His grip slipped, and his son fell into the void.

The White Rabbit watched in horror as his son disappeared into the black chasm. The last thing he saw was a flash of silver light. He screamed. His body crumpled. His instincts kicked in, and he scooted back to the fountain as debris from the brick buildings fell, many narrowly missing him. He used the edge of the fountain to pull himself to his feet. The quakes intensified, almost throwing him to the ground again.

He steadied himself, leaped over the cracks in the ground, and landed in front of the tavern. Staying outside was not an option.

He burst through the tavern doors into another mess of chaos. Patrons were scrambling upstairs and out the back door. Tweedle Dee was nowhere to be found, but his brother was shaking, curled up in a wooden chair, rocking back and forth.

The White Rabbit did his best to hold back the pain of his loss. He knew if he allowed it to consume him, none of them would have a chance. "Tweedle Dum, what happened?"

"The hand.... it came... from the—"

An emerald hand shattered the wood floor beneath Tweedle Dum and wrapped its massive fingers around his round body. In its grasp, the chair splintered. Only wood fragments remained after the hand ripped the Tweedle brother. The White Rabbit looked down, seeing the cellar and frightened eyes. There was no hole to follow.

The vision of his son being swallowed by an abyss swept through his mind. The lump in his throat threatened to spring free. He shook his head and sprinted out the door, dodging falling stones and bricks while maneuvering around cracks in the ground.

He turned down a small side street east toward the Hatter's cottage. The White Rabbit did not know what he would find when he arrived, but it was the only place he could think of going.

Creeping dread eclipsed the usual peacefulness of the woods. The White Rabbit's fur stood on end. When he turned and glanced at the Night Market slowly shrinking in the distance, something dark descended upon it and snuffed out all the light within. Whatever stole, the light followed him, and it was relentless.

He had to cross the chess fields before he got to the Hatter's place, and he hoped the White Knight and the rest of the armies were keeping the monster contained.

As he broke through the trees, he got his answer. The red and white armies were hard at work, frantically replacing magical wards. More physical members of the army were reinforcing the beast's prison. Relief left his lips as the White Knight nodded and waved him to continue.

The mayor didn't need more than that. He disappeared into the foliage on the other side of the chess field in just a few strides.

It was a relief to see the small white gate to the Hatter's front yard, which, as usual, was hosting a tea party. Before he could cross the threshold, the ground split around the perimeter of the property, a brilliant burst of green light springing forth before thick tree roots slinked up and back into the ground, gripping the soil as the massive black trees grew from the cracks, now lingering, staring down their somber limbs at the once serene cottage.

The ground crept in and closed around the new trees as if they had always been looming. It made the mayor uneasy. The quaking slowed, and he heard the commotion coming from the tea party—shouts between the March Hare and the Hatter. He went closer to the black trees to see if anyone was injured.

An extremely annoyed Hatter sat at his seat, and a terrified March Hare, Sir William of Grell, and Dormouse huddled at the cottage's front door. The White Rabbit pushed past the ominous trees and swung open the gate.

"Is everyone okay?"

"Ah! My old friend, it's been far too long! Please, sit and have a cup of tea!" The Hatter grabbed the teapot and poured the warm liquid into a cup. The White Rabbit just blinked at him.

Confused, the rabbit's gaze alternated between the group cowering at the door and the relaxed Hatter, offering him a cup of tea as if it were any usual cloudy day.

"Hatter, are you aware that a mass of black trees just surrounded your property, crawling out of the ground? Did not you feel the ground shaking?"

The Hatter glanced at his front gate, shrugged, and sipped his tea.

"As I told my guests, it's quite in your head. Now, everyone, stop this nonsense and come back to your tea. It's getting cold!" Irritation nagged at his voice.

The White Rabbit knew the Hatter well. He often dismissed things, claiming, "Nothing was happening," but even this was hard to ignore, yet he did. The mayor shook his head and walked toward the March Hare. He kneeled next to the cluster, pressing their backs against the closed door.

"The shaking," the Hare sputtered.

"I know. It's over for now. Is anyone injured?" The White Rabbit didn't make out any apparent injuries.

"Only mentally and emotionally," chimed the quivering Dormouse.

The White Rabbit stood and went back to the Hatter.

"Dear Hatter, your guests are a bit shaken. I would think a wonderful host would cater to making them comfortable, despite what may or may not be, yes?"

The Hatter paused, his hand holding the teacup to his lips. He responded with a simple nod and sipped his tea.

"You are correct, my dear rabbit friend. I've forgotten myself. Shall we continue our tea inside my cottage beside a warm fire?" He looked up, and tiny droplets fell onto his face.

The three on the porch almost broke the door to enter as the Hatter grabbed his ornate cane from the table.

"Shall we?" he asked, giving the White Rabbit a half-bow and gesturing to his front door. The White Rabbit sighed silently and headed toward the house. Once the two passed through the threshold, the Hatter clicked the door shut.

The moment the warmth from the fire tingled his senses, the anguish of what had occurred washed over the White Rabbit. He slumped on the Hatter's purple rug, his back against the couch. The mayor brought his hands up to his face and quietly mourned. The other four made conversation, their voices strained and almost a whisper in the back of his mind.


Grenin barely reached the top of the steps outside the citadel when the buttresses behind him cracked and burst, debris hailing down on those retreating from the citadel. The Master Apprentice hoped the building was empty.

Once he felt the grass of Gale Park under his shoes, he turned toward the crumbling building. He could only take in the destruction momentarily before his eyes caught a new commotion down the red street. The bricks split down the center of the road and ignited in a brilliant green flame. Munchkins, Pridyr, and humans scrambled for some escape, but few did.

The blue brick road ripped from the red one and forced those running to leap to one side.

A hand gripping Grenin's arm brought him out of his disbelieving trance. A familiar voice called him fully back to his senses.

"What happened?" Glinda said. Her voice was soothing even in the most tragic moments. The munchkin blinked a few times before he focused on her features.

"The spire," Grenin said, but he did not know how to continue. He had no answer other than that they had failed. "The Grand Magus is gone, and the spire..." He looked around the park and the crumbling streets. Down the steps tumbled the

Library's Pridyr statues, and screams erupted. The academy's roof burst into green flames, spreading fire to the neighboring buildings.

Glinda followed his gaze to the green brick road rupturing, raw earth swallowing the once vibrant path. "It's only a matter of moments; he'll be free."

"What do we do?" Another female voice said from the other side. The young munchkin's eyes were wet, but he saw a spark of hope within. Many students of magic and Magus Apprentices stood around them; all appeared hoping for some remnant of guidance.

"We try one last time," Glinda said, facing the crumbling citadel. The green light within the main spire grew more brilliant as the Emerald City collapsed around them.

"Glinda, there's nothing left. Our only option is to escape." Grenin looked up at her with a pleading gaze. "We have lost this battle."

"I know," she said. "Did you make it to the vault?"

He narrowed his eyes. "I did."

"Go."

"I will not just leave you or our people here to—" Her soft, worried smile stopped his rebuttal.

"Yes, you will. Now go!"

Grenin was about to plant himself firmly, but a strange crackling sound, as if someone had stepped on glass, caught his attention. The yellow brick road shattered into shards of glass, all reflecting the green bonfire engulfing the city. The shards hovered before turning in unison toward Grenin. Glinda was not wrong. He turned and sprinted toward the gates, the yellow brick road splintering as he flew past the falling buildings.

He kept his eyes on the gate but could hear Glinda and his students chanting and conjuring a protective barrier around themselves.

As the barriers climbed and formed a thick, iridescent shield, the yellow shards launched, the sharp tips targeting Grenin's back.

One grazed his left cheek, but the rest fell useless to the dirt when they hit the barrier. Some shattered into gold dust.

Grenin closed his eyes and whispered an incantation. It was an old teleport spell, simple but effective. He would teleport outside the gates and disappear into the woods beyond the poppy fields. He was thankful Scarecrow had been traveling from Munchkin City, so hopefully, he would meet him in between.

He heard the others running behind him, and as he ended the spell, he saw Glinda and the rest not far behind. Expecting the others to transport with him, he finished the spell.

A flash of green popped him out of his location and onto the spire, with the dead Grand Magus at his feet. Glinda and the rest came into existence beside him. Grenin and Glinda shared looks of terror and confusion. None of them waited to scale the fallen debris and ran toward Gale Park.

Once in the park, they attempted the spell again, only to be returned to their previous position.

"He's already too powerful," Grenin bellowed over the destruction.

The female Munchkin student tried again, but before the last words passed her lips, an ethereal green hand shot from the spire and wrapped around her. She struggled only for a moment before the hand drained her life force, and her clothing fell to the ground.

Grenin froze next to Glinda as more hands sprang to life, gripping each student until their clothes fell like dead leaves.

Grenin and Glinda teleported out, but the result was the same every time. Glinda fell to her knees, and Grenin took her elbow, his fatigue apparent.

A glaring light erupted from the central spire, forcing them to turn their faces away. Grenin's eyes darted about, looking for any others that remained. His heart sank when he saw no movement, remnants of clothing covered in dust.

Glinda stood, her eyes meeting the tip of the spire, Grenin's gaze following. Another brilliant green light exploded from the spire. The once-sturdy structure fractured, light spewing from the cracks. The rest of the spires bursting shattered their last hope. If it were not for what remained of the citadel, they would have been annihilated. Sparkling dust fell all around them, glittering in their defeat.

The light dimmed, and a shadow moved within the foyer of the broken citadel. It was a nightmare they had kept locked away for many years. True, menacing evil had returned to the Land of Oz, and nothing could be done.

The dark figure stepped out of the settling debris of the spires, each step with meaning. It reached the massive glass doors and raised its hand, palm toward the two. The glass shattered, spraying the steps with shining shrapnel.

A deep, melodic tone filled the heart of the crumbling Emerald City. A melody once sung by Dorothy Gale on her way to find the Great and Powerful Oz echoed in the destruction with malicious intent.

Glinda placed a shaky hand on her husband's shoulder, his own reaching up to grasp it. They watched helplessly as the towering presence slowly descended the stairs.

The figure moved past the last step of the citadel and firmly placed its feet onto the crippled brick road, its features sharpening. The man stood with his hands behind his back. His piercing gaze surveyed the city with almost a bored expression. His features were gaunt and harsh, accented perfectly by his groomed beard, matching his well-kept salt and pepper hair. Though the man looked like he was in his mid-fifties, the way he moved showed no physical limitations, making his demeanor even more threatening.

He studied the destruction as a king would his lands and finally rested his gaze on Glinda and Grenin. He ran his hand down the lapel of his black tailcoat jacket. On the left lapel was a symbol embroidered in silver stitching, matching the trim on his cuffs. His black slacks complemented his white shirt and purple tie. He looked like a well-respected businessman, but Grenin and Glinda knew better.

"I believe the last thing I heard whispered from your lips on the day of my imprisonment was 'monster,' was it not, Glinda?" The man's tone was calm and calculating, giving the two a sense of foreboding as his slow and deliberate steps closed the distance between them.

"I hate to disappoint," he said and gave the two a sinister smile. He snapped his fingers, and green flames wrapped around the citadel. Another explosion ruptured the foundation, bringing it completely to ruin. Only bits of the spires remained inside the citadel's rubble.

"I am, after all, the Great and Powerful Oz." His smile remained as he focused on Glinda. She clutched her stomach and crumpled over. Grenin dropped to his knees beside her, and she fell to hers, her body shaking.

Their eyes met, and she gave Grenin a weak smile. "It seems," she said, her breath labored, but before she could finish, a green hand burst from the ground and encased her. The dense hand dissipated, taking Glinda with it.

Grenin scrambled to his feet. "Glinda!" He bolted down the shattered yellow brick road to the park with only seconds to react. He could not help her dead, and what he carried was too important. The munchkin kept his eyes on the gate, trying to ignore the death surrounding him. He maneuvered around debris and corpses alike. A spell passed his lips, and he found himself just outside the gate, steps from the poppy fields. Only to be teleported back to the city.

He bellowed, and a green hand burst through the ground, trapping him. The Master Apprentice jerked, trying to free himself from the prison, but it was useless. Suspended in the stockade's grip, he stared down at his dead friends' remains.

"What have we done?" he whispered into his hands.

"Because you'll be locked away until you die, I will leave you with some company." Oz stated with a smirk. The remnants of ash billowed from where the clothes of the dead had landed. The Grand Magus's robes lay at the base of the green hand.

Oz walked up to the transparent fingers. "I will return with a gift just for you, old friend. Until then, enjoy my masterpiece." He gestured to the destroyed Emerald City.

Buildings exploded and caught fire as he walked to the gates. The entire city fell before the Great and Powerful Oz.

# Chapter 21

The wind whipped through the poppy fields, and Lucian's long black coat moved. He adjusted his felt fedora, slumping the brim slightly over his blue eyes. The cloud cover had swallowed all remaining light only moments before green flames burst within the city gates.

He quickened his pace to the edge of the fields and stopped. His pouch was hanging from his right hand, and he looked on in disbelief. The falling rain formed puddles and gathered at his feet. He stared at his horrified expression in the rippling water, searching for answers that would not come before looking back out over the city skyline.

Guilt and failure flooded his heart. "I shouldn't have left."

He gripped his satchel tight to his chest and slumped against the trunk of a large oak. All he could do was watch his beloved city crumble.

He could not shake himself from the scene unfolding before him. The once-proud emerald towers cracked, and the ground shook. The violent jolt almost flung him to his knees.

He heard screams and knew people were scattering within the city as green rays shot up and black clouds released into the air. Lightning flashed through the darkness.

A familiar form popped into existence and ran toward the tree line, but just a second later, Grenin was gone.

Lucian dug his nails into the wood. An eerie quiet choked the horrific scene, and the ground shook again. More explosions came from within the gates, another series of flames lighting up the clouds.

The ground under the poppies cracked and split, and an iridescent light shot up. Something reached forward, and the light pulled the poppies down.

Lucian attempted to move back into the woods, but the quaking was too intense. He braced himself against the tree and watched the Emerald City fall.

The poppy fields took on a new shape. Thick vines slithered out of the cracks and claimed the field as theirs. Large plants reached for the dark sky, and once they stood about six feet tall, they bloomed into brilliant-colored flowers. Though they were beautiful and looked innocent enough, something made Lucian drop to the ground and push away from them.

The fissures in the ground sealed together, and the iridescent light disappeared below.

As the shaking subsided, Lucian found his footing and brought his eyes back to the city. The screams gave way to silence. The light intensified, taking over the sky before disappearing into the heavens.

Behind the colorful flower garden, the smoldering city was something out of nightmares. When the closest flowers turned their petals toward him, he ran. He was unsure where to go, but the forest he usually avoided seemed familiar and safe to him. The only things he was sure of were that the world had changed and the Emerald City was dead.


Plates and steins tumbled to the drinking hall's floor. The Pridyr of the Plains were meeting about defenses when the ground began shaking, and it had progressively worsened. It felt as if the entire hall would come down on their heads.

Ragnus could barely find his footing as he took his mother's hand and pulled her toward the entrance. His father spun out of his throne and shouted instructions to his people. Being so close to the witch's old castle, they could take no chances that it was just a simple earthquake.

"I can make the rest of the way. Go help your father," Ragnus's mother said as she removed her cloak.

"What are you doing?"

"Getting the rest of the Plains' army. Don't worry about what I'm doing. Go now!" She shooed him as if he had interrupted her reading time and dashed for the door.

He always admired his mother's ability to stay calm in any situation. She had taught him when he was a cub that nothing comes from panic except poor decisions. She placed her paw on the door, and Ragnus turned toward his father.

A large jolt forced him to brace on one of the long tables. A stone shattered where he'd stood a second before, and it took everything within to embrace his mother's outlook. Though he appeared composed, memories of past failures seeped deep within him.

Ragnus shook his head and snarled. He dodged falling stones and skirted other debris. The last to file out the back of the hall, he took a quick once-over to ensure he was the last to leave. Satisfied, he let the door slam shut and spun out of the way just in time to miss a massive stone crashing at his feet.

"Ragnus! Take the Tundra Pride warriors to meet your mother at the west gate," the chief shouted as he waded through the chaos to his son.

"What's happening?" Ragnus reached over and plucked a large spear from a weapons rack. The spear had a wicked silver arrowhead fastened to the end of a thick black shaft carved from the trees in the Spectral Woods.

"I received reports this morning from our mystics of an energy surge from the witch's fortress. Whatever is happening is coming from there and one other location, but it's too far to pinpoint. Be ready for anything. The ancestors' whisper of evil awakening once more." He clasped his hand on Ragnus's shoulder. "I'm proud of you, son. Now go help your mother."

Ragnus clapped his massive paw on top of his father's, giving him a determined nod. They bolted in opposite directions. Ragnus went to the village's west end and helped some panicked villagers to safer routes leading to the fields between the village and the forest.

He was thankful that most of the Plains' Pride were warriors. There would be far fewer casualties because of it. He turned briefly to watch those fleeing to the tundra.

He spun and ran to the west gate, his attention falling on the mountains before him. This was the moment they had been fearing, but twilight was upon them, and they all knew exactly what had to be done.

The closer he got to the gate, the straggling soldiers found him, and he signaled for them to follow.

"Sir, they evacuated the villagers. All that remains are warriors, though some of our strong are helping get the innocents to the Tundras."

"That's fine. We have more than enough for our defenses," he said, pushing one side of the gate open. The Pridyr nodded as they passed, and Ragnus took the back, ensuring everyone had been evacuated.

He shut the gate and turned to see his mother standing at the front of a large formation in cherry-brown leather armor and a sword strapped to her hip. Other groups formed, most of which were a mix of other Pride warriors sent to help defend the land. He took his position in front and planted his spear into the ground. He looked down at his armor and snorted. It'd been so long, but some things always felt like home.

His mother held firm and faced the monstrous, foreboding mountains. The shaking had yet to cease, cycling from jolting to rolling.

A sharp cry from the formation came from behind his mother, and she jumped back.

The knee-high plains grass had shrunk away and shifted.

"A chessboard?" Ragnus said, looking back at his mother, hoping for some answers. She looked just as perplexed.

She gripped the hilt of her sword and spun toward the mountains. Lightning flashed through the dark clouds, lighting up the warriors' faces. Each expressed worry and confusion, and all Ragnus could do was mask his concern from the others.

Thick fog at the base of the mountains turned and swirled into frantic, human-like shapes. The mist dissipated, and Ragnus saw a group of men and women dressed in red and white plate armor running back and forth. A knight dressed in white sat on top of a white horse. Darting from one side of the massive group to the other, he waved his silver sword about.

"What's happening? Who are they?" Ragnus shouted.

His mother did not respond. It appeared the red and white armies were trying to contain something. She finally looked at her son.

"Whoever they are, it seems they have their hands full. We know what we must do. Let's not get distracted."

Ragnus let out a stressed breath. It looked as if they were attempting to hold something at bay, all focused on a particular rock formation.

The White Knight shouted, and Ragnus's blood chilled at the bits he could make out. Whatever they were holding back only had to bide its time.

Lurisa yanked her sword from its sheath, brandishing it high. Her steel flashed in the lightning streaking across the sky.

"We knew this day would come! Our duty, our right, is to protect the Land of Oz. No victory comes without sacrifice! By my teeth, by my blood, by my spirit!"

"By my teeth, blood, and spirit!" The divisions recited and raised their weapons above their heads.

With his spear high, Ragnus repeated the mantra, all his people following. The shield warriors surrounding the platoons bashed their weapons against their shields in rhythm, hooting after each line.

The rise of the Pridyr warriors' call drowned the shouts from the white and red army and the thunder that crashed above.

Ragnus expected to see the witch's minions descend from the sky and land. That he'd yet to see a flying monkey, or a goblin made him uneasy.

Many moments changed Ragnus's life, but nothing could have prepared him for the monstrosity that burst through the rock at the foot of the mountain.

The force flung the red and white armies back like discarded dolls. Shocked silence replaced the Pridyrs' chanting. The White Knight's horse attempted to bolt, but the knight kept his steed focused and urged him toward the settling dust and rocks. All the Pridyr warriors stood at the ready.

A high-pitched, squealing roar erupted from the newly formed cave. Something massive poked its head through the dust, and wings that blocked out the little light from the overhead lighting followed.

Another shriek echoed through the checkered plains. As the dust settled, more of the creature became visible. It resembled a lanky dragon. Its limbs were thin but far from frail, and the claws at the end of each digit were as long as a human leg. They sliced through fallen debris as they pushed out of the cave.

Its face was the most terrifying. A short snout with elongated teeth, stained yellow and brown. At the center of its head was one massive orange eye with a seething red pupil. Wisps of hair hung on the sides of its head. Fin-like appendages flared from its cheeks. It took slow, prowling steps. Its tail snaked and whipped around, slamming three red soldiers to the ground. Scales covered its back and the top of its head. Blue veins below the surface of its sickly white skin wriggled like dying worms.

The giant head reared back and snapped down at the prone soldiers. Their screams were a haunting overture. Ragnus gripped his spear and prepared for what was to come.


The ground in front of Flint fell away. Jumping back, the council members and apprentices missed the formed chasm. The shaking had started just moments before, and it had picked up speed, weaving in and out of the dense trees.

Flint grabbed Umiko before she fell into the gaping hole. She fell on her rear next to a tree.

"You okay?" He turned and kneeled, doing a quick check for apparent wounds on the young woman.

"A little shaken, but okay," she said, pushing herself from the leaves and dirt. She brushed off her robes and threw her suitcase to the ground.

Umiko wasted no time sliding off her bulky robe and shoving it into her bag. Underneath, she wore a simple sea-green sleeveless top and gray pants. Her black boots reached just below her knees, and they seemed to be made for tracking through the terrain.

The tremors continued, and flashes of green danced to the crack of thunder overhead. The light illuminated the surrounding forest in a ghostly jade hue.

"What in the three circles are you doing?" Balanor shouted.

"Adapting. Take the robes off." She looked back at the rest of the council, who stared at her.

"Now!" She startled them enough to comply, though they still looked confused.

Flint stared at the growing hole. Bits of the land crumbled into darkness as it crept toward the massive tree roots.

"We need to get out of here," Umiko said.

Flint turned about to head back the way they had come until loud shouts echoed around the hole, and dirt rose to the surface like a tide.

The space just above the hole looked liquid, like someone had suspended a watery surface over a newly planted flower bed. The voices became louder and more tangible. A generously sized cottage and garden, complete with a long table and toppled dishes, manifested in front of them.

Flint could barely distinguish the frantically moving bodies through the thick shrubs around the perimeter. He turned and walked in the other direction, signaling the others to follow him.

"What just happened?" Umiko panted as he picked up the pace.

"I don't know, but that's not something I'm going to wait around to find out. We need to get to General Ragnus. We may already be too late." He looked at the sky, still painted with green flashes, and drops of water clinked on his metal forehead.

Umiko glanced at the shaking cottage and dashing figures. A strong pull made her halt, but only briefly. Flint made no motion to stop. She had no time to waste, but she couldn't help peering back again to see if the people were harmed as she leaped over a group of gnarled roots, though the panicked voices confirmed they were alive.

The group picked up the pace to a brisk run, moving and dodging new cracks forming in the forest floor. The fine hairs on her arm stood on end, and a deep, sinking feeling grabbed her gut.

There was something more in these trees — whispers, voices intangible, yet mocking. She tripped and tumbled into a tree trunk, but she braced herself, her palms slamming into the bark.

A quick jolt flipped her around, and the whispers grew louder. A sharp, taunting giggle came from her left, and she stumbled away from the tree. The child's laughter continued, but nobody was present.

*They belong to us...*
*They belong to us...*
*They belong to us...*
*They belong to us...*
*They belong to us...*

The voices fluctuated from child to man, from near to far, from up to down, and from left to right. Umiko was in a state of mental chaos. She shut her eyes and covered her ears. The shaking ground brought her to her knees.

She tried to push the voices out, but the assault continued.

*They belong to us...*
*They belong to us...*
*They belong to us...*

"Umiko!" Flint gripped her by the shoulders and pulled her to her feet. He braced her back with his arm, scooped her legs up, swinging her bag over his shoulder with his.

Tin Man saw she was fighting something, and he knew the Spectral Woods' effect on people. The more distance they put between them and their current location, the better.

Flint urged the rest on. He knew the woods well and would have no trouble tracking them.

He clutched Umiko to his chest and balanced the two pouches on his shoulder. Being constructed of metal made these tasks far more manageable.

Flint ran toward the council members ahead, but just a few feet from the group, thunder crashed above. He skidded to a stop, with leaves and dirt flying up.

A green flash lit the forest enough for Flint to see the group's horrified expressions. Lightning struck a tree to his right, and the massive trunk rapidly descended toward Flint and Umiko.

He threw himself forward and rolled with her as the tree slammed next to them. There was no time to celebrate the minor victory. Umiko's eyes fluttered open.

"I heard..."

"I know what you heard, and it's not a good sign," he said as he helped her to her feet. "Are you okay?"

"Yes, let's get to General Ragnus." She took her bag from Flint's arm.

The shaking calmed down, but the storm was more violent. Flint pulled the axe from his belt as he stepped to the front of the group. He was taking no chances. They were not out of the woods yet.

# Chapter 22

Ragnus smelled the curdled breath of the monstrous creature. It pulled its scaly lips back, showing the old blood caked onto its steel-cutting teeth. He couldn't tell if it was plotting its next move or merely toying with the armies scurrying back like ants escaping a downpour.

The tail swiped so rapidly that no one had a chance to do anything other than accept their fate. It crashed onto the entire left flank. Of the few that took the full brunt of the blow, the rest remained motionless on the ground. The white army's armor turned red, and those already in red a deeper crimson.

A massive, clawed appendage slammed into the prone bodies, taking away any hope of survival. The creature plunged its total weight, creating a carnage puddle. It swung its long neck around to the other side, and the rest of the army recalibrated, their swords at the ready.

An older gentleman whipped his horse around and placed himself between the sea of red and white bodies and the monster. His sword caught a flash of green lightning.

Ragnus heard him shouting, but making out the words over the commotion was impossible. The general turned to his mother, who still locked her eyes on the massive creature. He'd never seen his mother freeze in the face of adversity. Dread washed over him, but his platoon's shaken expressions made his courage deep inside burst forth.

He tightened his grip on his spear and took his mother's arm gently. Her horrified gaze met his for a moment.

"Go," he said. She hesitated, but he roared over the chaos. "Go!"

Lurisa whipped around, shouting, retreat.

Ragnus bolted toward his father's platoon on the other side of their village. As he darted around the gate facing the mountains, the few guardians stationed on the cliffs sprinted down the narrow path to the plains. They flew past Ragnus's retreating troops and into the woods.

He wasn't sure if he wanted to know the reason behind such a response, but the Pridyr, particularly the Celehawk Clan, had a reputation for their bravery and mental tenacity.

His sense of dread summoned images of Flint, Lucian, Glinda, and Grenin through his mind, but they were short-lived. A swipe of the creature's tail crashed next to him. He dodged, rolled to his side, and pushed himself up.

The creature focused on the dwindling red and white armies. The White Knight feverishly swung his sword and kicked his horse, urging him into the face of death.

Chief Urvan had a far unique expression than the rest of his men. While the platoon shared horrified looks, the chieftain studied the creature, watching each move with the scrutiny a master does their pupil.

The monster was racing out of living bodies to snap and claw at, but as each soldier fell, the White Knight charged.

Chief Urvan pulled the sword from its sheath. "There's no winning this fight. This will end your story if you choose to stay." He shouted to his platoon over the creature's screech. The chieftain gave his son a sad smile.

Ragnus spun his spear into a ready position. "I'm not running ever again."

"I know, son. You made your mother, didn't you?"

"If we all stayed to die, what would be the clan's future?"

The chieftain's smile grew, his amber eyes glistening as a tear rolled down his cheek. He reached over and gripped his son's forearm and squeezed.

"I'm so proud of you, son. May we meet again in the shadows, General Ragnus." He lifted his sword, his head tilting to the storm above. He roared back and charged in to help the White Knight.

Few red and white soldiers remained, but those who did still fought desperately to drive the creature back. The White Knight swiped at the creature's front claw just as it was about to crush another soldier. The beast recoiled and screamed. It whipped its disgusting head to the knight, baring its putrid crimson teeth.

The knight raised his sword, and three soldiers took the same stance. A javelin soared over the knight's shoulder and caught the creature's bulbous eye.

He turned in his saddle and saw the massive lions running toward them, their weapons trained on the beasts. Relief and uncertainty flooded through him. He had only seen one lion-like creature before, but anything that would help him drive back the dreaded Jabberwocky was welcome. He lifted his sword again and shouted encouragement to his men and women.

The rushing lion army brought new life to those left in red and white, and their attention turned to the behemoth, its head snaking back for another violent attack.

Four Pridyr leaped up and pierced the creature's skin with their weapons. They used their claws for leverage as they climbed onto the thing. It spun and coiled into itself. Its snarling maw snapped at them as they made gaping holes in it.

The Jabberwocky's eye pulsed gray liquid that held the consistency of mashed fruit and smelled of weeks-old rotting corpses. The stink stung, but the Pridyr pressed onward, around the many wounds oozing the creature's strange lifeblood.

A male Pridyr's sword flung back, ready to come down for another attack. The beast's teeth interrupted it as they tore into his arm. He screamed and fell into the mud and sinew below, his arm landing next to him. Seconds later, the massive, clawed grip of the horror crushed his head.

The soldiers fought on, but it was not long before more fell. The Pridyr added to the bodies on the checkered grass, the once neatly tended field, now a sea of bone and blood.

The White Knight gave Ragnus a nod before he lifted his voice and sword, challenging the monster. He charged in with no intention of making it out. They had to stop the thing or force it to retreat. Either way, the knight would protect the land and those left on the field.

He noticed movement on his right and did a double-take as the most decorated lion bounded on all fours as fast as his steed. The lion focused on the Jabberwocky, and the knight kicked his horse. The monster turned from the soldiers to the two warriors.

The Jabberwocky's head whipped forward, but Chief Urvan stopped at the last moment. He stood and lifted his sword in time to slash the creature across the snout. The deep wound sprayed, and the monster screamed, reeled, and stumbled to the crumbling mountains.

Ragnus saw the opportunity and barked out orders. With a sweep of its tail, the creature spun and took the remaining red and white soldiers to the ground.

The general rushed forward and shoved his spear into the base of its neck. He stomped on the spear, thrusting the arrowhead farther into the creature. He leaped toward the thing's head and dug into the Jabberwocky's skin with his massive claws. Sickly blood coated Ragnus's fur, the smell making him lightheaded, but he pressed on.

Flashes of the past burst in the back of his mind—memories of his fallen brother and the times that led to his exile. Fear climbed up his throat, but he saw his father charge in, the White Knight fighting wordlessly by his side, and remembered he was not the victim of his past. He was the success of his failure, and he would not falter again.

General Ragnus pulled the spear from the creature's flesh, leaving a gaping hole in its wake. He slid down, braced his foot against the base of the neck, and positioned the spear for another strike. He thrust the steelhead into its skin. The monster buckled and spun, pulling its head away from Ragnus's father. His relief was short-lived. The Jabberwocky's maw snatched up his father. Rows of razor-spiked teeth bore into his body.

The chieftain struggled to bring up his sword as his teeth-torn form bled out of the side of the creature's mouth. Chief Urvan's head rolled back. With his eyes closed, his physical senses telling him his body was being shredded, his mind took him from the bloody fields to a serene picture.

Urvan watched his younger self interact with his two boys at the edge of the Spectral Woods. His boys ran out into the fields, picking up sticks and play-fighting one another. A rustling of leaves caused the chieftain to turn around.

It had been many years since he had looked upon Kurvan's features, and he stumbled. Seeing his youngest son's face, he knew his time had come. His late son was there to take him home.

"Seems I've found my battle," Urvan chuckled knowingly, his voice giving off an otherworldly echo. "Though it is lost."

"You're not done yet, Father. You can give the others enough time to escape." Kurvan's voice was distant but easily heard.

"I fear I have spent my last," Chief Urvan said, feeling himself severing from his physical form, but Kurvan closed the distance, embracing his father's spirit, and a surge of energy flooded his mangled body.

"Our battles do not end because we lose our physical forms," Kurian said.

Chief Urvan's eyes opened wide as he took in a labored breath. The peace of the fields left him, and the noises of battle rang through his ears. New life gripped his limbs, enough for him to pull back his sword and plunge it deep into the roof of the monster's mouth, the tip of the steel searching for the thing's brain.

This would have been the mark of death for most normal creatures, but it was a painful inconvenience to the Jabberwocky. It dropped Chief Urvan to the ground, but the damage had been done.

Ragnus heard the White Knight yell a string of obscenities before charging in. The creature whipped its head around and crashed into the knight's rib cage, sending him flying and smacking him hard against a tree trunk.

The thing coiled back again and turned its attention to Ragnus and the other three remaining Pridyr, who were attacking from different angles.

It spun its head and snapped a Pridyr from its back, its teeth clamping down, blood oozing from its maw.

"The woods! Now!" Ragnus commanded over the creature's screeching. He leaped from the monster's neck and rolled in the mud on impact. The other two followed.

The creature, finally overcome by the wounds, turned away. It spread its wings and took flight, retreating to the mountains.

The White Knight lay motionless at the base of the tree trunk. There was no helping him now, but Ragnus's father lay clutching the bleeding wound just below his chest. Ragnus ran over, lifted him, and threw his arm around his shoulder.

He braced his father as they made for the tree line. He heard the creature's shriek circling back, and the dreaded hum of its wings as it closed in on them.

"Take the chieftain." Ragnus said to the other Pridyr. They slid into place and continued bolting for the trees.

Ragnus's spear was still stuck in the monster's neck, and he was too far from the carnage to find anything useful. Accepting his fate, he stood with his paw-like hands open and claws out. That would be enough if he could at least distract the thing until they were in the woods.

The Jabberwocky lowered its head and aimed directly at Ragnus as it landed. Not losing any momentum, it ran at him. Ragnus was ready for the impact, but it never came.

The White Knight appeared on Ragnus's right, bending down and grabbing the first weapon he could grip. The knight swung the sword back, arching the thrown steel, aiming for it to stick directly in the thing's side. A screech from the creature told both the weapon had met its mark, the head flinging back in pain as the teeth gnashed violently at the protruding object in its side.

"Run! It wants me anyway!" the White Knight yelled to Ragnus, but he didn't want to leave the knight alone. "I won't survive long enough to keep it distracted if you just stand there and stare! Run, damn it!"

The Jabberwocky snapped at the White Knight, and Ragnus ran toward the trees. He pushed against the pain in his ribs and leg to make it to his father.

At the treeline, he glanced back. The monster picked up the White Knight with its teeth and slammed him to the ground. Ragnus expected to hear shrieks of pain from the man. He heard taunting laughter. Things turned eerily still; the only sounds were falling rocks from the mountains and cracking thunder overhead.

The Jabberwocky frantically looked around, then stared at the tree line, where Ragnus slid behind a massive oak. It turned and retreated into the mountains, leaving the plains a gruesome graveyard.

In a soft patch of foliage, Ragnus found the two Pridyr and his father, and his gasps for air were a sign of what was to come.

He knelt next to his father and squeezed his hand. "We've failed."

"We've only failed when we give up, son." He turned his head and hacked, blood splattering into his other hand.

"But our job was to protect the land," Ragnus began, but a look from his father stilled him.

"And you will continue to do so. I have faith in you. Bring us back to peace, Ragnus." The chieftain braced his back against the tree. He removed the emblem from his chest armor and placed it in his son's hand.

"By the bonds of the world, I now leave. I, Chief Urvan, declare my son, General Ragnus, the Cowardly, now redeemed, as Chieftain of the Celehawk Clan and protector of the Land of Oz."

"Father," he choked as he gripped the emblem.

"You know the way... son..." Chief Urvan's eyes closed. He stopped breathing and lay motionless.

The other two Pridyr dropped to one knee to honor the passing of their chieftain, their heads dipped. Staring at the still body of his father, Ragnus fought back the anger and raw pain welling in his throat. He allowed a tear to run down his nose and splash onto his father's cheek.

"We leave at dawn. Tonight, we will give my father a proper burial in our homeland." Ragnus took his father's arms and crossed them over his chest. "I'll prepare the grave. You two, build a small fire."

The new chieftain stood, grief gripping every step. He stopped at the tree line and stared over the slaughter that tainted their serene plains. Leaning against the tree, he looked for a burial spot for his father. One question repeated in his mind. *What now?*

Grenin rested his forehead on his knees, his arms wrapped around his head. He ran the last few days over in his mind. Was there anything they could have done to prevent this? They did everything possible, but the worst still came.

His eyes trailed over to the transparent portion of the jade hand, the shriveled robes the only thing visible to the Master Apprentice. Staring down at his dead master's remains in the scorched grass, he felt a pull at his chest and his throat.

He wondered what had happened to Glinda. Had anyone survived? Where was Lucian? Did Umiko make it to Flint before everything crumbled? Caged physically and mentally, these questions and the unknown ate at his thoughts.

He tried multiple times to escape the jade hand's grip, but the prison was too well constructed, and the magic was impenetrable. Forced into quiet contemplation, he mulled over anything they had overlooked.

The muffled commotion outside had ceased. He didn't know precisely how long he'd been detained, but the shaking had stopped an hour earlier. The raging downpour grew in strength, cleansing the ashes and washing away the remnants of his old friend, and it choked all light from the skies. It felt like the storm was feeding off the peril of the land.

Grenin shivered as he watched the last ashes become liquid and seep into the grass around the fractured yellow brick road.

"I'm sorry..." he said into his lap.

The rain ceased instantly. He lifted his head from the somber position and looked about the tiny jade enclosure.

"Tragic. Isn't it?" the voice mocked him.

A fire ignited in Grenin's chest. The munchkin unfurled himself, his expression dark. He had not heard that voice in years, but it still had the same effect on him.

"This is not over. As long as I breathe, you will always look over your shoulder," Grenin spat.

A melodic chuckle was the only response he received. The Master Apprentice settled back into the palm, his mind still racing, trying to find some weakness in the prison.

"I'm not completely uncaring. What kind of host would I be not to allow you a view of my masterpiece?"

The transparent part of the hand moved from next to where Grenin sat and slid up to show that the shattered spires had all crumbled into a pile of emerald waste. As the transparent portion settled, the base of the fingers became an impenetrable, fluid-like window.

Grenin recoiled in horror. Bodies lined the walkways, and the beautiful buildings were only rubble. Gale Park was on fire around his prison. Indistinguishable forms lay within the flames, never to take another breath.

"Devastation is a painful teacher, isn't it, Master Apprentice?"

Grenin was too stunned to respond. The restaurant Glinda and he had visited just two nights before was a smoldering pile of ashes and bricks. The Divination District looked more like a haunted village than the bright and inspiring place it once was. Tears stung his eyes. Everything he'd built and loved was discarded and turned into mulch.

"I am a rather busy individual, so I cannot show you all my glorious work, but I have one last thing..."

The image in front of Grenin shifted to a massive room with two large thrones, one obsidian and the other red, positioned at the end of a magnificent red and black carpeted walkway.

# Chapter 23

The witch felt hands that had seen hard work and better days gripping her skin. The clouds in her mind cleared, and her sight returned.

She lashed out, trying to grab whoever had her, but she had nothing left. Anger was the only thing keeping her conscious and her eyelids open.

The hands set her on her throne, and two of her soldiers stepped in front of her and bowed respectfully. Then, one on each side, they took their places at the base of the steps.

The queen, who had yet to come around, sat on her throne with a heart-shaped scepter in her lap.

"You have made us fools," the witch accused the air. When no response came, she shrieked.

The queen's eyes fluttered open. Once all the magic was gone, her skin and tattered dress faded. The woman's eyes were almost white; only tiny, dull pupils remained.

"His promise will give us power," the queen said through labored breaths.

The witch wasn't sure if it was an attempt to calm her rage or reassure her of their decisions. She growled. "His promise is empty. He used us. Don't you see that?"

"My love would never!"

The witch wrinkled her nose. "Your love?"

The door to the throne room flew open, stopping her before she could pursue the queen's declaration. Before them stood two large items covered with silk cloths. The one on the queen's side was a deep crimson, while the fabric on the witch's side was a striking obsidian.

Five soldiers stepped forward and took a knee at the base of the steps.

"What is this?" the queen asked.

"A gift," came the deep voice, but it did not sound ethereal.

The queen's eyes came alive once again. "I told you his promises were not lies!" She attempted to sit up but slumped back onto her throne.

"Easy, my queen. You shall have your strength and beauty again soon," the voice said, moving about the room.

"Enough games! We fulfilled the request. Now fulfill your part!" barked the witch.

The space between the two sheet-covered domes crackled with energy, and a tall, foreboding form appeared, his hands clasped before him. Oz tilted his head politely in their direction and offered both women a polite regard.

The foundation under his feet splintered and cracked, seeping forth a mystic green smolder. Flashes of electric current pulsed between the cracks. Magic around him settled, along with the blemishes in the ground, and the very air shifted and returned to normal.

The witch narrowed her eyes. "You!" she began but found her strength failing.

"Now, now. Let's stay focused, shall we?" Oz said. He smirked, placing each of his hands on the silk sheets. He removed the clothes in unison, and they floated like dead leaves to the ground.

The witch locked eyes with Glinda, who stood steadfast and defiant in her magically warded cage, chunks of her once beautiful dress missing, and dry tears caked on her cheeks. The witch's grin that spread onto her lips was one of nightmares.

In front of the queen stood Tweedle Dee and Tweedle Dum, also caged, but their expressions were more confused than frightened.

"I thought Alice had killed that old queeny, but look, Mr. Dee, she lives and breathes!" Tweedle Dum said, pointing a finger at the Queen of Hearts.

"Would you classify that as living, Mr. Dum? Or rather existing? There seems to be no life to be had in that one."

"You are correct. And what of the gray one? A new pet, perhaps? Or possibly—" Tweedle Dee reached up and grabbed his throat as he gasped for air. His panicked eyes met the queen.

A sparkling red mist poured from the heart-shaped crystal tip of the scepter in her raised hand. The fog rolled along the ground to the caged brothers, and their expressions turned from humor to dread.

"I think it's time we made an example out of those who defy me and taunt my beautiful ladies," Oz said. He gracefully walked over to the wall closest to the queen's throne.

The witch's venomous glare switched between Oz and Glinda.

The mist climbed up the Tweedles' feet rapidly, and once it fully encased them, it drained them. Their life and innocence fueled the fog, making it more vibrant. The two men's skin aged, and their bodies shrank and wasted away. The queen's skin turned smooth with youth as they died, and red flushed her cheeks. Her lips brightened to two pressed rubies, and from the top of her head down, the crimson returned to her locks, soft and bouncing, full of curls once again.

The two in the cage's eyes dulled, and the queen's sapphire orbs shone. She stood; her scepter pointed at the dying men.

"Your punishment for insulting my sister and me is a prolonged and agonizing end," the queen said as she descended the steps. Her dress wrapped tighter around her youthful form, the rips mending, the hearts turning deep red, and the white bright. The sleeves came to her wrists, and the corset around her waist cinched to fit her more diminutive form. Her red shoes were no longer covered in holes or missing their heels. They tapped slowly as her deliberate pace sang her approach and filled the Tweedles with the last emotion they would ever experience—fear.

Tweedle Dum reached up. "Please, Your Highness," he said, his arm limp around his brother.

"You seek forgiveness on the wrong day," the queen said, her blue eyes piercing into her victim's. She pointed her scepter at them again. Pain swelled behind the brothers' eyes. Visions of torture tore through their minds. The brothers didn't recognize their sibling; both were monstrous, but only to one another. Tweedle Dum saw his brother, full of health again, lunging for him with a brick in his hand, and Tweedle Dee saw his brother coming at him with a shard of glass.

In their last breaths, they strangled each other until they lay lifeless on the cage floor.

The queen's lips crept into a dark grin before she laid her scepter to rest on her shoulder. She turned to face the witch with insanity in her eyes.

"It is time for you to join me, sister. Take what is yours," she said as she climbed the steps back to her throne.

The witch remained seated but leaned forward and extended her arm, index finger pointing to Glinda.

"Bring her forward," she commanded. The soldiers grabbed the cage, but the witch waved her hand. "No, bring *her* forward."

Without hesitation, the soldiers unlocked the cage, ensuring the magical bonds around Glinda's hands and feet were firmly in place. They then lifted Glinda by her forearms.

As they dragged the Prime Minister up the steps, the Wicked Witch looked at Oz again. His smirk grew, and once Glinda was within reach, he nodded. The witch stared for a moment longer before turning her attention to the broken woman.

"Clever. I know about the two-part potion with the wine and bucket of water. I don't know what hurt more, dying or you letting people believe I could be killed by water," the witch said, her breath hitting Glinda's cheeks.

"Stop this... I beg you."

"Oh... you're going to beg."

The space behind the witch's throne split to give way to a mirrored surface. On the other side, Grenin clambered toward a similar surface. He tried to smash through the liquefied barrier.

"Glinda!" He banged his fist on the liquid glass, but it merely rippled.

"Grenin, listen to me. If there's hope, the light shall always chase the shadows into hiding. Even in the darkest hour." Their eyes pooled with tears.

The witch gripped Glinda's face, electric currents pulsing from her fingertips and deep into Glinda's pale skin. The Good Witch's body tensed as the power of the Wicked Witch coursed through her veins, her essence transferring to the gray hag.

Glinda's skin turned paper-like, and the small veins under her skin blackened. She looked like an old book burned by an invisible fire; her gaze never left Grenin as she felt herself fall away. He screamed and pounded on his prison wall.

With strength returning, the Wicked Witch's hair turned from ragged dark to a beautiful midnight black, long, full, and draping down to her waist. Her skin became pale as a bright full moon, now holding an iridescent emerald-green sheen, giving a subtle highlight to her refreshed appearance. Her youth restored, eliminating the wrinkles. The once tattered old dress shifted into a long, black, sleeveless V-cut gown. A wicked choker framed her long, slender neck, and her eyes shimmered a vivid emerald, sharp, and full of life.

Pastel wisps of light peeked through Glinda's cracking skin. Her eyes lost all color but remained on her husband. Her lips moved in a barely audible whisper.

"Grenin, hope. I'm forever in your heart." The last words, she puffed out ash as she became a disintegrating statue.

The Wicked Witch took the last of Glinda, and the Good Witch fell into a pile of dust on the steps. Grenin screamed, and the split closed on the desperate munchkin. The witch locked eyes with Grenin as the window evaporated from existence. She would get to him later. Now was not the time.

She lifted her head and turned, gazing around the room to see all the shocked faces staring back at her. The queen, gleeful during Glinda's death, stood with an expressionless gaze at her 'sister' in her new beautiful appearance.

Oz raised his left eyebrow slightly. "Unintended consequences."

The queen looked at Oz as he admired the witch's transformation. Then spun back to the witch with a scowl.

The witch looked around, noticing the expressions of those within the throne room. She gazed down at her hands, stunned and pulled them back to her side.

"Names from my past have no meaning to me anymore," she stated. "Yslene is the name I chose for my future."

She kicked through Glinda's ashes on her way to the doors.

"Where are you going, sister?"

"There is much to be done. These soldiers are not sufficient. I shall return."

The soldiers grabbed the handles and pushed the doors open. She stepped through to begin her wicked work.


With Yslene's returned strength, climbing to the cave high in the mountains was not taxing. After their two worlds merged, an ominous forest made its home behind the women's fortress, which was still nestled between the icy peaks.

It had been many years since she had made this journey. She pulled herself over a small ledge into the cave and looked around for signs of life. Though the outside seemed lonely, she knew better than to judge by her eyes alone. The creatures she sought were crafty and did not like to be disturbed.

She stood completely still and closed her eyes, listening for any slight sound carried by the harsh wind. Minutes passed without even the slightest noise. Then, a subtle scratch just inside caused the witch to open her eyes and walk in.

Entering such a foreboding cave would make most people cautious, but Yslene took each step with nothing but confidence.

She noticed small bone fragments cradled in holes carved into the rocks. A grin formed on her lips, and she pressed deeper into the den. She snapped her fingers and encased her hand in a brilliant green flame.

Near the heart of the cave, a winding path led into the mountain. The walls closed in at some points but finally expanded to give way to a massive ceiling with blue and green stalagmites that shifted their iridescent colors on the ice encasing them as she passed. The witch walked to the center and took a firm stance.

A chair carved from a large rock stood in the back, and deep holes pierced the cave walls, perfect hiding places.

She scanned the entire space; the silence was unbearable. After a few moments, she spoke.

"Gragskal."

The name held a power that only the witch had known for decades. The ancient call echoed off the cold stone, bringing life to the place. Rumbling came from one of the bigger holes from above, but the woman held her position, challenging the inhabitants to show themselves.

An imposing winged creature pushed out of the large hole far above the stone chair. Its enormous mass squeezed through the opening, leaping down and landing on all fours with a loud echoing thud.

The creature sat on its haunches, bringing its cold, beady, red eyes to rest on the witch it towered over. The Gragskal's fur was a mixture of black and silver, and the scars on its ape-like face showed the many hard years it had endured. Its bat wings unfolded to an impressive spread of seven feet, and it lumbered a few steps forward.

The Gragskal's eyes squinted as he rested his colossal weight on one fist and brought his face toward the witch's.

"You dare speak the ancient name of our kind?" the creature thundered, his canines showing pink stains and his breath hot and rancid from his last meal.

"Vak, you were but a child when we last met. Though your body has aged, it seems your mind is still that of a young chimp." She sneered at his disrespect.

"The Gragskals follow you no longer!" Other Gragskals stirred out of hiding, their faces peeking down.

"Insolence!" Yslene screeched. The flame in her clawed hand pulsed, and electric sparks surrounded her fingers. She flicked her wrist toward Vak, and he flew back into the stone chair.

Currents shot from her fingers and wrapped around his massive body, tying him to the chair. Green flames licked his face, and he howled.

"Who have you become?" the witch barked, closing the distance between them.

"Who I had to be when you died. Our king!" Vak wailed as the current strengthened.

The witch turned to face the gathered Gragskals.

"What a great king!" Yslene said to the gawking eyes. Her gaze landed on Vak again. "You are nothing but cave vermin without me."

She squeezed her hand like she was choking him. The electric current closed around his neck, and he clutched his throat.

"The Gragskal will return to my fortress and serve my will once again."

"Or?" gasped Vak.

"There is no *or*."

The cave filled with a flurry of panicked Gragskals flapping their wings and shrieking frenzied cries, adding to the king's pain-filled bays.

Yslene followed the last out of the cave. She stopped on the ledge that overlooked her fortress. Wickedness surrounded her black heart, and she let out a triumphant shriek of laughter as she watched the Gragskal return to the castle.

"Fly," she whispered into the storm.


When Yslene returned, she found the queen on her heart-shaped throne, admiring her scepter. Two guards stood steadfast at the bottom of the stairs and straightened as the witch approached.

She ignored their gestures of respect and slid into her obsidian seat.

The Queen of Hearts spun her scepter on the arm of her throne. "I take it your venture went well, sister?"

"Of course it did," Yslene replied with irritation. She looked out the window and saw several Gragskals perched on one of the fortresses' towers. "Our army grows in strength. The Gragskals have returned."

"I have been in a rather deep conversation since you've been gone."

"I don't find any comfort in that."

"Your comfort is not my concern," Oz said, stepping away from the body-length mirror on the wall.

Yslene had not noticed he was in the room. Disoriented, she focused her gaze on the man. "We have done what was asked."

"That you have, Yslene. Form your armies, for tonight we bring the Munchkin City to its knees." Oz regarded himself in the mirror for a long moment, then slowly strode toward the women.

"My monkeys will not be enough to confront the remaining resistance."

"They will not have to!" The Queen of Hearts leaped from her seat and skipped down the steps, enticing a disgusted look from the witch.

"I see my guards, goblins, and monkeys. What I don't see is your meaning."

"Ah, but you will!" She stopped at the bottom of the steps and grinned at the witch. Yslene's nose twitched. Her skin crawled, and her hatred flared.

"There are a few pawns to place on the board to guarantee the girls' return." Oz gave the queen a knowing smile, gesturing for her to continue.

The witch rested her elbow on her throne and leaned over her crystal ball, which swirled with shadows and fog.

"You have my attention. What needs to be done after the fall of the Munchkin City?" she inquired, waving her hand over the ball. Green flecks sparked life inside.

Oz stopped at the massive windows. Outside, large-winged creatures spread their shadows over the moon. The return of the creatures breathed life back into the castle. "Send your Gragskals out to retrieve what the girls loved most. We will incentivize them to return of their own free will."

"Who could mean so much as to bring the girls back?" the queen asked, skipping back to her throne.

The witch hoped the queen was not always like this. She may need to rethink this business venture. She pushed the thought out of her mind.

Random images of darkness and chaos moved through the crystal ball like a destructive cloud. Scenes of Oz and Wonderland inhabitants flashed until the ball focused on two individuals.

Yslene ran her fingers over the smooth glass surface and looked into Lucian's eyes. Her attention then turned to a man wearing a purple suit and aquamarine hair, sitting at a lavish table holding an orange teacup.

Curious, the queen got up and looked over the witch's shoulder. Her blue eyes sparkled.

"The Hatter. Of course!" She spun happily on her heels and bounced back to her throne, clutching her scepter to her breast. She laughed hysterically, and the guards glanced sideways at her. "Oh, how I have waited for the day to have that man begging at my feet for mercy. He's been nothing but a nuisance!" She perched on the edge of her seat, her legs bouncing.

Yslene's eyes remained on the Scarecrow moving through the trees away from Emerald City.

"Bring them here, and the girls will be yours," Oz said.

Though the witch was skeptical, the man had led her and the queen to succeed in what she thought was impossible.

She walked over to Oz, stood beside him at the open window and called for her Gragskals. Six flew to the window and slid in, following her to the crystal ball so they could study the faces of their prey.

"Bring them to us unharmed. I want them in good health before we destroy them," Yslene commanded. The six bowed and bounded out the window, taking flight into the night sky. She watched them disappear and stared into the brewing storm.

Yslene signaled to one of the armed guards. He ran and dipped his head low before her.

"Congratulations on your promotion to captain. Gather your men." He nodded as he stood and headed to the doors, and three guards followed the newly promoted captain out.

The witch heard heels clacking and watched the queen suspiciously as she left the throne room. The queen made no skipping or giggling motions, but an icy madness in her eyes piqued the witch's interest.

Yslene waved her hand over her crystal ball, and the swirling black mass swallowed the images of Flint and Hatter.


The Queen of Hearts stood at the bottom of the stairs leading to the castle. She looked over the frozen ground. Decaying trees reached the thick clouds as if they pleaded in their last moments, only twisted memories of what they once were. Freezing winds blew the falling snow into a blanket of white over the dead ground out back of the impressive fortress. She left a trail of dainty footprints behind as she ventured toward the forest, her red dress a terrifying contrast to the snow and black trees.

Halfway to the tree line, she stopped and turned her sinister sweet smile to Yslene. "You've done well gathering your soldiers and Gragskals. I feel it is time my soldiers join our cause and make our army whole," the queen said, her insanity-filled eyes moving to the snow.

She pointed her dangerous scepter toward the quiet ground. Dark red mist crept from the gem. The ominous mist seeped into the snow and disappeared under the white blanket.

The scene was serene.

A low rumbling disturbed the ground under the snow. The white above shifted, and black dirt stirred with the pure white.

A hand shot up, decayed by time, and searched with the fervor of the starved. More limbs broke the surface and pulled their headless bodies from the ground.

Yslene descended the stairs as many undead corpses crawled out of their graves, and an army of black, white, and red lumbered over to the queen.

"That is impressive," Yslene stated from beside her. "But they're missing their heads. Will they not need such a vital thing?"

"My dear sister, the important ones were buried with their heads."

The ground cracked just before them, and a muscular arm rocketed upward. A man in dull, bloodstained armor caked with dirt freed himself from his resting place. The hearts decorating his armor matched the queen's dress, but he was missing his head, just like the rest.

The King of Hearts reached down and gripped something with his fingertips. He lifted his head from the grave and held it to his shoulder. His eyes snapped open to reveal white, milky orbs. The tarnished crown on his head lay perfectly on his long, blonde, disheveled hair.

His army fell behind him, and the King of Hearts dropped to one knee. He lifted his head toward the two women, his grip tight on his hair.

"To serve is our purpose. Your wish is our will," he proclaimed.

The queen smiled and turned to the witch. "They get rather restless. I would hate to see such talent go to waste."

Yslene stared down at the shambling army of headless undead. She surveyed each one, weighing its possible usefulness.

"Send them to Munchkin City. That's a loose end I want to be tied for good. I will send some of my Gragskals to ensure destruction." She turned, sending her dress billowing out behind her, and climbed the steps to their fortress.

# Chapter 24

Over the past few hours, the mayor of the Munchkin City, Headmistress Virta, and the Master of Alchemy feverishly ran between the few remaining buildings. The school was one of the few that still stood and sheltered most of the surviving Munchkins.

Soft, pulsing white light pumped from Headmistress Virta's fingertips to the young girl's wounds. The girl's arm and leg were under falling debris when the brick roads cracked. The shaking had ceased, and strange foliage that was not common for their area in the Spectral Woods now tangled with what were once familiar trees.

Her eldest son came in and closed the door lightly so as not to disturb the wounded and those attending to them.

"How is City Hall holding up?" She whispered to him, her hands working over the girl.

"Stable, but we must make our way to the Emerald City." The Master of Alchemy said, his voice shaky. "We must evacuate; we have no choice."

His eyes told her all she needed to know, and she sighed. Fanning her hands downward, then up again, she closed the spell, and the wounds sealed.

"I was afraid of that. We have nothing salvageable left?"

"Fortunately, many survived, but most of them were wounded. Getting to the Emerald City will at least give us a safer place to consider our options."

Virta pursed her lips as she glanced around the room. It would take impressive magic and tenacity to evacuate every survivor, but it had to be done.

"Get everybody who's able to meet in the center of the city. We'll need to gather everything still intact and leave immediately," she said, grabbing her red satchel from a chair.

The Master of Alchemy held the door open for his mother. "I'm glad I came home early."

"No one is gladder than I am." A blast of wind whipped up, sending ice through her body, and she pulled her school robe around her.

There weren't many able-bodied Munchkins left; most were still recuperating from the massive quakes. The rest gathered in the city's center, dragging carts and filling them with provisions.

Virta lifted baskets of fruit and pushed them into a wagon until movement deeper in the forest just behind Dorothy's old house caused her to pause. Darkness crept down her spine like black ooze. And the smell...

"Corran," she whispered. Her son stopped putting blankets in the cart next to his mother. It was rare that she used his name rather than his full title.

A lumbering mix of red, white, and black cards, some missing heads, others either carrying them or having them sewn back on haphazardly, stepped fully past the trees and blocked their escape. They surrounded the city.

Virta almost fainted at the shriek that came from the trees. She fell onto her son, horrified. Just above, a winged monkey stretched its wings, ready to attack.

"Sh-she's back..." The headmistress got out before the Gragskals rushed from the trees and descended onto the munchkins below.

Cries of horror and confusion blared through the city, turning Virta's attention away from the creatures and those around her. Most grabbed at the closest thing they could use as a weapon to fend off the advancing forces. The survivors did not notice the circle of the headless army beginning to lumber closer to the desperate scene because they were focused on the aerial assault.

Virta grabbed the shovel leaning against a cart and smacked a Gragskal out of the air. It screamed and spun to the ground, slamming onto the broken brick road.

She turned on the headless army as they approached at a disturbing pace. Their lumbering movements were smooth and graceful as each pulled their steel, charging in.

Two older students peeked out the school's doors at the sudden chaos and froze, seeing the surrounding army of the headless closing in on the city. Though that was frightening, they reeled back when they saw the screeching Gragskal swooping and clawing over frantic munchkins and heard the shouts of the headmistress over the furor.

"Get the injured out! Any way you can!" she shouted, ducking a lunging winged creature.

The students' response was immediate action. They spun back into the school, shutting the door behind them before gathering those not beyond help.

Outside, clashes of steel and shouts told those within that a stronger wave of attackers had met the defending munchkins, driving them to a feverish pace.

A female Munchkin with long red hair in a recent graduate's black and green robes sprinted toward the statue of the man they knew as Oz from Dorothy's home.

She raised her hand and flicked towards the statue. The brass ball in the sconce lifted and floated to rest in her palm. She slid the ball into the hand of the marble statue and stepped back. The floor tiles' green and silver swirl pattern shifted, giving way to a spiral staircase underground.

She heard screams of the dying outside as she and the other students ushered the injured down the stairs and to the dirt floor of the caverns below. After the destruction of the quake, there was no telling what devastation was waiting for them, but it was their only chance of survival.

The school doors flew open, and the sounds of death reverberated off the rich marble of the entrance hall. The redhead watched the headmistress, the Master of Alchemy, and two others rush back as the headless descended on them.

"Myrra, go!" Headmistress Virta shouted over her shoulder. The girl froze momentarily, wanting to bolt forward and help, but she knew better than to ignore the headmistress. She always had a reason for what she did, even if it was not noticeable. Myrra flew down the stairs, hearing the four not far behind.

Corran, who was the least injured, gripped his amulet, and it blazed a deep amethyst. He focused on the shambling army. The headless Nine of Hearts swung wide at him, barely missing his head. The sword hit the tile floor with a spark.

"There's no fighting them," Virta said and grabbed the arm of the limping woman next to her. She slung it around her neck and quickened her pace.

"No, this will not be a fight," the Master of Alchemy said, his eye color changing from radiant blue to match the color of his amulet. Magic swirled in his pupils as he chanted. He finished the chant and shot his hand out. A blast erupted, and the army flew out of the school.

The headless and Gragskal attempted to push through the broken doors, but something unseen kept them out. They clawed at the impenetrable bubble, which moved like liquid with every violent hit.

Corran turned and escorted the other three to the staircase. "That will not hold long. I'll grab the orb."

He focused on the deteriorating barrier to keep it from dropping too soon. The headmistress and two munchkins descended the stairs.

Virta looked back up at her son. She knew the army would be on him as soon as he broke his focus. He had to make every second count.

Corran whipped his outstretched hand toward the orb, which flew into his grasp. The barrier broke, and the masses rushed in.

The floor sealed in a counterclockwise pattern, like dominoes falling into place.

Corran stepped back to the closing hole, the headless inches from him. He could feel the air from their swiping weapons.

The Nine of Hearts charged in, his mouth opening unnaturally large, and screamed victory. He arched his sword up and swung ruthlessly down. Corran took one step back and disappeared into the hole with the orb. The last tile sealed him and the others off from the army. He heard rage fill the chamber above.

The headless army and Gragskals ransacked the school and other buildings, destroying anything and everything in their path. Debris and bodies scattered across the city, leaving it a ghost town.

The Nine of Hearts walked through the city with the Four of Spades, Six of Diamonds, and Three of Clovers. The queen granted them the gift of their heads. They scoured the town for survivors or other secret passageways for those who escaped.

The Gragskals went through houses, taking shiny trinkets and magical items, and the headless ensured no living thing remained. However, the four stood, eyes locked on Dorothy's old house.

"I don't like this place," the Nine of Hearts said. Something about it repulsed him. Something was under the house, but he could not pinpoint the source of the discomfort.

"Leave it be. Nothing lives inside, and look," the Three of Clovers said, pointing to a plaque in front. "It's nothing more than a memory."

Satisfied, the Nine of Hearts nodded, and the four turned from the house, calling for the army to reconvene in the center of the dead city.

This war had only begun, and there was far more to do.


It had been hours since the shaking had stopped. Within the cottage, the White Rabbit kept looking up at the front door, hoping he would see his wife and kids come through. His family knew the Hatter's place was a destination to head for in case of a massive disaster. But as he clutched his tea, sitting on the floor by the fire, staring into the flames, he realized they wouldn't be coming.

He needed answers. *What happened at the Night Market? Where did all this come from?*

Now that the events had stopped, he felt a pull to head back to his burrow and find the rest of his family. The sight of his son falling into the black abyss had played over multiple times in his head, but he jumped to his feet this time. He laid the teacup on the small table next to the couch where the other three huddled together, still chattering frantically. There was no use in even saying goodbye; it would fall on frenzied ears. He slipped past the group and out the front door.

"Mayor! Have you joined me?" the Hatter asked triumphantly. He had returned to his tea party and sat at the table.

More teacups and cakes were on the ground than on the table, but that didn't bother him. Nor did the sudden appearance of the ominous black trees. He was more annoyed with his friends, who stayed inside instead of joining him.

"No, Hatter. I'm going to find what's left of my family." His somber tone caused the Hatter to lower his teacup to the matching saucer on the table, setting it down with a soft clink.

"Is this something you prefer to do alone?"

"It is." He walked past the Hatter, pausing briefly to lay his hand on the man's shoulder and squeeze it before disappearing into the unfamiliar woods.

The Hatter did not notice the strange, haunting noises echoing through the surrounding trees. "Have you three had enough of acting silly?" asked the Hatter, dipping a crumpet into his tea. He leaned back in his chair, chewing the crumpet, with an amused look.

"Do you not hear that?" The March Hare gave him a deadpan stare. "I know you're insane, but this is just ridiculous." The March Hare, Duke William of Grell, and the Dormouse's expressions were riddled with worry, and their eyes darted around.

"Rude."

"Mr. Hatter, the strange noises seem to be close," William of Grell said, his long neck whipping in every direction as the howling turned to high-pitched screeches. The Dormouse scurried between the Duke of Grell's long legs and darted back into the house.

The March Hare couldn't take anymore. If his friend didn't care for his own safety, he would. He urged William of Grell to follow the Dormouse under the stairs.

The Hare grabbed the Hatter roughly by his jacket and yanked him toward the cottage. The Hatter's chair toppled over, and his teacup flew into a hedge to his left.

"I must implore you, dear Hatter. Something is not quite right, and I ask you to trust us and make for your house at once!"

The Hatter rolled over onto his stomach and slammed the palm of his hand on the ground. "I lost my tea!" He brushed his hand over the grass, looking for his cane. He gripped the object and swung it up toward the Hare, careful not to strike him.

The Hare jumped back, releasing his grasp of the Hatter's jacket, and looked insulted. He grabbed the lapels of his coat and stuck his nose up.

"If you wish to perish, I cannot stop you!"

"It is all in your head!" The Hatter cried as the Hare ran to the cabin.

The Hatter snatched an overturned teacup and the half-full teapot and poured another cup. The howling and screams called through the trees, but he plucked a spoon from the table and stirred in a decent helping of sugar.

As he brought the cup to his lips to take a sip, his gaze met his terrified friends peeking out from under the stairs. He shook his head. These silly noises were all in their heads, and the Hatter would not give in to such absurdity.

Could the shaking ground turn the entire party on its side? So, what if sudden ominous trees shot out from the ground to surround his house? So what if they heard strange noises? It is a forest. It was just a different perspective of the same reality, something the Hatter was more than used to.

He took a long, thoughtful sip from his partially cracked teacup and looked about his front yard. It looked like a party of hippos performed an entire musical number on the table, but it was not enough for him to stop enjoying his tea.

The Hatter huffed into another drink as he looked through his open front door. He heard his friends' muffled, strained voices, no doubt seizing rations from his kitchen and finding hiding places. It wasn't very sensible. There had not been another incident for.... He glanced down at his silver-chained pocket watch.

"Three hours! Fools! The lot of you! To ruin a perfectly happy tea party with such nonsense." The Hatter took another drink as a dark shadow crept over the table, the light from the lanterns overcome by some presence. "Nothing is happening!" he shouted and tilted his head.

He thought a giant cloud might have been the cause, but saw the horrified expressions on his friends' faces as they peeked from behind the front door. Concern washed away his relaxed demeanor.

He turned in time to see three Gragskals slam onto the table, breaking the thing in two. The remaining dishes shattered, and silverware went flying.

Unable to comprehend the creatures, the Hatter dropped the cup; the object made a dull thud in the grass. He jerked to run to the house, but clawed hands gripped his shoulders and lifted him swiftly into the sky.

His friends watched in desperate grief and heard him struggling in the distance.

"Okay! Something might be happening!"


The Gragskal dropped the Hatter onto the throne room floor unceremoniously. His once neat aquamarine hair was disheveled, and the fall tore his suit in many places. The creatures had given several traumatic blows to his face and body, so when he came eye-to-eye with the smiling queen, blood dripped from his broken nose and cracked lips.

The Gragskals bowed, and the witch stood.

"I said unharmed," she growled.

"He became quite... mouthy, mistress. It was an unfortunate measure that was needed," one of the larger said.

A raspy chuckle came from the not-quite-broken man. He attempted to stand, but the Gragskals subdued him. He held the queen's gaze. Down on his knees and propped up with his arm, he ran his other hand over the damage to his ribs.

"Couldn't stay away, could we, queeny?" He hacked out a cough and spat blood onto the throne room floor.

The Queen of Hearts returned with a wicked smile, the calm about her unnerving to all but Yslene and the Hatter. She stood and descended the stairs, every click of her heel on the marble flooring echoing. She took her time, twirling her scepter, the smile still plastered on her face.

The queen walked over to the bleeding man on the floor and placed the heart-shaped tip of her scepter under his chin, forcing his head up and making him look her in the eyes.

"I have waited *so* long for this," the queen said softly, almost lovingly. Red tendrils of smoke flowed from her scepter. They caressed the Hatter's cheeks and swirled as if he had taken a significant hit from a hookah. Once it reached his eyes, the smoke became tangible and clung to them, coating his vision red.

"You destroyed my world by helping that girl," the queen said, a maniacal look in her eyes. "It's time for me to return the favor, Lovie."

The smoke acted like a mask on his face, and it propelled him into a dark world of fire and chaos fueled by the queen's influence.

He sat at his table, the furniture and dishware looking normal, but his guests were crude mockeries of his friends. Elongated teeth dangled from their mouths, their eyes a haunting yellow, and their nails twisted in wicked black claws.

The corrupted March Hare clutched a broken pocket watch in his teeth, with black goo oozing from the watch. The duke indulged a lifeless white rabbit while sipping a strange green glowing liquid from a tiny bird's skull.

The Hatter stood frozen. He looked frantically around for the Dormouse but was sorry when he saw the creature lumbering by the March Hare, over ten times its original size and sporting the same features as the other two.

They were talking to each other as if they didn't notice the Hatter's presence, but it was in an odd guttural language he couldn't make out.

He watched in horror and went to make a move, but three pairs of yellow eyes turned and focused on him.

He stopped. His eyes darted around for a way out, but the perimeter, usually surrounded by a cute, hedged fence, was spilling out fiery flames.

The figures' lips curled into snarls, black ooze dripping from their fangs. The only sign of their attack was a twitch of the March Hare's long ear. They sprang, and the Hatter tucked into himself. Claws ripped his skin.

Everything evaporated into a red mist, and he found himself on the throne room floor, his screams bringing him back to reality. At some point he had curled into the fetal position and was gripping his own arms, hugging himself tightly.

The sweat on his brow made his hair cling to it under his torn hat. He shivered and panted as he focused on the queen. Her wicked smile had only grown wider.

She gestured to the guards next to the steps, and two came running over.

"To the dungeon with him! That was just the prologue, my dear Hatter. Our story is far from over." The queen laughed as the two guards picked up the Hatter, his eyes glazed over, and dragged him out the doors.

The guards tossed the Hatter onto the straw in the dimly lit dungeon. He landed on his broken ribs, forcing the wind out of him. He crumpled on the floor, gripping his face with his fingers, still feeling the red smoke creeping over his skin. It had long since evaporated into nothing, but its effects lingered. He didn't want to move.

Many moments passed before he lifted his head to view his new cage. Grime and age covered his prison's stone walls and bars, but despite this, they held firm. He could never break out of his cell, especially in his weakened state.

The Hatter dragged himself across the dirt and straw and leaned against the stone wall, resting his head back, every ounce of energy sapped from his body and mind. His breath was rapid, and the pain swelled in his side. He saw blood caked on a nasty wound after pulling his hand away.

The Hatter gulped in a huge breath, his dazed eyes landing on the dim corridor outside his cell. He was close to a dream state and couldn't tell if his body had hit the breaking point or was still under the queen's influence, but the flicker in his vision brought him back to brief clarity.

A flash of an ethereal needle formed in his blood-covered hand as he sank to the ground. He could have sworn the fabric of reality shifted with the movement of his hand for a second. There was no time to contemplate the event since everything was rapidly going dark, but as the sweet serenity of unconsciousness wrapped about his mind, a croaked whisper of a long-lost memory escaped his lips. "Alice..."

# Chapter 25

"Alice," the soft male voice came beside her, but her mind was far from the gym. Her body may have been doing countless reps of pull-ups, but disturbing images in her thoughts kept her from noticing the rather good-looking man who had approached her.

She dropped gracefully, sweat dripping off her forehead, leaving glistening streaks dancing down her neck to her shoulders. She picked up the towel that she'd tossed over a large bottle of water on the ground and wiped the sweat from her brow. Her bright blue eyes finally acknowledged the man.

"I'm sorry, what?" she asked with a bit of sharpness to her tone. He winced a little, his chest caved slightly, and he took a more defensive stance.

"I-I'm sorry, your name is Alice, correct?"

"It is. Can I help you with something?" Alice bent and grabbed her water, giving him an impatient look. Her blond hair, pulled tight in a ponytail, made her appear even more stern.

"I was just wondering if—"

"No." She pushed past him and drank deeply as she headed for the locker room.

The man slung his towel over his lowered shoulders and walked toward the free weights room. Two men leaned against a mirror next to the dumbbells, chuckling, their heads shaking, but there was some sympathy in their mocking.

"You two enjoy watching a guy strike out?" he asked, irritation riddling his voice.

"Naw, man." One waved him over. "You must be new here."

"Yeah, just moved to town, but I've seen that girl whenever I'm here. What's her story anyway?"

"We've guessed she's a hardcore athlete or something. CrossFit, maybe," the other man said. "But every guy who asks her out, she shoots down, and it's never pretty."

The young man looked over toward the women's locker room, where she had disappeared, and sighed.

"Sounds lonely."

Alice squeezed the steering wheel of her silver Mercedes. It never failed. Every time she went to the gym, a meathead interrupted her workout. If she had lived in a larger place, she would have made a home gym so she wouldn't have had to deal with unwanted interactions. It's bad enough she was already in a relationship she wasn't sure she wanted to be in, let alone the time to herself being intruded on—the annoyances of what had happened plagued her gut.

It was past 8:00 p.m., and she was supposed to have met her boyfriend an hour earlier. Her phone buzzed with another agitated text message, and she barely glanced at it.

Alice turned the corner to park in her space and noticed her boyfriend's car in the guest parking a few spaces over. He was leaning against his car, his posture stiff.

She zipped in and pushed the button to shut the engine off. She slid out of the car and shut the door. He was already at the front bumper, his hand gripping his phone so tightly that his knuckles were white.

"I thought we were going to meet at the restaurant." She sighed and brushed past him to the locked door of her high-rise.

"That was an hour ago," he said.

Alice slid the keycard into the slot. It flashed green and beeped. She opened the door and walked through, not waiting for him to follow, but he did anyway. The elevator ride was silent and awkward. The only sounds in the hallway to her condo were the dull thud of their shoes and the rustling of their clothes.

He almost slammed the door shut behind them. "This has got to stop."

"What exactly, David?" She moved without pause into the bedroom. She flipped on the light and removed her workout clothes.

"This!" he barked at her bedroom door. He folded his arms across his chest. "I'm tired of not being a priority!"

She stopped and tilted her head up. Despite the lack of chiseled features and muscle, the man was far from unattractive. His brown eyes accented his sandy blond hair. He had a delicate, handsome face, and he kept his hair cut in a businesslike, clean style—perfect for marriage.

She went to the bathroom and turned on the shower, returning a moment later wearing only her sports bra and boy shorts. The chain from her necklace caught the light, and the metal fragment on her sun-kissed chest sparkled.

"I'm sorry, but it's probably best if you go." Alice went to turn from him again, but he gently touched her arm.

"Please. Why will you not open up to me? I've bared everything, and you have always kept me at a distance."

She turned to face him, and his hand trailed up to her side and hovered over the shard. Alice ripped her arm out of his grasp and whipped around.

"See! That's what I mean! What the hell is so important about that damn thing around your neck?"

"It's a reminder."

"A reminder of what?" he yelled.

"I've outgrown you. It's time for you to move on," she said, heading to the bathroom.

"You'll be alone for the rest of your life."

She paused, suspending a cold, calculating thought. She turned her head slightly in his direction.

"It's best that way," she said. "Now, if you'll excuse me, I have a mandatory meeting at work I need to get to. You can let yourself out." She shut the bathroom door behind her.


Upon arriving at the electronics store, the district manager. The stocky older man offered her a plump, splotchy hand, and she gripped it with the same direct, business-driven attitude she met every life situation with.

Alice knew exactly what this meeting was about. She owed him an answer, and he was there to force her into a corner. She knew he would not like her response, but it was best not to make long-lasting commitments, and taking his position was just not in her long-term plans.

Alice greeted her employees briefly as they walked to the large store's back office. Her silver skirt and white blouse accentuated her lithe form and long blond hair. If she unfastened her tight ponytail, her hair would have reached past the middle of her back, but she kept it that way only at home.

She passed through the office's threshold, followed her boss, and sat across from him. He sat in the chair, the leather complaining with a hiss.

"I need you to take this promotion."

She looked at him for a moment before responding. "It's not something I would be interested in. I'm perfectly fine with staying manager of the store. Have you considered Jackie?"

"Jackie doesn't have the business sense you do and spends far too much personal time with the staff. You must take this promotion. No one carries the respect you do and can handle this pressure. You know I only have a month before I retire, and I need someone to keep everything from falling apart." He folded his hands on the oak desk and leaned forward.

"It's a store. It was here before me. It will be here long after I'm gone," she said, turning for the door.

Her boss let out a heavy sigh. "Alright," he said before she left the room.

She had a habit of going through the departments on her way out to ensure everything was as it should be. As she went through the store, she touched base with her department leads, cleaned, and adjusted things.

She spotted Jackie in the back, laughing and carrying on with a few of her much younger male employees, and Alice shook her head. As she walked through the television department, a thirty-six-inch flat screen was askew, as if it might topple to the ground at any minute. Irritated that none of the employees had caught the obvious issue, she went over to fix it.

She bent, gripped the upper two corners, and began pushing it back. Loud explosion sound effects from the action movie blasted in her ears, and she wrinkled her nose. Static seized the screen, and the movie jumped around.

She brought her full attention to the exploding building on screen.

Shaking off the disturbance as if it were nothing, she moved the television to its rightful place. The static took over the screen for fifteen seconds before returning to the movie.

She took a step back; her eyes still locked on the television. She watched a masked superhero dash across the screen but caught an oddly familiar thing. A large, toothy grin flashed over the character's face. Alice let her eyes linger momentarily before she walked out of the store.

Alice removed her business attire and headed straight for her closet. She felt something she could only describe as electricity creeping up her spine, and the fine hairs on her neck stood on end.

She picked out a pair of blue leggings, black flats, and a white baby T-shirt. Her head tilted slightly when she noticed one of her items next to the vanity mirror was out of place.

The small bottle with the fading words *"drink me"* etched across the glass had fogged with age. Her gaze trailed from the displaced bottle to the worn copy of *Machiavelli's The Prince* and *Sun Tzu's The Art of War*. She ran her fingertips over the broken spine and the sun-bleached cover. She let the pages flutter open, old, dog-eared pages brushing her memory of the contents.

She inhaled and closed her eyes before moving to the next pile of old books, all coffee-stained and tattered from being read repeatedly. The lessons within were vivid in her mind.

A soft padding came from near the bathroom door. The light caught the metallic surfaces of her trophies that lined the wall. Awards from cross-country and Spartan races to college debate competitions stood, the expressionless human figures staring down.

Her lips tightened as she turned back to the mirror, but her gaze looked beyond her reflection.

"Enough with the games."

A gray-striped tabby cat lay on the bed behind her, spread out on its side, its indigo, mischief-filled gaze staring at her.

"If I need to go back, let's go," she said.

The cat rolled into a seated position and absently licked its paw.

"I'm guessing it's the same way."

After more grooming, the cat leaped from the bed, landed beside her, and jumped up onto the vanity. He knocked the bottle over and made straight for his reflection. The glass rippled and wrapped around his body as he passed through. A human-like hand covered in gray fur pushed back through the glass, its palm turned upward like a gentleman would offer a lady.

She took the hand and slipped into an unknown future, her eyes grazing *The Art of War* before the icy cold of the other side grabbed her senses.

It was a challenge to keep up with the familiar tail as it darted through a time and space utterly foreign to her. The Cheshire's agile form leaped from odd-shaped rooms to vast spaces with swirling nebulas.

The cat occasionally glanced back, but she could tell it was more amusement than concern. If she hadn't followed him closely, she would have gotten lost, and the cat wouldn't have returned to find her.

She grunted. "I don't remember it being this complicated," she said, following the cat through a small cottage window. She saw nothing but floating furniture, yet her feet were firmly on the floor.

"We can only return through an intact mirror," the cat said. Alice stayed close as he bounded up the stairs.

They entered the main bedroom. "How long have we been searching? It feels like we've been moving for hours." Alice reached out and poked the hovering glass vase that held a single red rose. It spun slowly in place.

"For you, probably only a matter of minutes or hours. For my world, it could be years," the cat replied. He jumped onto the floating vanity in the corner. It bobbed with the extra weight but did not move beyond that.

She watched him curiously as his paws moved up the glass. She knew time moved differently in Wonderland, but her head still reeled with repressed memories surging to the front of her thoughts.

Alice shut her eyes. This was real. She was standing in the gap between realities. There was no prescription for such craziness, so it had to be authentic.

She opened her eyes at the deep sigh from the cat. His paws trailed down the wooden surface. "There's a crack on the other side. We'll have to find another one." He turned and leaped onto the floating bed and out the window.

Alice followed.

Where there should have been grass or dirt, she saw nothing but stars. She hesitated to step down until he cleared his throat amusedly.

"It's solid."

Alice put her foot firmly on the stars, and the cosmos rippled. Tiny specks of light moved about her feet, but as inviting as the sight was, she met the Cheshire's gaze and nodded for him to continue.

Another hour of wandering through the stars had to have passed before the ground broke in front of them. The towers of a stone castle pierced through the surface. Once the structure stilled, he pounced to the nearest window and looked inside. His tail stiffened, and he froze.

"There," he said, his head gesturing to a small mirror above a long dining hall table.

Nothing was out of place in the castle. It looked like a historical museum in Europe.

Cheshire slipped in first, and Alice was close to follow. He crawled onto the cabinet below the mirror and moved his paw over the glass.

"This is it," he said. He sat back on his haunches and stared at her, his tail twitching.

Alice climbed up and placed her hand on the mirror. It shimmered and liquefied at her touch. A cold, strange sensation passed over her form, and she welcomed being on the other side.

She jumped off the cabinet and looked about the room. It was nothing like the castle, which was odd, but considering the source, she shrugged it off.

She turned to see Cheshire slip through the glass, landing gracefully next to her, and change into a humanoid cat. He gave her a devious smirk and adjusted his tailored cuffs.

"You alright, dear?" he asked, chuckling.

"You're different from what I remember," she said, pushing past him.

"Things always change. You can never go back." Her brow furrowed as she made her way to the front door of the tiny house.

You can never go back? There was the familiar talent the cat had with words. She reached for the brass doorknob, but the sound of shuffling made her stop. Something sat on the fireplace in the room to her right—a large purple hat and a bright orange porcelain teapot.

Alice entered the room. Nothing looked out of place. Everything was tidy, from the maroon couch and matching chair to the collection of teacups on the end tables and wooden coffee table. She picked up a framed picture of the Mad Hatter and the March Hare at the head of their tea party, the Dormouse on the table, and a strange flamingo from the mantle. When she finally looked at Cheshire, he was leaning on the doorframe, arms crossed and an eyebrow raised.

"You realize—"

"Yes, I do, and no, I do not know."

Another shuffling noise came from the staircase in the entryway. Alice placed the picture back on the mantel and brushed past Cheshire, who maintained his relaxed demeanor.

Alice looked all about for the source of the hushed voices, and when she walked down the hallway to the kitchen, she saw a small door under the stairs. She rapped it gently. Someone returned with more timid tapping, and she opened it to see the March Hare and Sir William of Grell curled up in the corner and the Dormouse rocking back and forth, holding his knees to his chest.

Alice fell to her knees, relieved and possibly more concerned than before.

"Hare?" He winced at his name.

"Th-they came in. The shaking." He just stared at the wall across from him.

"Who's they?"

"Flapping and wings." "The ground wouldn't stop."

Sir William of Grell babbled about judgments, and the Dormouse said nothing.

"Where's the Hatter?" Alice said as calmly as she could.

The Dormouse started crying, and the frantic Hare faced the corner. No one was going to help here. They were beyond traumatized, but one thing was obvious: The Hatter was gone.

Alice rose and left the door open. It slammed behind her, and she shook her head.

"So, what are you going to do, Miss Alice?" Cheshire prodded, giving her a sarcastic smile as she passed.

"You'll tell me what happened, and we'll go from there." She jerked the front door open and stepped through. The destroyed tea party and a towering, ominous forest hugging the property met her. If she was at all unnerved, she hid it well.

She slowly walked around the overturned chairs and fallen dishes, scanning for anything that might give a clue what had happened. Short of the thick roots coming up through the grass, nothing else was obvious.

"Well, we won't be able to do anything from here. I'll explain on the way." Cheshire stepped to her side, and she shivered. He opened the gate and offered an exaggerated bow.

She knew she had to play his game to discover what was happening, so she walked through. He closed the gate and sauntered into the woods as if taking a pleasant afternoon stroll.

"Okay, Cheshire, what's going on?"


A shadowy figure watched from a safe distance as Alice maneuvered through the forest with the Cheshire Cat. He had been trailing them since they left the Hatter's house, lucky to have his path cross with theirs.

He had been wandering the woods looking for more signs of what had changed in this world, and when he heard the creak of the gate, he ducked behind a tree and waited.

The man kept back far enough to follow without being seen and could still hear Alice and the cat.

Cheshire had run in the same circles. He remembered seeing him in a tavern, some twisted sanctuary in the less savory parts of Wonderland. Most there played to their own tune but acted as if they were interested in helping those in need.

The cat — he was never sure about that one. One moment, he stole some items to make more coins; other times, he acted as a hired guard or escort through the woods. He was entirely self-serving, but he wasn't surprised either. He wondered if his female companion was aware, though it looked as if this might be an old friend. Friends could change someone's motivation.

The woman, though, is obvious from the suburban world. The place was weird and so bland. He didn't care for it and had only briefly gone there to see that the place existed. With despair comes hope, and he'd heard stories of a girl who had once set things right and came from such a place. Two girls existed, and they were from a world where magic was sparse and people lived their lives always focused on the smaller picture.

The ones who broke from the mold usually found themselves in extraordinary situations. Alice was no exception, but hers was not the only name he had heard. Dorothy graced the lips of many, and he knew the stories of Oz far better than those of Wonderland.

He stilled as Cheshire gauged their next direction. The dark forest had a talent for turning people around and sending them where they had not intended.

The woman's annoyance with the humanoid cat was clear because most of her expressions were hardened and her gestures sharp. Cheshire's smirk never left his face.

After following them for over an hour, he stopped for a while. He knew their destination and could find them easily.

The man grasped the loose strands of his long black hair and tied them over his shoulder to look more presentable. He had no stomach for looking haggard or disheveled. His long midnight-blue coat slid off his shoulders, and he placed his black pack on the ground and draped the coat over it.

He made sure nobody had discovered him while checking his surroundings. Satisfied, he ran a hand down his black shirt, smoothing out any wrinkles he might have created while traveling. His shirt looked pirate in nature, billowing in the middle along the long sleeves and decorated with thin silver trim and bright hook-like cufflinks. Black pants made from a thick material made ventures such as this far more manageable, and he was pleased that he could keep them clean.

Alice and Cheshire's footfalls faded. Other than that, the forest was eerily peaceful. A thankful break from the creatures that surfaced and made a sport of tracking and killing those who tempted fate within the dark, clawed boughs.

He bent to retrieve his coat, his long hair draped over his left shoulder. His teal eyes scanned the area as he slipped his arms into it. He adjusted the sleeves before pulling out a small vial with green swirling liquid from his pack. He popped the cork and downed the contents.

The man's form shimmered momentarily and gave off a dull glow. He tossed the empty vial into the pack and threw his bag over his shoulder just as his body faded. He headed away from the direction Alice and Cheshire had gone, leaving only footprints he pressed into the dirt.

It wasn't often that he could use this potion, but he needed to move without the possibility of being seen.

If Dorothy had come back as well, he needed to know.

# Chapter 26

Nature blazed by in angular blurs, in dark blobs of ominous colors as Lucian dodged low branches and thorny shrubs. Monstrous wooden claws reached out, determined to slow his pace and fling him into the gaping maw of his relentless pursuers.

He sought refuge in the forest and tried to find Flint, but Flint's cabin was deserted. He traveled under the cover of night to Ragnus, but when he reached the tree line of the Celehawk Clan's territory, he saw nothing except an abandoned village and a stinking battlefield of blood and rot. At that moment, hope drained from him, and it drove him to stay tucked within the Spectral Woods.

With the shrieking horde at his heels for days, closed two steps to his one. He had never known such guile from an unknown danger.

In his rushed wake, branches that had relented to his passing gave way and snapped back into place. Still, nothing but a silhouette of a black wave spread through the trees, and the only thing that alluded to this thing being a creature was the sound it made. Occasionally, Lucian could hear the bark of a command, some intelligence through the chaotic wail.

His long jacket snagged on a thick branch. The wicked grip shredded the cloth as he yanked away from the wretched embrace. The momentum sent him spinning, and panic gripped his throat. He tripped over a tree root and toppled to the ground. Dead foliage and rich soil filled his mouth.

His palms helped break his fall, but the sticks and debris sliced his hands—not painful, but annoying. He pushed himself up and regained his hurried pace. His legs pumped him deeper into the dark forest. His fall gave the black mass behind him time to gain an advantage, though he doubted he ever had a lead on them.

He leaped and slid over a fallen trunk. The jagged wood caught his pant leg and shredded it. His slacks were not the best choice for the affair, but after years in rows of books, anything more durable seemed wasted and uncomfortable.

Something lumbered close to him. At that point, he couldn't outrun it. He swung himself over an overturned trunk that was leaning against a tree. Lucian crouched in the crevice with his back pressed against the standing tree. He stilled his breath and clutched his chest as his new lungs burned. It was a strange sensation in one of the latest additions, a gift from the council and a few other organs he had gained from them over the past year.

A branch creaked overhead. Something significant in the tree he braced against forced the branch to groan, and he heard the limb threatening to snap. If it did, whatever the thing was would fall into Lucian's lap. He stiffened. He never liked physical confrontations, and he was severely outmatched.

Another creak sounded from above, and whatever had perched there most likely moved on. He looked up and saw nothing.

Lucian was smart enough not to give in to the false sense of ease. He merely listened to his surroundings and surveyed the area. He glanced around the tree trunk and saw that the flowing black mass had dissipated, but it didn't bring relief. If anything, more worry flooded his senses.

Things were far too quiet for creatures in a heated pursuit. Lucian kept his low crouch and slowly ventured out from his hidden trunk cubby. Second-guesses plagued him, questioning his quest for greater knowledge. Was it better for him to have remained just a simple straw man in the middle of a field? Possibly, since he faced far more complex ideas. Suffering, despair, disappointment, happiness, and love.

An unexpected wave of confusion washed over him, and he froze. His thoughts lingered on the distant past, and his new heart thumped in his chest. Lucian sighed and pushed on.

He wondered how people lived with all this uncertainty as he stepped to another tree.

The knowledge that something terrible could happen and that victory may be impossible, no matter the effort. Knowledge was a bittersweet gift. Was it possible to be smart enough to stay ignorant?

He sized up his following escape path and started another dash for freedom. A sharp gust of wind came from his left. The breeze from large wings almost blew off his fedora, and his hay-and-leaf-like hair whipped about his sewn features. Lucian braced his hat on his head, but his coat lashed in wicked protest against the cyclone of wings and teeth.

There was not much light between the cloud cover and canopy, but what the Scarecrow could make out of the creature that landed next to him was familiar from many years ago. Memories of Dorothy and flying monkeys came back as the thing pressed forward. Lucian saw hunger in its eyes, which had not evolved with time, but its body looked far more solid than he remembered. He hadn't seen these creatures since the night the witch died. His eyes widened, his mind raced, and he stepped back.

A loud thud to his right gave way to the entrance of yet another winged monkey, both stalking as they slowly closed the distance.

Lucian had read about these creatures during his time in the city. Gragskals are a creation of dark magic.

The creatures grunted in a foreign guttural language, and Lucian took another step back.

The destruction of the Emerald City, the light being snuffed out, and now the appearance of Gragskals.

"No," he whispered to himself. "It can't be."

The creatures seemed to be deep in an argument. One thumped his chest toward the other, and Lucian slid another step away. He tried to steady his mind.

The witch was dead. He saw it with his own eyes. "It simply can't be."

As the exchange between the two Gragskals became more heated, he turned to go and almost ran into the chest of a third, slamming to the forest floor. He dodged the creature's attempt to grab him and ran.

The creature roared, and the other two halted their disagreement. Three Gragskals took flight, hot on Lucian's heels once again.

The closest Gragskal landed just behind Lucian, its large hand hitting his shoulder. Lucian slammed against the ground.

He skidded, digging a line into the dirt before he flew over a pile of fallen leaves and twigs.

The Gragskal leaped into the air and came thundering down with a massive swipe. His claws hit Lucian on the shoulder, shredding his coat and cutting his skin.

The Scarecrow flipped over and pushed himself against a tree. The creature dove in and swiped again.

They hadn't given up their position if the other two were nearby, and Lucian focused on the present threat. He put his hands up and braced for the impact.

A curious image flew into his mind. A crow appeared out of nowhere, and then another, and yet another, until there was a barrage of shadowy crows screaming and aiming for the Gragskal's face. They swirled about him, turning the thing's world on a different axis.

Lucian stood and took off deeper into the forest. He hadn't seen the other two beasts but wouldn't search.

Once all the commotion was far in the distance, he took a moment to look about the area for any sign of more shadow-like crows, but only an eerie silence greeted him.

Of all the books he had read, he had never come across such a strange phenomenon. He brought his right hand up to eye level and then examined it before running the palm over his lacerated shoulder, looking to see how bad the damage was.

A shocked yelp escaped him when he saw the deep gashes mending together by a shadow-laced thread. He stared at his body fixing itself, and a dark figure flapped into his mind again.

Lucian raised his hand, and the crow entirely took shape. It burst from his hand and disappeared into the trees above.

He turned his hand over and studied it.

"What is happening?" he whispered. "The world is not the same."

Approaching grunts and growls brought Lucian's attention back to the forest, and he continued into the trees. Only a few moments passed when he noticed structures in the distance. He'd wandered the woods for so long without direction, and he never would have expected to find something familiar. He saw the destroyed yellow bricks and realized it was Munchkin City.

He rushed in, and an overwhelming sense of dread gripped him. There was no life to speak of.

He ran to the nearest building and peeked his head in the window. No one. There was no movement, no signs of any life, just empty structures. The city was in ruins, and only carnage remained. He recoiled.

Seeing the recognizable bodies sent a shiver down his spine, somber dread gripping his heart. He took a deep breath and searched for a sign of what had happened. The old phrase of curiosity and cats goes a long way, and in this instance, the Scarecrow should have listened.

He heard a noise and rushed deeper into the city. It was once a cute, tiny home, most likely belonging to an older grandmotherly type. The structure was pink, and the shutters were sporting a soft green color with little yellow flowers painted on them.

He crouched, opened the tiny green door, and peeked in. Nothing had overturned or was out of place. The tea set was still on the kitchen table as if the occupants had needed a cup of sugar, and they had simply gone next door to borrow one.

He looked around for anything that might give a clue to the noise. He grunted as he pushed inside the structure. The buildings were small, but not to where he could not fit.

Lucian was careful not to disturb anything within but searched for any clues. He got down on his hands and knees and looked under the kitchen table.

Not a thing. He stood and expected to see pictures hung on the off-white walls, but a headless corpse in red and white armor stood between him and the rest of the room.

Lucian retreated out the door, and the headless corpse lunged after him. He stared in horror. The lack of its head didn't burden it, and it moved with unnatural speed.

The Scarecrow turned to escape back to the forest, but a black, red, and white sea surrounded him. Armored dead shambled toward him, closing all hope he had.

Despair is another one of those feelings he had learned and experienced. He dropped to his knees. There was nothing to be done. He lifted his chin to the sky, unleashing his anguish. Raindrops caressed his face as the one name that plagued and soothed him for many years danced on his lips, but fear stole his voice.

The King of Hearts raised his head with his arm and promptly placed it back onto his shoulders. "She wants him alive."

Everything slowed. The survival instinct rushed in, and Lucian stood, ready to fight impossibility itself. Unfortunately, he did not have eyes sewn to the back of his head and did not see the abominations flanking him. Unlike the Gragskals, who had sheer mass, these things had numbers and unity.

After the King of Hearts barked a command, Lucian was on his knees in seconds. The headless army swarmed him. The first attack came from behind, knocking him to the ground— soldiers piled on top of him, exposing only his face.

His only hope — the name of the woman he could never forget — persisted on his lips. In a few moments, he would be completely incapacitated.

He strained to keep his face exposed. The sea of death, the rain pouring onto the desperate scene, and a mass of shadowy flutters flooded his mind.

"Dorothy!" he screamed to the storm, unleashing a black mass of spinning crows wrapped around her name as if embracing a long-lost friend. The shadowy crows flew in a violent cyclone from his mouth and disappeared into the clouds.

Lucian collapsed. His head rested on the broken bricks. Darkness enveloped him, but he felt the Gragskals thud as they landed nearby. There was a verbal exchange between the creatures and the King of Hearts, but the Scarecrow could not make out the words before everything went black.

Dorothy's calm weekend turned into more nightmares. Every time she slipped off to sleep, it was the same thing. She was in the Land of Oz, but a child, and unlike before, she was alone, wandering the dark forest. She didn't remember how she had returned. It was not the tornado and the falling house. She just woke up to chaos and old demons, with not a friend to speak of.

That voice and laughter haunted her and were the last things she heard before jolting awake, sweat plastering her hair to her face. She panted, looking about the room.

Anguish lingered in her waking world, which made her annoying existence worse. She swung her legs from under the sheets and rested her feet on her black sneakers. It took her a few moments to believe she was safe in the hotel room her aunt had left her in two days before. She had one more night before she had to check out. Dorothy wanted to enjoy it, but she would not be allowed such a luxury.

She looked at the clock next to the bed, which read 10:30 p.m. Flopping back onto the sheets, she groaned softly and rubbed the sleep out of her eyes. "Might as well go for a walk." She huffed and reached for the clothes lying on the lounge chair in the corner. Ankle socks and black leggings, along with a forest green V-neck shirt, completed the outfit.

Dorothy slipped out of the lobby and onto the sidewalk. The hotel was in a lovely little suburb. Despite being outside the city, there was plenty of traffic, and people enjoying the local nightlife. An abundance of coffee shops, pubs, and clothing stores populated the two streets. She took a deep breath, sighed, and looked at the traffic lights. The corner of Dove and Cherry was busy.

The crowd pushed past; her existence was nothing more than a street sign. She watched the Cherry Street signal blow in the icy wind.

A storm had rolled in since she had fallen asleep a couple of hours before, and the clouds above covered the stars.

Dorothy shivered and crossed the street. Far too lost in her nightmares, she didn't pay attention to time passing and found herself on the outskirts of town at the edge of a peaceful meadow. She'd visited this suburb several times but didn't remember coming across such a lovely place.

The city night ambiance faded, and she let go of the horrid dreams. Stepping into the knee-high grass, she had some semblance of calm. The clouds turned a soft orange as the sun peeked over the horizon.

She wondered how long she'd been walking, but the sun's warmth, the peace she hadn't felt since she was a young child, pushed the idea from her mind, and she embraced the scene before her.

She flopped back onto the soft grass, her eyes closing. Tilting her head toward the light, she took a deep breath, and her body relaxed into the welcoming meadow.

The sound of a car screeching and swerving didn't bring Dorothy out of her delusion. The front tires barely missed her head, and it veered into the wrong lane, hitting another car head-on.

Screams erupted from the crowd, which stopped and stared at the collision and the woman lying at the intersection of Dove and Cherry; her eyes closed, and a serene smile on her lips.

A small girl gripped her mother's hand outside a coffee shop. Next to them, a man in a brown suit pulled out his cell phone and called emergency services while another recorded the incident. Her mother looked like she wanted to help but was balancing a coffee and holding her six-year-old tightly.

A large crow perched atop the Dove Avenue streetlight; the child saw it as she craned her neck at the gawkers. The bird moved slowly and left wisps of shadow in its wake, and she blinked multiple times. The little girl yanked her mother's hand, but her eyes never left the strange crow.

Too engrossed in the scene, her mother could do more than hold on to her daughter and didn't hear her tiny words in the sea of shouts.

All the cars had stopped. People slowly exited their vehicles and hung on their doors for a better look. The crow fluttered again and jumped into flight, leaving a wake of shadow behind it, and the clouds above growled. Thunder shocked a cry out of some, but the chaos on the street stole the show.

The first officer ordered onlookers to move away from the pile-up and the woman in the street. Everyone moved back to the sidewalk or their vehicles.

He approached cautiously, but seeing no signs of a weapon or movement, he took a few steps forward. He reached out to her, but something violently knocked him back and slammed him against the grill of a Ford Fiesta.

Drawing his firearm, he looked around frantically, then grabbed his radio on his shoulder and shouted for backup. His gaze landed on the woman in front of him. She hadn't moved, but nothing else presented itself.

Two more police officers showed up, and they moved cautiously toward Dorothy. The original man braved a closer step, and when he was about arm's length from her, a loud crash sounded from above, accompanied by a blinding flash.

Something screeching swooped at the officers' faces, and they jumped back. A cyclone of shadows spun in from the clouds above.

The police scampered back and ducked behind open car doors, guns drawn, but with absolute confusion on their faces. Shaking, they watched a shadowy mass dive in and envelop the woman. The sky above opened, and the storm returned. A downpour and violent winds forced everyone to retreat to cars and buildings. Lightning streaked across the thick clouds, and thunder shook windows. Those who had been recording checked their videos after finding shelter only to be greeted with static disruption.

Dorothy felt like a gentle cloud was lifting her, the soft caress lulling her into a peaceful trance. She sighed, utterly content with her dream.

She felt a soft fluttering brush over her face. Dorothy squeezed her eyes shut. She didn't want to wake up or let go of the peaceful dream, but a jolt and the feeling of falling snapped her awake.

Wrapped in a tornado of shadowy flapping wings, her world spun. She was rapidly approaching a canopy of trees and stiffened, ready for impact.

The crows spun her to the ground, and she landed with a dull thud on the forest floor. Trembling, she attempted to push her face from the dirt, but it was too much. Her sight clouded, and unconsciousness pushed itself to the forefront, but the voices...

# Chapter 27

Drip... drip... drip... The cold smack of the small droplets had no source, but the White Knight could feel them. Darkness surrounded him, and a searing pain in his ribs and right leg caused him to stiffen and twitch when he moved.

His consciousness tunneled into the world of the living. He opened his eyes and blinked at the cold drops hitting his forehead.

The skies, still black with the storm, had taken an interlude, and as his sight focused, he found himself on a fallen tree trunk, a thick branch hovering over his body. Impaled above him was one of his men. The blood leaking from his chest wound continued to drip onto the knight.

Remorse flooded him as he looked from the soldier above him to the mud-covered bodies of the fallen warriors. The red and white army mixed with the still forms of lion-like men.

He rolled off the trunk and landed on his hands and knees. He fought through each painful move and labored breath.

Thunder cracked overhead, but the knight paid no attention. His focus turned to the abandoned village in the distance. He forced himself to grab his sword and stand.

He limped as he picked his way through the carnage to the village. The lion people might have left some rations, and he hoped he would not find much resistance barging in. He couldn't fight in his current state.

He passed through the open gates and stumbled. Pain surged through his leg, and he leaned against a wooden cabin he assumed was once someone's house. There was no sound inside, so he pushed open the door and rummaged for anything useful.

Taking from the village did not sit well, but survival pushed him to do things he wouldn't normally do.

The knight hobbled between a few buildings and gathered food, blankets, a water canister, and things to help build a fire. He found what he assumed was a healing hut. The magical-looking items were foreign and frightened him, but some natural healing remedies he recognized. He grabbed jars and vials and threw everything into a sack, hoping he was right about the content's effects. He could barely manage the load as he swung it over his shoulder and stumbled, supporting himself briefly on another wooden structure.

It took some time to calm his labored breathing and muster the energy to push off the wall and head out the back gate toward the trees. Once he met the treeline, he turned, shifted his weight onto his better leg, and surveyed the new land.

The foreign mountains now cradled the checkered plains with the abandoned village, which also had materialized out of nothing. He twisted to face the massive and unfamiliar dense forest. The lion people were kind and brave enough to help defend his soldiers and the land from the Jabberwocky. He considered it in his best interest to see what they might know and followed them.

He tracked the lion creatures deep into the woods. It had only been hours, but each painful step added days. The heavy rain hit the thick canopy above and created an eerie mist at the base of the trees. Some raindrops made it through, which washed some gore from his face and armor, but enough remained to remind him how alone he was.

It had been many years since he had traveled alone, but he had trained for combat and survival since he was a boy. Those lessons hadn't faded with age.

Night settled in, and he found a dense thicket to take refuge beside and built a fire. The White Knight moved around the perimeter of his camp, checking for danger or anything else living in the area. He would only remain until dawn — enough time to eat, apply healing remedies to his wounds, and get some rest. He needed to return to the lions' tracks as quickly as possible.

Satisfied that this campsite was as secure as possible, the knight removed his helmet. His long silver hair, still tied back with a black piece of leather, fell down his back. His face, though worn from many battles, had robust features. He looked like he hadn't shaved in a few days, with silver scruff on his face. Despite being in his late forties, he remained well-fit for combat.

He groaned, reaching into the bag beside him, and removed a green vial. He drank the contents and made a disgusted face. It tasted awful, something between an earthworm and mold, but he already felt his wounds mending.

He tossed the empty vial back into his bag, and a rustling noise drew his attention to a pile of leaves. They moved, and the knight got to his feet, wincing as he stood.

He placed his hand on the hilt of his sword. He could not fend off an attack if it were a dangerous foe, but he advanced with caution. As he moved closer, he heard murmuring.

Guardedly, he craned his neck to view the other side of the tree. A woman in her late thirties lay sprawled. Mud caked her clothes, and she whipped her head about as sweat poured from her brow. The knight hurried to her side as best he could.

Thinking she was in a feverish nightmare, he grabbed his bag and limped back to the fire. He dropped it next to her legs and kneeled. He searched for one of the smaller vials of herbs. Some markings on the bottles were plants he knew to have calming effects. He hoped the lion people used them the same way, but trying something was better than letting her suffer.

He was all too familiar with bent reality; how real it could get if not addressed. The man had had enough interactions with the Queen of Hearts to see the worst of it.

The White Knight tilted her head back to soothe the floral concoction down her throat. The woman's speaking slowed and stopped, and her breath turned light. Her limbs stilled, and she lay as if she were in a peaceful slumber.

There was no way he could carry her and track the lion people. He conceded the possibility of having this campsite for a few days. It was as safe as they were going to get. They had plenty of turned-over trees and shrubs to nestle into.

It was no simple task, but he lifted her upper half, looped his arm under hers, and pulled her to the warmth of the crackling flames. He laid a blanket out and placed her down to rest. The herbs seemed to have a positive effect as her brow dried, and she stayed asleep.

The rain had stopped, making the small camp more welcoming. If the storm had continued, they couldn't have kept the fire going, but they got a slight reprieve. The knight tossed in more kindling. It was enough to keep the two of them warm within their small shelter.

Vigilant, the knight sat with his back against one of the fallen trunks. He reached over into his sack and pulled out dried meat rations. There was no telling how long they would have to stay in this spot, and his rations would only last a few days of traveling. He bit into it and took a long-needed drink from the waterskin.

He felt warmth wash through his body, and his wounds ached and tingled some. A thunderclap above reminded him they were on borrowed time before the rain began again.

His crystal blue eyes reflected the dancing flames as he looked down at the sleeping woman. He adjusted his seating position, closed his eyes, and rested his head on the dead tree. He hoped they would not be seen, but it was a risk he had to take.

The warmth of the crackling fire relaxed him, and the herbs worked on his broken bones and skin, but despite these minor comforts, behind his eyelids, he saw the dead man he'd woken up to on the battlefield.

"I'm sorry," he whispered as he drifted off, a tear wetting his cheek.

# Chapter 28

The King of Hearts flew open the imposing throne room doors, his headless captains and lieutenants behind him. Gragskals that filled the rafters above followed them.

"Your Highnesses." The king bowed, and the rest of the headless fell to one knee before both women, who sat steadfast with their chins raised.

The Queen of Hearts swept her eyes over the headless army. She did not notice one missing captain or lieutenant, and a dark smile spread on her lips.

"Report."

"The Munchkin City is ours, my lady," he said, keeping his head bowed.

"And the vermin?" Yslene spat the question as if she'd found a hair in her wine.

Standing, the Nine of Hearts moved forward, and went back to his kneeling statue. "The Master of Alchemy and the school's headmistress escaped with some of the injured. The City Hall was silenced and ransacked. Those from the school were the only survivors."

The witch's expression remained taut, but her eyes narrowed on the Nine of Hearts. The lack of response made the headless visibly nervous.

He attempted to make himself as small as possible. "Would you like us to pursue the survivors, Your Grace?"

"No! The only two concerns I have will have their hands full with the injured. Their hearts bleed for others, and it will keep their attention. The land is already ours. They have failed."

"I'm glad to see your confidence has been restored." The atmosphere next to the witch's throne cracked and shifted, and Oz moved from otherworldly to solid form.

"My confidence has never failed me. It was brashness, and I will not make the mistake again," the witch said over her shoulder.

The room resounded with Oz's deep chuckle as he descended the stairs and went to the window.

A spark from within the witch's crystal ball caught in her peripheral vision, and she turned her head. Black and gray smoke swirled about, masking the visions below. The queen's mirror quickly mimicked the appearance of Yslene's ball. The fog billowed away, and a scene rose to the surface—a wandering Alice and Cheshire navigating the woods.

The witch's rage surged to her throat as her eyes focused on her crystal ball, but she held it down, knowing the time would come. Dorothy slept beside the dying embers of a fire, with an unfamiliar form next to her.

Oz faced the mountains, a smile coming to his lips. "And now, ladies, we begin."

www.ingramcontent.com/pod-product-compliance
Lightning Source LLC
Chambersburg PA
CBHW060403310726
48976CB00003B/924